Uncharted

PAGE STREET
PUBLISHING CO.

PAGE STREET
PUBLISHING CO.

First published in 2018 by
Page Street Publishing Co.
27 Congress Street, Suite 105
Salem, MA 01970
www.pagestreetpublishing.com

Distributed by Macmillan, sales in Canada by The Canadian Manda Group.

22   21   20   19   18   1   2   3   4   5

ISBN-13: 978-1-62414-593-3
ISBN-10: 1-62414-593-0

Library of Congress Control Number: 2017963331

Cover and book design by Page Street Publishing Co.
Cover image © Ayal Ardon / Trevillion Images

Printed and bound in the United States

To my mother Josephine,
the bravest person I have ever known.

Prologue

England, 1794

Elizabeth Mayville did not hold with premonitions, déjà vu, or any other superstitious nonsense. Never before had she had the feeling that she was being watched or followed. Never, that is, until now.

Pulling on her cloak to conceal the package clutched to her chest, Elizabeth walked out her door for the very last time. Although the Royal Mail would soon be closing, she didn't dare go straight there. Taking the circuitous route she had practiced, she stopped outside the millinery and sliced the hem of her cloak with the small knife she kept strapped to her calf. She purchased a new cloak with a hood to cover her blonde hair and left her old one for mending. Then, as the clerk tended to another customer, Elizabeth dashed out the rear door, hoping her disguise would buy her the time she needed.

Her heart beat in rhythm with her heeled boots clicking on the cobblestones as she rushed to the square. With a quick look over her shoulder, she darted inside the Royal Mail. Several long minutes later, it was done.

Elizabeth sat on a bench perched along the river, tugging the gold link chain that encircled her neck like a noose. She longed to run as fast and as far as her long legs would take her, but she needed to see for herself that the package was loaded onto a boat heading for America. She had planned to deliver it herself to her older brother, but now, with the Serpent Society bearing down on her, she had to let it go—lest they catch her with it. Hopefully, she could join her brother in America, someday, where the Serpent Society would never find them.

In the encroaching darkness, a cold mist crept up the bank of the river, chilling Elizabeth to the bone. Pulling the unfamiliar coat tightly around her, she watched and waited until finally, the mail barge set sail.

Her heart hammering, Elizabeth took off at a run, her breath coming out in silver bursts as she raced down the narrow alley toward the station. If she was very lucky, she just might make the eight o'clock train to London.

A cold hand of dread pressed against her chest as two men stepped out of the fog, their faces hidden beneath hard red masks. Elizabeth skidded to a stop. From behind her, the heavy tread of boots sounded like a death march.

She couldn't risk being taken alive. She had to protect the secret.

Elizabeth blew out a long, shaky breath, but her hand was steady as she quickly opened the Celtic knot clasp of her locket and retrieved a tiny vial.

"Let it end with me." The words seemed to carry down the alley in an unearthly voice as Elizabeth tossed back the poison in one mouthful.

But Elizabeth knew that prayers were seldom answered and a secret worth dying for was, by its very nature, also worth killing for.

CHAPTER *One*

Maine, 2017

It had been three years, two months, and six days since I'd accidentally killed my mother. Hers was the last funeral I'd been to, and I wasn't sure I could make it through another one, let alone two.

My hand shook on the door handle of Dad's sedan as I stared up at the church looming at the top of the hill.

"Annabeth," Dad said, the tell-tale staccato seeping in between the syllables of my name, as it did whenever he was worried, "are you sure you want to do this?"

I was sure I *didn't* want to go his friends' funerals, but Dad needed me, and ever since Mom died I'd promised myself I would do everything I could to make his life easier. Nodding, I forced a smile, hoping it masked how I really felt: like a hollowed-out pumpkin.

"You have nothing to prove," Dad said. "Just say the word and I can drop you back off at your dorm."

Oh, how I wanted to say yes.

After a stretch at McLean psychiatric hospital, my doctor and Dad both thought I was doing better—back in school, able to focus and be "present." Yet the tightness in my chest had increased with each passing mile that brought me farther from my safety zone. Now, I would be with people who knew everything about me; I couldn't hide behind my books or my paintings. But I pushed aside my worries and wrapped myself in the blanket of numbness I'd worn since the night Mom died.

"I'll be fine," I said, trying to convince us both as I climbed out of the car. "I know how much Malcolm and Sarah meant to you."

I had spent many summers and holidays at their house, Bradford Manor, along with the other Magellans—members of the Magellan club that Dad had belonged to in college, which was dedicated to investigating myths, legends, and unsolved mysteries. Every time I'd been there, Mom had been with us. I tried not to think about the memories that would be waiting for me around every corner.

"It just seems so ironic and sad that for all the traveling the Magellans did to exotic places, Malcolm and Sarah drowned in the lake right behind their house. An accident at home, just like Aunt Kathy and Uncle Paul."

"Tragic is what it is." Dad gave my hand a squeeze as we walked up the stone steps. "Thanks for coming. It helps more than you know. And Richard and Griffin can't wait to see you."

Since Griffin's parents were now dead, his uncle, Richard, was stuck raising a teen alone, just like Dad. "The last time I saw them was at Bradford Manor when I was about thirteen."

Dad closed his eyes, his face softening at the memory. "That was a great weekend. The whole gang was there, all of us Magellans, and your mom, of course. You and Griffin had a ball."

Griffin Bradford was a year older than me, and *him* I remembered. Clearly. He was bratty and incredibly irritating. When he discovered I was terrified of spiders, he snuck into my room and shook a jar of them into my bed. My shoulders squirmed just thinking about it.

Dad took a deep, steadying breath as he opened the door to the church. Since he'd gotten lost along the way—

no big surprise there—we were late, so we slipped into a pew in the back where I could tune out most of what was going on.

The burial was a different matter. I had to force myself to get out of the car, force my legs to walk, force myself forward, when all I wanted to do was turn around and go home.

But even home was no longer a sanctuary. After Mom died, it became a memory-filled house with no heart and just another reminder that I couldn't go back, yet I couldn't seem to move forward. This in-between world was like living in purgatory.

As I followed Dad down the meandering path to the burial site, I wrapped my blazer tightly around myself and rubbed each of the seventeen charms on what had been my mother's bracelet. I hoped the ritual would calm my frayed nerves. It didn't. The closer we came to the dark wooden caskets, the more it felt as if I were walking in quicksand. Stopping, I told Dad I was going to hang in the back while he said hello to Richard and Griffin.

Griffin was far from the gangling kid I remembered. I stared at his profile: a cleft chin, sharp cheeks, and full red lips. If it weren't for his familiar crooked nose, I might not have even recognized him. His suit was pulled taut across his broad shoulders, his body tense as he stood rigidly gazing down at the caskets. He glanced back and stared at me with bloodshot eyes.

Shuddering, I took a step back on the soft spring grass, and then another, and another, until my view was blocked by a flowering pear tree. Two police officers hovered in the back with me, their eyes trained on Griffin.

"Terrible, isn't it?" Startled, I turned and saw a girl about my age with wild red curls and bright purple glasses.

I nodded. "Just awful."

"Are you family?" she asked.

"No." My voice was cracked and dry. "Good family friends. You?"

She shook her head. "I knew Dr. and Mr. Bradford from the hospital, and I used to know Griffin. No one's seen him much since they got back from Europe a couple of years ago—except for now, since his face is splashed all over the newspapers. Not that anyone minds staring at that face."

"Why is he in the papers?"

"You haven't heard?" She pulled her curls behind her ears and leaned in conspiratorially. "Who goes for a boat ride at one in the morning on a cold rainy night? My father's the sheriff"—she jerked her head toward the older policeman—"and he's sure that Griffin knows more about his parents' so-called accident than he's letting on. Griffin may be named a suspect."

No one could fake the grief I saw in Griffin's face, no one. "But my father said the coroner ruled their deaths an accidental drowning."

She quirked an eyebrow. "That doesn't mean it was one. Summer's the busy season around here; an open double homicide investigation isn't good for home sales or business. But the Bradfords were worth millions and Griffin inherited everything. Dad doesn't trust him."

I hadn't seen Griffin since he was fourteen, but the boy I had known adored his parents. How much could he have changed in four years? I swallowed a bitter laugh. I knew the answer to that all too well. Plenty. I barely recognized the girl I used to be—she was long gone. I knew that Dad thought I'd be "cured" when I went back to the *before* me, but Dr. Harrington said that wasn't how things worked and that *I* needed to stop comparing myself to her. Easier said than done. That me was fun, outgoing, strong. I am her foil, in every way. Even I liked her better.

The girl practically knocked me over when she whipped around to see what the police were doing. "Sorry! I'm Holly by the way, but I gotta go. Dad's talking to Deputy Clarke, and I want to know what's going on."

"Why does it matter to you?"

"I intend to find out what happened to the Bradfords. They were really good to me. When Mom had cancer, we couldn't afford the experimental treatments, but Dr. Bradford made sure everything was paid for."

"I'm so sorry about your mother."

"Oh, she's fine now. In remission."

Holly's tone was light, as if her mother had chicken pox. It made me want to shake her. "She's lucky. And so are you."

She let out a hollow laugh. "Yeah, real lucky. Apparently along with her new lease on life came an epiphany—she didn't want to be stuck in the boonies saddled to a policeman who worked long hours. So now I see her and her new husband—her oncologist, by the way—every other weekend."

What I'd give for every other weekend.

Holly handed me a card with her name, cell phone number, and title: *Investigative Journalist, Laketown Daily News.* "Call if you want to talk, or if you think of anything."

"You're a reporter?"

"An intern, at least for now. All I need is my big break—and this case could be it," she said with a gleam in her eyes.

I wasn't sure what to make of Holly, but the scales were definitely tipping away from like. Since I'd probably never see her again, and I didn't want to be rude, I shoved the card in my pocket, knowing I'd never call her.

Once the burial was over, I headed for the Dunkin' Donuts across the street while the police roved around Griffin, Dad, and his friends—the four remaining Magellans. I thought about the four who had died—along with Mom—and a cold shiver scuttled down my spine.

By the time I emerged with my coffee, Dad was waiting by the sedan. "You drink too much coffee. Although, if that's all I have to complain about, I guess I should consider myself lucky."

My smile faded as I slid into the passenger seat. As if that was all Dad had to complain about. He never blamed me for Mom's death—not once. Sometimes I wished he would.

I took a long sip of my coconut iced coffee while Dad drove through town and turned onto a twisting country road, singing the wrong words to an Eagles song on the classic rock station and stealing anxious looks at me when he thought I wasn't looking. Not for the first time, I felt like an exotic animal at the zoo.

"We've been driving for over half an hour. Shouldn't we be at Bradford Manor by now?" I could've sworn we'd already passed that BRAKE FOR MOOSE sign. "I think we're going in circles."

Dad shook his head. "I'm sure this is the right way."

"I'll just double-check." I picked up his phone, but it was dead. "Where's the portable charger I gave you for your birthday?"

Leaning over, Dad ran a hand through his thick sandy brown hair and absentmindedly patted down his cowlick. He was in definite need of a haircut. Of course, that would require leaving the house. "I could have sworn I put it right there."

I fished around the middle console—it was stuffed full of papers, gum wrappers, change, a broken garage door opener, and assorted sticky notes with reminders to get gas or go to an appointment or buy dog food despite the fact that Argos had died a few months before Mom—until I finally found it.

"You should have veered left a few miles back."

Sighing, Dad made a U-turn.

We crossed a bridge that straddled foaming water and drove deeper into the forest while dusk settled in all around us. Ancient trees stood like sentinels, blocking out the light from the star-strewn sky. Branches and vines crept into the dirt road, making it even narrower, as if it was closing in on us. I took a deep breath and dismissed the unsettled feeling that was slithering like a snake in the pit of my stomach, reminding myself that we weren't traveling to a haunted house but to Bradford Manor, where I had spent many weekends.

The road ended in front of an elaborately-carved black iron gate. Attached to a stone column were three signs:

NO TRESPASSING

PRIVATE

NO ADMITTANCE

"Real welcoming," I muttered. If the signs had been there before, I hadn't noticed.

Dad pressed the intercom button recessed into the column.

"Is that finally you, Sam? We were about to send a search party."

Dad waved at the security camera. "Sorry. We got lost."

As we drove up an incline, the vista completely transformed: The woods receded, and acres of lawns and gardens spread out before us. In front of the clapboard mansion replete with turrets and multiple stone chimneys was an elaborate alabaster fountain, and behind it was a lake glistening in the moonlight. It wasn't quite the fairy-tale castle of my childhood memory, but it was close.

Richard ushered us into a cavernous foyer. He was thinner than I remembered, with receding salt-and-pepper hair, but he still had a warm smile and kind dark blue eyes. He pulled me into a hug, telling me how sorry he was about Mom. Richard, along with the Bradfords, had been on a remote island when she died, so they never came to the services. Not that I would have remembered either way, since I fainted three words into Dad's eulogy.

"How's Griffin holding up?" Dad asked.

Richard scrubbed a hand across the back of his neck. "Not good. I've been a doting uncle his entire life, but I'm not prepared to be a stand-in parent. I've read a dozen books on parenting and grieving, but to tell the truth, I don't know what the hell I'm doing. I owe it to my sister to get this right   I just wish I knew how."

Dad gave Richard a knowing smile and patted his shoulder. "I'm sure you're doing fine."

I cleared my throat, wishing I was somewhere—*anywhere*—else.

"Annabeth was accepted at her school's summer art program." Dad beamed at me. "So I can spend as much time here as you need."

"Thanks, Sam. I'll take you up on that. Griffin's been very emotional, so don't be surprised by his behavior."

As if any teenage behavior could surprise Dad at this point.

"But he's really looking forward to seeing you both."

I was sure that was only half true, but I followed behind Richard and Dad nonetheless, my Keds squeaking on the polished marble. We passed a study and a dining room with a table that could easily seat twenty, before coming to a large but cozy combination kitchen/family room that was exactly as I remembered: white cabinets and a driftwood backsplash Mom had painted with mermaids, sea monsters, and whales. I smiled sadly as I remembered eating breakfast on the bluestone patio beyond the French doors with all the Magellans and their kids, playing chase around the kitchen island and doing puzzles at the oversized pine coffee table. Without the others, the house felt ominously quiet.

Griffin, along with Camila and Jack—the other surviving Magellans—came in from the patio. Griffin had always been tall, but now he had six inches on me. I reached up to give him a hug, telling him how sorry I was, and his back stiffened beneath my hands.

As soon as Griffin pulled away, Jack had his arms around me. "So good to see you, darlin'!" he exclaimed in his Texas drawl. He hadn't changed a bit since the last time I saw him, though now I was about his height. He was still stocky, with brown hair and an easy smile.

Camila, on the other hand, looked like she had aged ten years—her skin was sallow, and her purple-black hair had lost some of its luster. She pulled me into a tight hug. "Annabeth! Look at you! You are the spitting image of your mother."

I flinched, although I was used to it. Everyone said I looked like Mom. We had the same blue-gray eyes, wavy dark hair, seemingly too many teeth for our mouth, and a ski-jump nose (as we had called it) that turned up a bit too much at the end.

"Are the boys still in Cuba? They posted some great pictures," I said.

"No, it was just a short trip to visit their abuela. They wanted to come, but they're both doing the summer session at Tulane," Camila answered.

Richard shook his head. "I still can't believe they're in college. Griffin will be going this fall—and next year it will be you, Annabeth. I still remember the kids all running along the beach in their diapers. Seems like it was yesterday."

I didn't remember that. I did, however, remember Griffin *chasing* after me, wagging a dead fish in his hand that resulted in me slipping off the dock, cutting myself on a rusty nail, and getting a tetanus shot. Thanks to him, I can add trypanophobia—fear of needles and injections—to my list of medical conditions.

"I can't believe you're the same skinny girl who was so adventurous—always climbing something and off exploring. I was looking through old photos"—Richard chuckled—"and in every one you're bruised or bandaged. You drove your poor mother crazy!" He caught himself too late. We all stood there, surrounded by an awkward silence that screamed.

"Anyway, I'm so grateful to have all of you with us during this difficult time," Richard continued, a quaver in his voice. "My dearest friends, I just wish we didn't keep meeting at funerals."

Leaning against the wall to steady myself, I regretted not returning to school when I'd had the chance. I wasn't sure how I was going to survive the next few days. I glanced at Griffin, who was clenching and unclenching his hands, and noticed three of his fingers were partially amputated. None of the cuts were straight, and each finger was of a different length. I wondered when in the last four years that had happened—and how.

It occurred to me that I didn't really know Griffin, not anymore. A lot could happen in four years—I knew that all too well. There must be some reason the sheriff didn't trust him, some reason the police might name him a suspect.

I didn't like the idea of Dad spending a lot of time at Bradford Manor.

CHAPTER *Two*

The walls of my suite were the softest blue, almost the same shade as the fog hovering over the lake. The fabrics were all varying shades of white, in contrast with the rich walnut bed, nightstand, and armoire, carved with flowers and swirling vines, which age had mellowed to a golden hue. I crossed the gleaming wooden floors to the window seat in the turret overlooking the patio and watched clouds roll over the forest, extinguishing the starlight. Leaning my head against the glass, I listened to the gentle *tap tap tap* of the rain against the pane, and the night Mom died came flooding back to me as it sometimes did, like a movie playing inside my head that I'm unable to stop. I shut my eyes, hoping it would go away . . .

Hey, Mom—

Finally, you call back! The "pillow in the bed" trick, really? You tell me where you are right now!

I'm . . . in the park.

Mom inhaled a sharp breath. You're with that boy, aren't you?

Yes, and . . . well, the cops are here, too.

Oh, Annabeth.

You have to come get me.

The silence seemed to stretch on and on before Mom answered: *We'll talk when I get there.*

Only she never came. She was exactly one point two miles from the park when she was hit head-on by a drunk driver.

Tonight, I was losing my battle with the sorrow that haunted my thoughts, constantly looking for a foothold, so I needed to do what I always did when that happened: read.

Remembering that Bradford Manor had a beautiful library, I crept down the kitchen stairs and turned down the hall. I passed the butler's pantry, basement door, and mudroom before finally coming to the wooden pocket doors. As soon as I crossed the threshold and inhaled the musty smell of old parchment and ancient texts, reassurance covered me like a soft blanket. Here I would find my escape, my safety net, my sanctuary. A wooden trestle table stood in the center of the room, piled high with thick tomes, while long blood-red velvet drapes hung on the windows on either side of the stone fireplace. I walked past a paneled wall decorated with travel photos and another with old maps, finally finding a dozen books about King Arthur that I had already read. Sliding out my favorite, *The Mists of Avalon*, I returned to my room. As I immersed myself in Camelot, my sadness receded into the corners of my mind where it lurked like a shadow, waiting to pounce again.

I woke up later than I intended to the sound of laughing on the patio. Reluctantly, I tugged on my jean shorts, threw on my least wrinkled T-shirt, and joined Dad, Camila, Jack, Richard, and Griffin outside. Richard introduced me to Suzette—their cook and house cleaner—who was replenishing a buffet table with an assortment of delicious foods: quiches, pastries, bacon, and sausage. Suzette, who was painfully thin and wore a pinched expression, looked me over from head to toe, frowning.

I grabbed a coffee and a chocolate croissant and sat down. Scattered across the long wrought-iron table were photo albums; Richard and Camila were pulling out pictures of Malcolm and Sarah for the memorial celebration. Having no desire to see photos that I was sure would include Mom, I pulled my bare feet beneath me, leaned back in the chair, and inhaled the heady sweet fragrance of the lilacs while half-listening to Richard and Dad talk in best-friend shorthand—laughing at snippets of sentences they had no need to finish. I remembered having a friend like that, a best friend.

"Annabeth? Richard asked you a question," Dad said.

I turned to find all of them staring at me expectantly. Griffin was leaning toward me, his hands on the table. Once again, I stared at his fingers. It was so strange—his pinky was cut on the diagonal. Why would the surgeon do that? Griffin scowled when he caught me looking and quickly folded his arms across his chest.

"Annabeth?" Dad said again, his forehead wrinkling.

"Sorry. Can you repeat the question?"

"I was just saying I hear you've become quite the artist," Richard said. "I'm not at all surprised, though. From the time you were old enough to hold a crayon, you've always been coloring. Even before Malcolm, Sarah, Griffin, and I left for Ireland, I remember Jill saying she was hoping you'd go to the Rhode Island School of Design like she had. Are you still interested?"

"I'm working on my college list."

"I can't believe I've never been to Ireland," Dad said, his voice a touch forlorn. "Kathy said the trip you all took after college was life-changing. I wish I could have gone."

My mom's sister—my Aunt Kathy—had always referred to the trip as "the expedition," and it had been her favorite topic.

"Hey, you were the responsible one, Sam, getting a job," Camila said. "But there's no reason we can't all go back together."

Except of course, it could never be the same. Half of the Magellans were dead. "You were gone over a year, weren't you?" I asked.

Richard nodded. "Still, it went by in a blink of an eye. We survived primarily on what we could catch or pick and the thrill of adventure: not knowing what's over the next hill or beyond the horizon. Best trip of my life. Even better than looking for Sasquatch or chasing the Nazca Lines in Peru." Richard wore a wistful expression. I knew how that felt—knowing the best years of your life were behind you.

"I've never seen this one." Dad pointed to a picture of the Magellans in a jungle somewhere, with monkeys hanging from the limbs above their heads. All the Magellans except for Richard were in it—even Dad, who met up with them to write a magazine article on the disappearing rainforest—and each of them had the same cool tattoo of a circle dissected by a horizontal line and a vertical arrow.

"I didn't know you all had the same tattoo." I tapped the sleeve of Dad's T-shirt. "So, Dad, I guess the story you told me—that it was supposed to be a compass but the tattoo artist messed up—is a load of crap. What does it really mean?"

Dad laughed. "Honestly, the memory of that night is a little foggy. Do you remember, Richard?"

An unspoken look passed between the old friends before Richard cleared his throat and responded: "Malcolm designed it. It was so long ago I don't recall what it stands for, either."

One thing about Richard hadn't changed at all: He couldn't manage a poker face to save his life. So why was he lying about a tattoo?

I looked over at Griffin to see if he was buying this, but he just sat there with his arms crossed, staring off into the woods. For some reason, he feigned aloofness, but every muscle in his face was tense and alert.

"You all got a symbol tattooed on your arm and none of you can remember what it means? Long night of drinking?" I asked.

"Yes, to tell you the truth." Dad laughed again. "I vaguely remember it having something to do with a symbol Malcolm kept seeing on those old maps he collected. He thought it might be related to that phantom island—"

"Antillia," Richard said, interrupting Dad. "Also known as the Isle of Seven Cities, from an old Iberian legend. Now I remember."

Camila pulled up Dad's sleeve. "I can't believe you still have the tattoo, Sam! You promised me you'd have it removed. We all did when we discovered it was an obscure symbol of the occult. Besides, my doctor said the ink used could be harmful. I guess wandering drunk into a tattoo parlor at two in the morning wasn't the best idea we ever had. You should have it taken off right away."

"I've been meaning to."

Dad could add it to the long list of things he'd been meaning to do. I bet I could find a sticky note that read *Call doctor about removing tattoo* in the car.

"Meaning to isn't good enough. It needs to go." Camila leveled a look at Dad that made it clear she wasn't taking no for an answer. "Honestly, it was an easy procedure. I'll take you to our doctor in New York. Come for a few days. We'll see a ball game, do a karaoke night—"

Dad shook his head. "Not after last time!"

"—and have that tattoo removed. How about you come back with us on Sunday?"

"No can do. Annabeth's summer session starts on Monday."

"I'll take her!" Griffin interjected. "I've been meaning to visit a friend in Boston anyway."

I had no desire to spend several hours in a car with Griffin, yet I could hardly refuse all the eager faces staring at me expectantly. Besides, if the ink was dangerous, that tattoo needed to come off as soon as possible. I forced a smile, which, I was pretty sure, was as close to natural as I got. "Sounds great."

Within ten minutes Dad's appointment was scheduled with Camila and Jack's surgeon, Red Sox–Yankees tickets were bought, and reservations were made—all while I flipped through an album titled *Expedition*—safe, since it was Mom-free. "Did any of you actually discover anything on your trips?"

Griffin nearly choked on his water.

"Annabeth," Dad scolded.

"I don't mean to be rude. I just can't fathom solving ancient mysteries and finding undiscovered territory, especially when it seems like there's a McDonald's in every city and Mount Everest is littered with trash."

"Ah, but you're wrong." A smile played at the corners of Richard's mouth. "Only about five percent of the ocean has been explored and scientists estimate we've barely identified ten percent of the ocean's creatures. Who knows what's down there? And there are remote mountains, volcanoes, and jungles that no man has ever stepped foot on. There are many mysteries yet to be discovered and some that never should be."

"Science and legend are not mutually exclusive," Camila said, helping herself to more coffee. "And as a matter of fact, I did discover something—something that is now used in almost every hospital in the country."

Dad loved to tell the story about how Camila fell in the jungle, sprained her wrist, and scraped both legs pretty badly. Sarah was shocked when Camila's cuts healed faster than they would have had she seen a doctor, and then she realized it was due to the incredible healing properties of the plants Camila had fallen on. The experience inspired Camila to found her own biotech company.

"That's what brought us together," Jack said. "All of us Magellans were scientists *and* dreamers. Especially Malcolm," he added softly.

Griffin's dad could always make it seem like dreams were plausible and myths were true. I remembered sitting on the beach around a roaring fire while Malcolm mesmerized us with tales of his adventures—real and invented. "I loved listening to Malcolm's stories. If I close my eyes, I can still imagine the winged water horse gliding into the water, the lake monster rising from the mist, and the giant squid skimming the surface . . . I can envision islands covered in gold."

Leaning back in his chair, Griffin stared at me with narrowed eyes. "That's all they were—stories meant to entertain children. My father was a biologist, doing important research. Cryptozoology is a serious scientific pursuit. Stop talking about him as if he was a mad scientist. In fact, can we *please* stop talking about expeditions, phantom islands, and mythical horses?"

I was so surprised by both his outburst and his harsh tone that it took me a minute to respond: "I didn't mean to offend you or insult your father. I always liked him, very much."

"It's fine, Annabeth. You said nothing wrong." Richard shot Griffin a warning look.

"Hey, here's a photo of the last time we were all together," Dad said. "Jill and Sarah were so busy talking that they burned all the hamburgers and hot dogs, so we had peanut butter and jelly s'mores for dinner."

Dad's attempt at a change in subject backfired. Both of us sat there, our eyes glued to the picture. It was so easy to be transported back, to remember the smell of suntan lotion, bug spray, and the acrid smoke of a crackling fire . . . the chorus of tree frogs and laughter from the grown-ups . . . the stars blazing across the sky as I lay curled up at Mom's feet. We'd all been so happy then—it was hard to believe that five of the people in the photo were dead. Even harder to believe that my mom was one of them. My hands began to shake.

Dad slammed the album closed. "I'm sorry, honey," he whispered. "I know this is hard on you."

"It's hard on all of us. And I'm the one who's sorry." And I was sorry. Every. Single. Day.

A light rain began to fall, prompting Camila to dash

inside with the albums. Everyone else jumped to help clean, leaving Griffin and me to grab the last two platters.

"Annabeth?" Fisting a silver tray, Griffin rocked back on his heels. "Sorry about before. Talking about Dad, looking at those photos . . ." He raked his uninjured hand through his dark wavy hair. His expression was heart-wrenchingly sad and I wondered if that's how I looked when I talked about Mom. I shook my head at the thought, because I only talked about Mom with Dr. Harrington and only because he made me.

I nodded. "I get it." Maybe I should give him another chance. As Doctor Harrington was always saying, everyone responded differently to grief. I was hardly the queen of charm, myself.

Jack poked his head out the French doors, his eyebrows drawn into one thick line. "Griffin, you better come in here. Right now."

Griffin dropped the pastry dish with a long *clang* and raced inside. I followed right behind him, a sudden chill snaking down my back. In the foyer, the two policemen I had seen at the funeral were arguing with Richard. Two more cops stood in the hallway.

The sheriff strode into the kitchen, holding an official

looking paper. "Griffin Bradford, since you are the legal owner of this house, I am here to inform you that we are executing a search warrant."

Griffin snatched the warrant out of his hands, and as he read and reread it, the scowl on his face transformed into a look of sheer and utter panic.

"What on earth for?" Richard demanded.

"We're investigating the suspicious and untimely deaths of Malcolm and Sarah Bradford."

CHAPTER

Each one of us seemed to be holding our breath. Camila grabbed Jack's arm with both hands, her eyes wide and her mouth gaping. Jack put his arm around Camila protectively, as if the police were there to arrest her. Richard stood frozen; only his eyes moved—darting from the sheriff to Griffin.

"You can't do this." Griffin's voice had a fierce edge to it.

"My lawyer will hear about this!" Richard whipped out his cell phone.

The sheriff stood with his hands on his wide hips. "Call whoever you want. In the meantime, we *will* execute this search warrant."

Griffin slammed the document onto the marble counter. "The hell you will!"

The sheriff narrowed his brown eyes. "What are you afraid of us finding?"

"Nothing, because you will search this house over my dead body. Or yours." Griffin was wound tight, like a coil ready to snap.

"Threatening a police officer? You're lucky I don't arrest you right now. You two, upstairs." The sheriff jerked his head toward the pair of policeman in the hallway. "Clarke, you'll search the basement. I'll take the first floor."

In one sudden movement, Griffin darted down the hall and blocked the basement door with his broad shoulders, his expression dark. "There are dangerous chemicals in the lab. You could get hurt."

Deputy Clarke—who looked like he could have been a marine or a football player—spoke in a calm voice, but he had his hand on his belt, right next to his gun. "I appreciate your concern, but I'll be just fine. Now stand aside, or we'll have to take you in."

Griffin spread his arms out and grabbed on to the doorjamb. "No! I won't let you down there!" The wooden molding splintered and cracked beneath his fingers, yet Griffin held on even tighter.

I stepped backward. How did he do that?

Richard dropped the phone. "Griffin, let go and come here."

"Listen to your uncle. If you don't move, we'll have no choice but to arrest you." As Deputy Clarke unclipped the handcuffs from his belt, Griffin shoved the officer, sending him reeling into the wall. Griffin mouthed something at Richard, then darted outside.

All hell had broken loose.

Jack charged after Griffin, but Griffin was long gone— I'd never seen anyone run so fast. Richard and the sheriff engaged in a long, heated argument, with Richard insisting that the sheriff hold off on the search warrant until his attorney could file an emergency motion, but the sheriff was having none of it. He demanded Richard unlock the basement door, or he was going to arrest both him and Griffin and break it down. After more shouting, Richard finally acquiesced.

Richard shadowed Deputy Clarke, Dad went upstairs to watch what the policemen were doing, and Camila followed the sheriff around the first floor. While all this was happening, I sat at the counter wondering what the heck was in the basement that Griffin didn't want the police to find.

A couple of hours later, Deputy Clarke emerged with boxes of documents. Richard trailed after him until his phone rang. He asked me to take his place while he answered the call, which was about the last thing I wanted to do.

"Are you a relation of the Bradfords?" Deputy Clarke asked as we walked to his cruiser.

I introduced myself and explained how Dad and I knew them.

"When was the last time you saw the Bradford family?"

I opened his car door. "Four years ago. And before you ask, I don't know anything about Malcolm's and Sarah's deaths, other than the fact they drowned."

He frowned, his bushy eyebrows almost touching, and deposited the boxes onto the back seat. "If you come across anything suspicious or unusual, it's your duty to alert the police." He handed me his card, with his cell phone number scribbled across the back.

"Why are you investigating their deaths? Just because they were out boating so late?"

Deputy Clarke's frown deepened. "Hardly. I shouldn't comment on an ongoing investigation, but suffice it to say the circumstances surrounding the accident are suspicious."

I wondered what he knew that I didn't as I followed him into the library. When I crossed the threshold, I gasped. Every framed picture had been taken off the wall, and piles of books were scattered on the floor.

"I didn't find a thing," the sheriff said to Deputy Clarke.

"As I told you would be the case," Camila said through pursed lips. "Which means you trashed the library for nothing. The governor happens to be a friend of mine, and his wife is on the board of a charity I founded. He will be hearing from me, and I will see to it that you don't get away with this. That's a promise."

A shadow crossed the sheriff's face. "I'm just doing my job, ma'am."

"What did you expect to find in the pictures?" I asked.

"Not that it's any of your business, young lady, but people hide many things in frames, particularly thumb drives." He shifted his gaze to Deputy Clarke. "What did you turn up?"

Deputy Clarke scrubbed a hand across the top of his dark crew-cut. "Hard to tell. There are a lot of documents to go through."

"Finish up here and go over the security footage again. I'll meet you back at the station."

Camila followed the sheriff as he thundered out the door.

Deputy Clarke heaved a sigh. "What a mess. Let me give you a hand picking up."

While Deputy Clarke re-shelved the books, I got to

work on the framed photos. Struggling with an oversized photo of the Magellans, Deputy Clarke grabbed the other end. "This group sure did a lot of traveling. Where was this one taken?"

"Madagascar. Dad said we'll go back some day and he'll show me the Tsingy de Bemaraha Strict Nature Reserve. He said it's the most amazing place he's ever been." But even as I said the words, I couldn't imagine him leaving New England again, let alone the country. His adventurous side seemed to have died along with Mom.

Deputy Clarke looked closely at the photograph. "My father moved to Dublin when I was a teenager to take a job as a librarian. When I visited him, I toured around the U.K. Never been to Madagascar, though."

My eyes swept across the dazzling pictures of jungles, deserted beaches, snowcapped mountains, and volcanoes, and I sighed. "I've hardly ever left New England."

Deputy Clarke laughed. "You have your whole life to see the world."

Having rehung the photos—hopefully in the right places—I turned my attention to the antique maps scattered across the table. Deputy Clarke pointed to several with damaged frames. "Damn it, I told the sheriff not to do that. There's no reason to come in here like a bull in a china shop, making people even more upset, yet he always does."

"I'm really not sure people could have been *more* upset," I said as I tried to guess where the reproduction of the *Hereford Mappa Mundi*—the largest medieval map in existence—went. I had loved studying it because it not only included geography, but scenes from mythology, too. I ran my finger over the spirals of the labyrinth—built to contain the Minotaur, a bull-headed, man-eating monster.

Deputy Clarke smiled. "I believe it goes right there." He pointed. "A bit out of your reach. Want me to hang it?"

"Thanks."

"Do you know what the Bradfords were doing in Europe a few years back?" he asked as he straightened it.

"Malcolm was a visiting professor at Trinity, in Ireland, and Richard had just retired, so he went with them."

"Curiously, after Malcolm's tenure was over, the family was scheduled to return home, but they never did. In fact, I can't find a trace of where they were for almost a year. Strange, don't you think?"

I shrugged. "Not really. Dad's whole group of friends liked to travel to remote places." I picked up a map of the British Isles, but the frame came apart in my hands.

Peering over my shoulder, Deputy Clarke cursed under his breath. "That one looks like an antique, too. What a shame. I can take it to be fixed."

"Get the hell out of my house. Now." Griffin loomed in the doorway.

"I was just trying to help clean up," Deputy Clarke said. "I can take whatever was inadvertently broken to be repaired, courtesy of the department."

He left out the part about questioning me, but it was clear from the ferocious look on Griffin's face that he wasn't buying it anyway.

"Inadvertently?" Griffin snorted. "How about you get your hands off my things and get out."

Deputy Clarke folded his arms across his wide chest. "I still need to look at that security footage."

"Follow me," Griffin said through clenched teeth.

Not long after, I heard raised voices from the foyer, followed by the slamming of a door. I went to see what was going on now—half expecting to find Griffin being led away in handcuffs for threatening the police again—but stopped dead in my tracks. Richard and Griffin were alone, and Richard was consoling Griffin.

"Don't worry. It's fine." Richard put his arm around

Griffin's shoulder. "Although I think I lost ten years off my life."

Griffin's entire body seemed to exhale.

Not wanting to interrupt, I returned to the library and carefully laid the maps with the broken frames on the table. Two were reproductions, but the map of the British Isles was an original, dated 1776 and signed by the cartographer. It was itself a piece of art, with beautiful hand-drawn illustrations of ships, sea serpents, and a lute-playing merman. The map was so old the parchment had yellowed and frayed, and some of the letters had faded beyond recognition. I couldn't believe how many small islands there were: Lindisfarne, Isle of Arran, Walney Island, Rathlin Island, Hy-Brasil, Inis Mochaoi . . . there were at least a hundred.

Looking closely, I saw that the frame wasn't broken; the wood just needed to be worked back into place. I pulled on a pair of gloves I found in a tray on the table, and then I cautiously removed the map. After fixing the frame, I laid the map back down and spied faint scribbling on the back. I picked up a magnifying glass from the tray and held it over the small, flowing script.

The Serpent Society has found me. Rest assured, I will never disclose the location of the island. If I do not join you, know that our secret died with me.

Yours always, in life and in death,

Elizabeth

My breath caught in my throat. Next to her name, Elizabeth had drawn the same exact symbol as Dad's tattoo. The paper below it was thin and rough, as if something had been rubbed out.

Who was Elizabeth—was she involved in the occult? What was the Serpent Society? What island?

What kind of secret would be worth dying for?

CHAPTER

I was restacking books when Griffin returned. His shoulders slumped, he collapsed on one of the red leather armchairs flanking the stone fireplace. "They're finally gone. I take it Clarke interrogated you?"

"He asked some questions about your family, but as I haven't seen you in years, there wasn't much I could say."

Griffin narrowed his sharp green eyes. "What questions, exactly?"

While I recited as much of our conversation as I could remember, Griffin rubbed his creased forehead, his frown deepening. When I finished, he let out a long, disgruntled sigh.

"What's wrong with what I said? None of it was exactly top secret," I snapped. "And besides, I couldn't exactly lie to a policeman."

"No, I suppose not." He sounded both defeated and exhausted. "You didn't say anything wrong. I'm not pissed at you; I'm pissed at Clarke. I'm pissed the police barged in here and trashed my house. I'm pissed . . ." Griffin pursed his lips, biting back the words: *I'm pissed my parents are dead.*

Join the club.

Sighing again, Griffin got up to rearrange a few travel photos I had hung in the wrong place. I couldn't help but stare at the eight Magellans smiling on a deserted beach somewhere, their arms all looped around each other, looking so young and happy. They were only a few years older than me at the time. "It's strange that half of the Magellans are dead. It's like they're cursed or something."

Griffin rubbed a thumb over the image of his mother, her light brown hair bleached blonde by the sun, a hundred freckles scattered across her cheeks and nose. "I wish I could blame it all on a curse . . . If only they hadn't disrupted that ancient burial ground or opened that tomb. Then I would have something to blame besides . . ." He swallowed hard. "Your aunt and uncle died because some idiot didn't clean the fireplace properly. It was an accident. Mom and Dad . . . that was, too. A terrible, awful accident." His voice was raw and choked.

Closing my eyes, I took a deep, shuddering breath, trying to push aside thoughts of that dreadful night Mom died. There should be another word for it besides "accident." How can a word used to describe spilled milk also apply to losing the person you loved most in the world?

Griffin walked over to the table, cursing softly as he surveyed the broken frames. "Damn him. These maps are antiques. Dad collected them."

"I think I fixed this frame," I said, pointing, "but check before you hang it. Did you know that there's a creepy note on the back of the map?"

Griffin turned it over and stayed still for a long moment as he stared at the eerie message from Elizabeth. When he finally looked at me, his eyes were cold and hard. "Why did you take an antique map out of its frame? Do you have any idea how valuable it is? Or how delicate?"

"I told you, I was trying to fix it and I was very careful. It's strange, because Elizabeth drew the same symbol as the tattoo. Do you think it has something to do with the occult? Or with that island, Antillia?"

Griffin didn't roll his eyes, but I could tell it was with great effort. "Antillia is a mythical island, so no."

"What's the myth?"

"The legend goes that during the Muslim conquest of Hispania in 714, seven Christian bishops fled to Antillia— an island off the coast of Portugal. Except, of course, it isn't there."

I stared at the message again. "If the symbol is related to a mysterious island near Portugal, why would she put it on a map of the British Isles?"

As he picked up the map, the muscles in Griffin's jaw tightened, accentuating his dimpled chin. "Who knows? The map and note are clearly old, so why do you care so much?"

My hands clenched, I tipped my chin and met his hostile stare. "Who said I care so much? Look, I was just trying to help put things back when I saw the message with the same symbol as the tattoo and thought it was strange. I get that you've hated me since we were little, but back off. I don't want to be here any more than *you* want me here."

Griffin's eyebrows knitted together. "Hate you? I've never hated you."

"Oh, come on. The spiders in the bed?"

A sly grin supplanted his confusion. "Payback for crashing my fishing trip with Zach and Lucas. I couldn't stand it that they'd rather hang out with you than with me."

I shook my head. "That's because you were a brat."

"Yeah, I guess I was." His grin widened. "Is it too late to say I'm sorry? Maybe you'd accept a blanket apology. I'm sorry I was a jerk then, and I'm sorry I've been a jerk since . . ." His smile faded and his face crumpled. He opened his mouth, but what came out was a cross between a sigh and a moan. "Clearly, I'm not handling their deaths well."

Was there a good way to handle losing your parents? I didn't think so.

"Thanks for trying to fix this, but I'm going to have it checked out, just in case."

"Don't forget the other ones," I called after him.

Griffin swiveled his head around. "What?"

"The other broken frames."

"Oh yeah. I'll come back for them."

I found Dad sitting alone in the kitchen, texting someone.

"What the hell was that all about?" I asked. "Griffin totally lost it. I thought he was going to rip the doorjamb off the wall with his bare hands." I walked down the hall to the basement door—once again locked—and gripped the wood, but it wouldn't so much as budge.

Dad put his cell on the counter. "I'm sure he's a bit stronger than you, hon. And I'm not surprised Griffin was upset about the search warrant. How would you have felt if someone went rifling through your mother's things?"

"Not happy, but I'm pretty sure I wouldn't have ripped the molding off the door and threatened a cop. Doesn't it bother you that the police are investigating Griffin? What do you think he's so worried about them finding?"

Tapping his fingers on the marble, Dad finally said, "Listen. Keep this between us, but Richard, Malcolm, Sarah, and Griffin were working on groundbreaking experiments—there's a fully equipped lab in the basement—so of course Richard and Griffin don't want the police, or anyone else, going down there."

"Is that why Malcolm and Sarah were out on the lake—research?"

"Yes." Dad stroked his chin, his expression pained. "*Highly* confidential research. I don't know much about it, but it had something to do with genetics and mutation. I didn't ask for details. Even if I had, they wouldn't have told me. They were concerned about it falling into the wrong hands."

I felt a flicker of foreboding as I poured myself another

mug of coffee. "Are the experiments dangerous?" I looked up at Dad and splashed piping hot coffee over my fingers. "Ouch!"

"Careful, hon." Dad jumped up, turned on the faucet, and ordered me to keep my hand beneath the cool water. "All experiments can be dangerous. Generally, the more complex the experiment is, the higher the risks involved."

As I stared at my bright red fingers, my thoughts turned to Griffin's amputated ones. "Did Griffin injure his fingers in an experiment?"

"No. It happened in Ireland," Dad said as he finished making my coffee—doctoring it with a lot of stevia and a splash of almond milk. "He was riding his bike home in the rain when he was clipped by a car and thrown into a stone wall. The bastard who hit him didn't even stop. Malcolm called me at two in the morning. He was a mess. The doctors didn't think Griffin would make it."

Dad's phone buzzed loudly as it skipped across the counter. He grabbed it, his face set in concentration as he read the message.

"Who are you texting?"

Without looking up, Dad said, "Some of my law enforcement contacts."

Before I could ask a question, Richard raced down the kitchen stairs, his face ashen. "Where's Griffin?" There was a note of panic in his voice.

As I explained about the broken frames, Camila stormed through the French doors, fists clenched and eyes wild, as if ready for a fight. Right behind her was Jack. He was fiddling with a leather rope around his neck, his lips pursed. Seeing Jack—who was usually the jokester of the group—looking so shell-shocked made my stomach quiver, and the sense of foreboding returned.

Dad stood and put his hand on Richard's shoulder, clarifying for everyone that his contacts said it wasn't unusual for the police to get a search warrant since Malcolm and Sarah were very wealthy and had died unexpectedly. Dad wrote—or used to write—the Doctor Dan Danger series, about a forensic investigator, so he knew a thing or two about case work.

Still, no one looked very convinced.

"Don't even get me started on the police," Camila said, scowling. "Our house was broken into a couple of months ago and the police seem to think it's all in my imagination."

"Was anything stolen?" I asked.

"Travel logs," Jack answered. "They didn't touch Camila's jewelry or take any pieces of art, which is why I'm sure it was corporate espionage."

Camila rubbed her arms. "Ever since the break-in, I can't shake the feeling that I'm being watched. Followed. Like I'm a big cat on a game reserve. But when I turn around, no one's there. I hardly go anywhere alone."

Jack put his arm around her waist. "Which is why I barely leave her side. Can't be too careful. Success can draw out the crazies."

There was a pregnant pause as all eyes shifted to me for a beat and then quickly away. I knew what would come next—someone would start talking, often rambling, about something else, hoping I didn't notice Jack's slip. If only people realized it wasn't the casual comments like "crazy" that bothered me, it was how everyone reacted afterward. As expected, Camila immediately started in on the police again, complaining about the sheriff and assuring Richard that she had already spoken to the governor, who promised he'd call the chief of police himself.

I had a strong feeling that the sheriff was going to regret crossing Camila. As I thought about the investigation, I rolled over what Dad had said in my mind again. It explained a lot, but not why the Bradfords had been on the lake in the middle of a cold rainy night. What kind of experiments couldn't wait until morning? One thing was clear from Griffin's reaction: There was much more to the story than he was letting on.

I went upstairs and pulled out my laptop, reading everything I could find on Griffin and his parents. The newspaper articles had little information beyond what Holly had already told me, but there were also posts by cryptozoology bloggers. They had a field day—each one of their pieces was more outlandish than the one before. One blog even alleged that Malcolm was tracking Bigfoot and the creature had killed him.

I crossed the room and pulled back the linen curtain. The view before me was like a scene from a fairy tale: cerulean blue water glistened in the afternoon sun; birds swooped in and out of the trees, warbling to each other; and bountiful hydrangeas spilled their flowers onto the stone steps. But just like in a fairy tale, things weren't what they seemed. I didn't suspect that Richard or Griffin killed Malcolm and Sarah, not for one second, but something just wasn't adding up about the night they died. Something was going on at Bradford Manor, something secret, something dangerous. I could feel it in my bones the way Mom's joints ached when it was about to rain.

Fishing through my bag, I pulled out Holly's card from the pocket of my blazer. Maybe Deputy Clarke couldn't talk about the investigation, but Holly could. I called her and we struck a deal. She'd snoop around and tell me anything she uncovered, and if I found out anything, I'd do the same. I felt a twinge of guilt for betraying Richard and Griffin, but I pushed it aside. I had no choice.

I didn't like Dad being mixed up with whatever the hell was going on, which is why I had to get to the bottom of it.

By dinnertime, the focus had shifted back to the memorial celebration. Richard claimed that Griffin had a migraine, and I wished I'd thought of a similar excuse. I would have much preferred reading in my room than going through the photo albums again. Mom was in many photos—at Malcom and Sarah's wedding, at Griffin's first birthday, at the holiday bash with all the Magellan families, and at the trip we had all taken to Lake Champlain in Vermont to search for Champ, the alleged lake monster.

"Honey, you're white as a ghost," Camila said as she felt my forehead with the back of her hand. "And you're clammy. I think you might have fever."

"I'm fine, but if it's okay, I'm going to sit outside. I need some air."

"Are you sure, hon?" Dad asked, his forehead creasing.

I nodded and forced a smile.

"The alarm code is 2951413," Richard said.

Dad laughed. "Pi backward."

I was holding in so many emotions that I couldn't even manage a smile. Guilt, anger, and sorrow all swirled inside of me, as if I'd swallowed a storm cloud, which was another reason to get outside as soon as possible. Dad deserved to enjoy a night with his friends without worrying about me.

After pushing the numbers into the keypad, I unlocked and unbolted the doors. Sitting down on an uncomfortable iron chair, I pulled my arms around my knees.

"What's wrong?"

I whirled around to see Griffin's cat-like eyes glowing from the other end of the patio. "Nothing."

"Sure." He slid into the chair beside me. "Memory lane pretty much sucks."

"That it does."

He covered his face with his hands. "What a shitty day. First the police, now all this reminiscing."

"I know. I saw some photos of Mom and nearly lost it."

Lifting his head, he stared at me with harrowed eyes. "It's still that hard? It's been . . ."

"Three years," *two months, and seven days*, "and yes, it is." We sat in silence for a few minutes.

"Don't suppose you want to sit by the beach. I could make a fire. And no need to worry, I don't feel well enough to be an ass. Just promise we don't need to talk about my parents or expeditions, or traveling in general for that matter."

I looked in the window at the four Magellans, still gathered around the photos, laughing. They were clearly going to be a while. "Well, how could I refuse such an inviting offer?"

Griffin let out a low laugh. "One sec." He returned with a bag of marshmallows, and we walked down the steps. The moon shone softly through the shredding clouds, bathing the shore in a warm glow. It was so peaceful that I *almost* forgot about what had happened earlier. Instead, I scanned the beach, water, and surrounding woods, and took one last reassuring look back at the house—bright and cheery, like an oversized Christmas ornament.

While Griffin started the fire, I found two perfect roasting sticks. I handed one to him and sat down on an Adirondack chair. The wood was still warm from the sun, and so worn it felt as soft as silk against my skin. I angled my stick over the orange flames that were flickering in the darkness and listened to the water lap rhythmically against the beach, like the percussive beat of the night music. Not to be outdone, a chorus of tree frogs and cicadas joined in, followed by an owl, the lead singer, who called out loud and clear.

"Ah, I see you're a golden-brown toaster," Griffin said, holding up his black charred lump.

"How can you eat that? Yuck!"

He grinned. "I'm not very patient."

I leaned over and handed him mine. "I'll make another. Dad said that you were homeschooled in high school, but you graduated. Are you going to college?"

"I'm going to Bates in the fall. It's about an hour from here. They have a great science department."

"You're into science, too? I guess it runs in the family."

"Family curse," he muttered.

"Why?"

He shrugged.

I figured he was thinking about the experiments that took his parents out to the lake, so I steered the conversation to something safer. "Do you know who your roommate is?"

"I'm commuting."

"Really? You don't want to live at school?"

He leaned back in his chair. "For now, I need to live at home."

"I think it would be good for you. It's easier at boarding school, where everything doesn't remind me of Mom."

He shook his head. "What's good for me doesn't matter. I still need time to . . . figure things out." Despair flitted across his face before he schooled his expression.

"Your parents wouldn't want you to hide from the world," I said softly.

"My parents tried to protect me from the world. There's irony for you," he added bitterly.

"My mom did, too. But they can't protect us from everything." God, I sounded just like Dr. Harrington.

Griffin shook his head again. "You don't understand. And that's a good thing, believe me."

I understood more than he knew.

An awkward silence fell between us. Maybe coming to the beach with him wasn't such a great idea. I was about to get up when Griffin cleared his throat. "Enough about me. So, you're an artist—a painter, according to Richard. What do you paint?"

"Landscapes, usually. Sometimes I paint scenes from

books I love, like *The Lord of the Rings*—although that's a secret," I quickly added.

"Why?"

It was my turn to shrug.

"Well, your secret's safe with me. You're thinking of studying art in college?"

I rotated the marshmallow. "I'm not sure I can. My level of talent depends on who you ask. My art teacher thinks I have potential; my dad thinks I'm the next Monet."

"Potential isn't bad."

"Yeah, it pretty much is. I go to a private school that costs a small fortune. Students are either amazing or they're showing real potential. Parents don't want to spend a pile of money to hear that their kid is average."

Griffin leaned toward me, wearing the same wicked grin he had when he was a kid. "You're not average. You've never been average."

My pulse quickened and about a thousand warning bells went off in my head. Griffin's smile widened as he watched me sitting there, tongue-tied. "Mom collected landscapes, did you know that?"

I shook my head.

"Her favorite ones were by the Hudson River School

artists. Mom was never much into jewelry, so for special occasions Dad usually bought her a painting. She had a few by Cole and Church, and later, Dad bought her a Hopper as an homage to Maine. Would you like to see them?"

I gaped. "They're here—in this house?"

Griffin nodded.

No wonder they had a state-of-the-art security system. "Sure, I'd love it." I took Griffin's outstretched hand, letting him pull me up. He gave me a pleased, mischievous look that was completely disarming. "Wait a sec, this isn't just an iteration of 'would you like to see my etchings,' is it?" I teased.

Griffin cocked his head to the side, watching me intently. "And what if it is? Would you still come?"

Was he kidding back—or was Griffin actually flirting with me? My palms went clammy, including the one he was still holding, and my cheeks burned. A cool breeze blew off the lake. I wished it would sweep me right back into the house and away from this situation.

He held my hand a little tighter. "Well?"

I didn't know whether to laugh it off, leave, or go with him. What did he expect me to do? What did he want me to do? What did he *mean*?

I shook my head at my own foolishness. This was

Griffin, after all. Fish-chasing, spider-catching, annoying Griffin. Of course, he was teasing me.

Laughing, I snatched my hand away and swatted his arm. "You're ridiculous."

"Annabeth, Griffin, you out there?" Dad yelled from the patio. "We're calling it a night and Richard needs to lock up."

"Be right up!" Not a moment too soon. "Rain check on the paintings?"

"I doubt Camila will be marching us up to bed anymore. I can still show them to you tonight. It's barely eleven."

Part of me wanted to go with him. I was surprised to find I was having a good time with Griffin, a very good time, if the funny sensation in the pit of my stomach was any indication. Yet the other part, the stronger part, told me to retreat to my room and read.

"Another time," I said firmly.

"Sure." Griffin turned away, but not before I caught the disappointment in his eyes.

We put out the fire in another awkward silence. I knew without looking that he was watching me, but I kept my gaze fixed on the ground as we walked across the sand to the steps.

"Annabeth?" he said, stopping halfway up the stairs.

"You're wrong about me not wanting you here."

The wind stirred, blowing the hair off his high forehead, and he stared at me expectantly. I thought about telling him that it had been nice to talk to someone who was as heartbroken as I was. That it had felt good to give advice, instead of always being the one to get it. That it felt good—beyond good, *wonderful*—to laugh and flirt with someone who knew me, knew what I'd been through. But I didn't. And the moment drifted away like smoke on the breeze.

CHAPTER *Five*

Thunder roared throughout the night, disturbing my dreams—or rather, my nightmares. I imagined Elizabeth, dressed in the garb of the 1700s, hurrying down a cobblestone street, furtively looking over her shoulder as she mailed the map before disappearing down a foggy alley . . . and then it wasn't Elizabeth at all, but my mother, climbing out of the fog and into her car . . . and each rattle of thunder sounded like someone veering across the lane and smashing into her. In real life, the crash was even louder, the sound reverberating through my body even though I was over a mile away. As soon as I heard it, I somehow knew it was Mom. With each minute that ticked away and she wasn't at the park, I became more and more certain, so much so that by the time I heard the sirens, I was huddled in a ball in the dirt, which is where Dad found me.

Bolting upright, I hugged my knees to my chest and rocked back and forth. I had that all too familiar churning sensation in the pit of my stomach, as if my insides were being twisted into a knot. Unzipping my overnight bag, I retrieved the pillow that Mom had embroidered for me with Christopher Robin's words to Pooh—*You're braver than you believe, and stronger than you seem, and smarter than you think*—the words she had said to me every night before I went to bed for fourteen years—lies, as it turned out—and closed my eyes tightly, trying in vain to force back my traitorous tears.

By the time I woke from my fitful sleep, the storm had passed. Looking out the window, I saw Dad, Richard, Camila, Jack, and Griffin eating breakfast on the patio again. I rubbed my forehead as if I could push away the thoughts that haunted me and surveyed myself in the mirror, scowling at the shadows that rimmed my eyes and my wild hair. Two nights down, one to go. I pulled on my shorts and tank top, attacked my hair with a brush, and made my way outside. After I said hello to everyone, I grabbed a chocolate chip muffin and a coffee and sat in the empty seat between Dad and Camila.

"Will Manuela be coming to the service?" There was a slight quaver in Dad's voice.

I swallowed my grin. Dad was not a fan of Camila's twin. Although the sisters looked exactly alike, personality-wise they couldn't be more different. Whereas Camila chased her ambitions as the head of a successful biotech company, Manuela spent her days either on the golf course or searching for husband number four. One suggestive look from Manuela and Dad turned scarlet and fumbled over his words.

Camila laughed. "No need to panic, Sam. Manuela's at a golf tournament my company's sponsoring for Rescue the Rainforest. She wanted to come, but I needed a board member there. I've heard from so many of our college friends . . ."

As I drank my coffee, I tuned out the conversation about the memorial service and listened to the soothing pitter-patter of last night's raindrops being shaken from the tree canopy by the breeze. Although it was morning, it was already warm, and the waves sparkled in the sun like broken pieces of glass scattered across the pavement.

"Annabeth?" Dad said gently. "Are you listening?"

Everyone was staring at me. "Sorry."

Richard smiled sadly. "I was just saying that I had a statue commissioned to mark the spot where they drowned. I thought we could take the boat over there before everyone gets here."

Camila tucked her long dark hair behind her ears. "I'd love to see it."

"You all go ahead without me," Griffin said.

Camila leaned across the table and put her hand over Griffin's. I couldn't help but stare at his fingers. He must have seen a plastic surgeon because he bore no scars at all—the skin was completely smooth. "We can go another time, sweetheart," Camila said.

"I'll be fine. Really. You all go."

Camila shook her head resolutely. "I am not leaving you here alone."

"I'll stay," I offered.

"You sure, hon?" Dad said.

I nodded. As the four of them headed to the dock, I tried not to think about how small the group was, how quiet it was without the others.

Griffin poured himself a glass of water, tossed back a couple of pills, and then refilled my coffee cup.

Inhaling the strong, rich scent, I smiled at him in a

gesture of thanks. "Do you own the whole lake?"

Griffin leaned back and took another swig of water. "Yup. It's a glacial lake."

"And all the woods around it?"

"Up to the town campground to the east"—he jerked his head to the right—"and the conservation land at the base of the mountain. The mountain was a ski resort, but the lodge burned down and it went out of business a long time ago."

I had never been on the lake in June without the sound of summer humming in my ear. It was undeniably peaceful, but I missed the shrieks of laughter, the roar of motors, and the crisp snapping of sails in the wind. "As a kid, I didn't realize how isolated your house was. Living in the middle of the woods like this would freak me out. Especially in the winter."

"The lake and the forest are beautiful all year, but especially in winter. If I recall," he said, his mouth curling slightly, "you used to pretend it was Narnia."

I laughed. "With the whole gang here over the holidays, it sure wasn't quiet. Didn't you use to have a house in Portland, though? Why did you move up here year-round?"

He looked away. "Dad retired from teaching when we

got home from Europe, and this is closer to the hospital."

"The experiments he was working on, was that for a company or just his own research?"

The muscles in Griffin's square jaw throbbed. "You don't need to stay and babysit," he said roughly. "Or quiz me."

The sudden shift—in his tone, in his expression—jangled me. Maybe I shouldn't have mentioned the experiments. I certainly didn't mean to bring up hurtful subjects, but he didn't need to lash out at me either. I wasn't going to let him get away with treating me like he did when we were kids, like *I* was the one who was a pain in the ass. "Seriously? Neither of us wanted to go on that boat ride. Staying here with you was just a convenient excuse, and frankly, you're not that interesting, so don't flatter yourself."

Griffin's eyes darkened as he pushed his index fingers into his temples. "Excuse me. I feel a migraine coming on."

"Funny, I do, too, and I don't even get them."

He stormed into the house.

Now suddenly alone, I lost the struggle with my dark thoughts and they pushed their way to the surface: If it weren't for me, Mom would be here with her friends. I took deep, steadying breaths and focused on the mundane—one of the strategies Dr. Harrington and I had developed. I was rubbing my charms while running through Latin declensions when my phone vibrated loudly on the wrought-iron table. I assumed it was Dr. Harrington. Other than Dad, he was the person who texted me about ninety-nine percent of the time. But it was Holly, and she wanted to meet at the campground. I jotted down a quick note to Dad, explaining I was going there to paint.

The beach at the campground was bustling with families. Kids were swimming and splashing, and the lake, much smaller than the one at Bradford Manor, was filled with boaters. While I waited for Holly, I pulled out the box of art supplies I kept in the car and tried to capture the gorgeous day. The sun shone down brightly from the cloudless sky, turning the water a clear cobalt. In the right-hand corner of my canvas I added a sailboat gliding along the waves and in the background, distant mountains presided like guards over the valley.

When I finished, I took a step back and examined it. It was perfect—absolutely perfect—like a postcard in a souvenir shop. It had no soul. I was about to toss it in the rusty blue pail by the picnic table when Holly called out to me.

"Why are you throwing that out? It's beautiful!" She bent down to get a closer look.

I shook my head. "It's garbage. It looks like a greeting card."

"If you're going to throw it away, can I have it?"

I clutched the edge a little tighter, really wanting to say no, and my charm bracelet clinked against the canvas.

"Oooh, I love your bracelet. You have so many charms."

"It was my mother's. Dad bought her most of them. I never take it off."

"Are your parents divorced, too?"

"No." As the silence seemed to stretch on and on, I cleared my throat. "My mother died."

"Oh. Sorry." She shifted her weight uncomfortably, her Birkenstocks crunching in the pine needles. I was used to that. "How did she—?"

"I can't stay long. The memorial celebration is later this afternoon," I said, interrupting her before she could finish. I was quite sure she didn't really want to know how Mom died.

"I can't, either. It's a Mom weekend and I'm grounded for one goddamn C. I kept telling my mother that I was having a hard time with trig, but did she listen? Noooo. 'Just try harder, Holly.' I mean, do you think that's fair? I tried my hardest."

"It seems pretty harsh."

"And my stepbrothers and stepsisters—all straight A's. Which makes me a constant source of disappointment to my mother."

I wondered if Mom and I would have fought if she were still alive. If I would have been a disappointment to her. Frowning, I pushed those thoughts aside and held on to the way I always pictured it—the pair of us shopping, watching movies, and going out for lunch. In my imagination, she was my best friend and confidant.

Holly plopped down on the mottled brown bench. "She even took my phone. As if with no phone to keep me busy I'm going to do friggin' math in the summer. I mean, have your parents—father—ever taken your phone?"

Shaking my head, I sat across from her. Although to be fair, I hadn't done anything that warranted punishment in over three years. How could I? The last time I broke the rules—three years, two months, and eight days ago—the punishment was swift, severe, and without mercy.

"So then how do you have your phone?" I asked, watching Holly Google something.

She flashed a self-satisfied grin. "Investigative reporter, remember? I know all her hiding places. If you give me that painting, I'll have a contingency plan, too. If she realizes

I snuck out, I'll have the perfect excuse. Tomorrow's her birthday and she will love it."

"A painting for information is a fair trade. What do you have?"

Holly's eyes lit up as she opened her notebook. "So, Dad's convinced Griffin wasn't sleeping when their boat sank, as he claimed. He's sure Griffin and Richard both know why they were out on the lake—and Dad's convinced the reason involves Griffin somehow—like maybe he was trying to leave Bradford Manor and they were trying to stop him."

I rested my chin on my palm. "Why would he think that?"

"About a year ago, some kids were playing with their father's rifle and a little boy got shot. Dad was the first on the scene and followed the ambulance to the hospital, where he ran into Dr. Bradford. They got to talking about the shooting, then about Mom's cancer and how hard it was to watch someone you love suffer. Dr. Bradford explained that she had to keep Griffin isolated due to some medical issues, which wasn't easy, but she'd do anything to protect him. At the time, Dad thought maybe he had an immune disorder or something, but now he's convinced that Griffin's dangerous—volatile—and the Bradfords kept him locked up to keep him from hurting anyone."

After the way Griffin reacted to the search warrant, I could hardly blame the sheriff for thinking Griffin was volatile.

"An entire year the family was off the radar—no one has any idea where they were, and Richard and Griffin refuse to say," Holly continued. "Dad and Deputy Clarke are wondering if Griffin was hospitalized somewhere. They're hoping the documents will uncover something—like a psychiatric disorder, or what meds Griffin is given, stuff like that."

I was quiet for a moment as I considered this. If Griffin was hospitalized for a psychiatric disorder, wouldn't Dad have told me? Which brought me to a disturbing question: Did Griffin know *all* about my past? I hoped he didn't. It wasn't that I was ashamed or embarrassed, well, not entirely . . . it was the way people treated me once they knew.

"So, what did you find out?" Holly asked.

"Richard, Malcolm, Sarah, and Griffin were working on groundbreaking experiments," I said softly, as if whispering the words would make me feel less like a traitor. "That's why the Bradfords were on the lake in the middle of the night."

Holly threaded the pencil through a coil of her copper

hair and pushed it behind her ear. "Really? What kind of experiments?"

I shrugged. If Richard, Sarah, and Malcolm were so worried about their discoveries falling into the "wrong hands," then the sheriff's daughter was the last person I should be telling about this.

Holly steepled her hands, her eyes hooded in thought. "Interesting. Hmmm. I dug up everything I could on both Dr. and Mr. Bradford. Mr. Bradford wrote a college thesis that was presented at a couple of cryptozoology conferences years ago. He said it formed the basis for his life's work. Have you seen it? The title was 'Myth, Legend, or Fact.'"

I shook my head. "I did some research, too, and I didn't see anything about that."

"I work for a newspaper, remember? I have access to things you could only dream about." Tapping her pencil against the picnic table, Holly sighed. "I'd love to get my hands on it—it might hold a clue as to what type of experiments he was doing. So until we know more, let's focus on Griffin. Maybe he had some kind of violent outburst and killed his own parents?"

"No way. Griffin's devastated by their deaths." One thing I was was an expert on was grief, and I was absolutely certain Griffin wasn't faking.

"Maybe it was an accident? Maybe the guilt is killing him. It can eat away at a person, you know," Holly said nonchalantly as she brushed her curls off her freckled shoulder.

Clearly, she didn't know. Not at all.

When I didn't say anything, Holly quirked an eyebrow at me. "I get that he's totally gorgeous and all, but I hope you're not falling for him."

I shook my head—adamantly, this time. "No worries there. I'm not looking for a boyfriend or anything close to one."

"Still reeling from the last one?" Holly laughed. "Believe me, I get it."

She so didn't. My last boyfriend, Bobby, was only a year older than me, although he seemed far more mature. First real kiss, check. First drink—straight vodka out of a water bottle—check. First cigarette—check. Mom was onto him, though, and wouldn't let me see him anymore after she caught us smoking pot in my tree house. It was Bobby who had convinced me to sneak out that fateful night, though to be honest, he didn't have to try that hard. Turns out, he wasn't so bad after all. He came to both the wake and the funeral and called me over and over again, but I never answered. His tousled blond hair and deep brown eyes used to make me feel like there was a hummingbird fluttering around inside of my stomach, but after Mom died, the sight of him made me nauseous. Every time I looked at his face, all I could think about was the fact that Mom had spent her last hour on earth worried sick about me, while I had spent it blissfully making out with Bobby.

"Boys suck. Especially the hot ones," Holly said, shoving her notebook in her back pocket. "My friend's family owns Burkes—they do party rentals and stuff—and they're setting up a tent and tables for the memorial. Since they were short-handed, my friend asked if I wanted to help serve. In addition to getting me out of the house since responsibility is good for me," Holly said in a mock serious voice, "it's also a perfect opportunity for snooping at Bradford Manor. I'll see you later today."

"Okay."

Holly started to get up, then sat back down, chewing on her bottom lip and adjusting her glasses. "Annabeth, maybe I'm wrong, but do me a favor and be careful at Bradford Manor. Stay away from Griffin. He's not the kid I used to know. He changed in Europe. Something's not right about him."

CHAPTER *Six*

My thoughts were scattered as I drove back to Bradford Manor. Was it possible that Griffin was involved somehow in his parents' deaths? If so, why would Richard protect him? He wouldn't, I was sure of it. Besides, he'd never invite us all to stay if he was worried about Griffin hurting someone.

I parked and walked across the lawn, past an alabaster fountain depicting three Muses with water gurgling from their hands, and around the back toward the patio. A minute later Griffin joined me, holding a bright pink cardboard box. I found myself staring at him, as if being unstable would leave a mark. You'd think I'd know better.

"Hey, I'm really sorry I was a jerk. Again. I'm going to have to get used to talking about my parents." He cleared his throat. "Anyway, I couldn't help but notice you drink about a gallon of coffee a day, so . . ." He put the box on the table and held out a plastic cup. "I bring you a peace offering. There's a bakery that makes amazing coconut iced coffee and I remembered that you love coconut. I also bought a box of brownies and cookies. You can't have changed that much."

But I had. My love of sweets was about all I had in common with that girl. My gaze shifted from the coffee to his face—he was looking at me with teasing green eyes and a lopsided grin, his forehead free of the creases that customarily squiggled across it—and he suddenly looked like the fourteen-year-old boy that I had known so well. But he wasn't. He couldn't be that boy any more than I could be that girl.

"Thanks, but I'm not hungry." I took the coffee and walked toward the house.

"Wait. Please."

Something about the way his voice cracked when he said *please* made me stop and turn around.

Tucking his thumbs in the pockets of his striped khaki shorts, Griffin looked at me sheepishly. "You don't like me very much. I get it. Hell, I don't really like me very much. Since they died, I'm not the same person." He blew out a long whistle of a breath. "Sometimes I don't even recognize myself."

There was something familiar about his expression—a sadness behind his smile, and I realized it was the same image I saw in the mirror—the markings of a fellow inhabitant of the land of *since*. Just like that, my anger evaporated. I had no right to judge him.

I sat down at the table, opened the box, and picked up a gooey brownie.

Griffin sat beside me. "I know it's hard for Richard, being stuck with me, but if he tells me one more time that I'm not acting like myself, I swear I'm going to lose it. How can I joke around, practice lacrosse, and scream at the television when they're dead? I couldn't give a shit if a bad call costs the Bruins a game."

"I know the feeling." Before the accident, I had been social. Since, not so much. Dad was always making subtle—and not so subtle—comments to that effect, and my old friends clearly preferred Annabeth-*before*. Would I always be measured against her and found lacking? Sometimes it felt like I had a twin sister who disappeared, and everyone wanted her to come back and wanted me to vanish. But when I tried to vanish, they wouldn't let me.

Griffin ran a hand through his dark hair, sweeping it off his prominent brow. "If you give me another chance, I'll try not to be an ass. Although," he said, smiling at me shyly, "I'm afraid I can't make any promises."

I took a big bite out of the double chocolate brownie—it was delicious—and smiled back. "I'll make sure to let you know when you mess up. And that *is* a promise."

Griffin threw his head back and laughed and I couldn't help but join him. He laughed so rarely that when he actually did, it was special. Then I realized that I never laugh, either. I used to laugh all the time, at least a dozen times a day, but since Mom died, I probably only laughed a dozen times a month, maybe a dozen times a year.

As Griffin talked about college and how much he was looking forward to being with people who didn't know about his parents or what had happened, I found it hard to believe what Holly had told me about the guy sitting next to me.

"So, why were you homeschooled when you returned from Europe?" I asked.

The smile disappeared from his face. "A few reasons. The public school isn't great and Mom didn't want me to board somewhere. I was hit by a car"—his eyes flashed to his injured hand for a beat—"and now I have to be careful about infections and stuff. I also get bad headaches, from the concussion."

I was relieved at the simple explanation as to why his mother kept him isolated. Yet I wondered why he didn't tell me that last night, when I asked him about living in the dorms. "Is that what you need to figure out before you can live at school?"

Picking up an oversized chocolate chip cookie, Griffin opened and shut his mouth in a series of false starts. "It's complicated."

"Oh." I hated it when people pried into my health issues, so I let it go at that.

"Did Deputy Clarke ask about my homeschooling?" Griffin's voice was flat, but I could see the accusation in his eyes.

"No, he didn't," I said, bristling.

Sighing, Griffin rubbed his forehead. "Sorry. It's a knee-jerk reaction at this point."

I quirked an eyebrow at him.

"The suspicion. You wouldn't believe how many people have struck up conversations with me, only to try to get information. I barely leave the house anymore."

Guilt twisted like a knot in my stomach and I was glad I hadn't told Holly any more than I did.

Shielding his eyes from the sun, Griffin looked out at the lake. "They're about to dock. I told Richard I'd bring down a cooler."

"I'll help."

Under Suzette's watchful eye, we packed a cooler full of drinks and snacks and carried it to the wide crescent beach, which was already decked out with chairs, umbrellas, and towels. It made the town beach look like a sandbox.

I sat on a chair beside Camila and Jack, who were sharing a chaise lounge. As Jack rubbed sunscreen on Camila's back and arms, I saw the small scar on her upper arm where the tattoo had been and thought about the map. "How did you guys figure out the tattoo was a symbol for the occult?"

Camila absentmindedly ran her finger over the phantom symbol. "Soon after we returned from the expedition, Malcolm came across it in his research. I had just started my company, and I needed to go to so many formal functions in evening dresses. I thought it was better not to have a mark associated with the occult on my shoulder. Besides, I was tired of explaining it."

Her voice had a ring of truth, but her glance at Jack

indicated there was more to the story.

"I love your necklace," I said, pointing to a gold locket with an intricate Celtic knot as the clasp. "Aunt Kathy had the same one."

Almost reverently, Camila ran a finger over the dull, mellowed gold. "A very good friend we met traveling gave them to me, Sarah, and Kathy as gifts. They were my dearest friends. I miss them so much, especially on days like this. They should be here. Your mom, too." Camila's soft voice quavered.

She should. Blinking back tears, I quickly excused myself. I couldn't do it anymore . . . it was all too much. Grabbing *The Mists of Avalon* from my room, I plopped down on the smaller section of the patio on the other side of the sunroom, hoping to go unnoticed. No such luck. I had only read a couple of chapters when Dad sat beside me. "I never get tired of that view."

I looked up from the page. Thin silver clouds wrapped around the sky, stealing the warmth of the sun. The lake was still and gray and desolate. I suddenly had the urge to paint it.

"You okay, hon? Want to talk about anything?"

"I'm fine, Dad. How are you doing?"

Putting his arm around my shoulder, Dad gave me a sad smile. "Terrible. I miss Malcolm and Sarah so much. But I'm lucky to be going through it with people I love. It helps." He planted a kiss on top of my head. "Everyone's headed in to get ready for the memorial celebration, so I guess I better shower. Can I get you anything? You didn't have much for breakfast."

"I'm all set. But I still need four more pieces for my portfolio, and the light on the water is calling to me." Not to mention that when I painted or read, the real world sort of faded away.

"Once you're done applying to schools, I'd love a painting of the lake."

"You got it." With my watercolors in tow, I headed down to the now empty beach. My fingers swept across the paper, and the amorphous mist that hovered over the lake sprang to life as a dragon skating across the water. I was just about to paint a boat with Merlin at the helm when I stopped myself. If Dad saw it, he would worry and watch me constantly for some misstep, some indication that I was losing it again. For no reason. I didn't agree with Dr. Harrington's assertion that I relied on fantasy worlds to avoid dealing with my grief in the real world. I'd tried to explain to him a dozen times that I'd always loved fantasy and mythology—it was a passion Mom and I had shared. Sometimes when I painted scenes from the stories she and I had loved so much, I did feel closer to her. And I wasn't going to let anyone take that away from me. I had already lost enough.

I held my breath as I heard someone walk down the stone steps, but it was only Griffin.

"Wow. I can't believe you just painted that," he said. "It's amazing. I love how you play with shadow and light. The fog looks almost alive. It reminds me of a place, a place that's special to me." Griffin stood transfixed, a far-off look in his eyes.

"You can have it if you want. It's not good enough for my portfolio." Besides which, I'd have to hide it from Dad, but he didn't need to know about that.

"Really? Thanks." His words were casual, but he stared at me as if I'd just given him a Renoir. "Your father wanted me to tell you that everyone will be here soon. I need to pull out the kayaks and canoes for the party. Can hardly wait."

I looked down at my paint-splattered shirt. "I guess I better change. Look, if it gets unbearable, find me, and we can sneak off somewhere for a break, okay?"

His furrowed brow softened. "Thanks."

As I darted up the steps, Richard called to me, asking for help mounting a photo collage to a long lattice wall that had been erected on one side of the patio. While I fastened a picture of the Magellans hamming it up on top of a volcano, I noticed that Camila, Kathy, and Sarah had the tattoos, but they weren't wearing the necklaces. I scanned the many pictures and found that in the ones taken after the expedition, none of them had tattoos, but each of them had the gold link chain encircling their necks.

In every single photo. That was strange.

By the time I changed into a sundress and came back downstairs, the first of the guests had arrived. Under the guise of being helpful, I was continually in motion—clearing, fetching, replenishing—basically doing anything to avoid being sucked into conversations that involved Mom. Too bad avoidance wasn't a class—or better yet, an AP exam—I would ace it. Holly was busy trying in vain to please Suzette, so I brought her a plate of cookies and an iced tea.

She finished off the drink in a few gulps. "Thanks.

Looks like I won't be doing much snooping. Do me a favor and search for that college thesis, okay?"

"Sure." I did want to read Malcolm's paper for my own information, just to be absolutely certain there was nothing in there that could make me worry for Dad. But I had no intention of ever showing it to Holly. I felt bad misleading her, I really did. She wasn't like my peers, who talked incessantly about college applications, as if their lives would be ruined if they didn't get into the right school. It took all my self-control not to roll my eyes at lunch. I knew what destroyed lives, and that wasn't it. In many ways, Holly and I were opposites. I was fighting to get through each day, while she was fighting for the big future she wanted for herself, and I admired her tenacity. At the same time, I couldn't help but wonder where Holly's line was—what she wouldn't sacrifice to get there. I couldn't let it be Griffin and Richard. Besides, if Dad was convinced the experiments should be kept from the police, it was good enough for me.

Holly went back to work, and I ducked into the library. As I crossed the worn carpet, embroidered with faded scrolling leaves and vines in autumnal shades of red, gold, and ochre, I wondered where Malcolm would put his thesis. A long line of bookcases housed the reference titles, so that's where I started. Then I tried the alcove, where the nonfiction materials were kept. After climbing the oak ladder, I slid it slowly across the rail, lightly running my fingers along the bindings until something caught my eye: a maroon hardcover that looked like a book at first glance, but it didn't have an author or a publisher on the binding, only "Independent Study, BIOL" in faded gold letters. I opened it, and beneath the thesis information, was the title: "Myth, Legend, or Fact."

My fiery excitement faded to ash as my thoughts turned to Dad. He was so happy with his friends, more relaxed than I had seen him in years. I hoped there was nothing in this paper to make me worried about him hanging out at Bradford Manor.

I climbed down, and sitting on one of the ladder rungs, I flipped through the pages. Although the chapter headings looked interesting—"Lake Monsters," "Aonbharrs" (which, from the illustration, appeared to be water horses), "Sasquatch," and so on—it was actually very dry and scientific, with endless pages on the evolution of prehistoric animals. Clearly, this had nothing to do with the experiments. I was about to shut it when I came to the chapter titled, "Mythical Islands of Atlantis, Antillia, and Hy-Brasil."

Strange. Hy-Brasil was on the map with the weird message from Elizabeth, so why did Malcolm refer to it as mythical? Intrigued, I read the summary:

The phantom island of Hy-Brasil takes its name from the Irish "Uí Breasail," meaning descendants of Breasal, the High King of the World in Celtic mythology. Hy-Brasil first appeared on maps as early as 1325, when the Genovese cartographer Angelino de Dalorto placed it to the west of Ireland. Both Saint Barrind and Saint Brendan reported finding Hy-Brasil on their respective voyages in the tenth century, and in 1674, Captain John Nisbet claimed that he and his crew spent a day on the island. After 1865, the island appeared on few maps since its location couldn't be verified. Many myths and legends surround the island: that the roads are paved with gold, that the Fountain of Youth is located there, and that the inhabitants are immortal.

Now that was interesting. Pulling out my phone, I looked up Hy-Brasil to see if there was anything more recent, but there wasn't much else besides legends, including a far-fetched one involving aliens and the coordinates to a UFO.

I went back to the paper, eager to learn more about the next island, Antillia. It was fascinating stuff. The legend went that seven Christian bishops, along with their parishioners, escaped the invading Muslims by settling on Antillia, where they established seven cities. In 1475, King Afonso V of Portugal actually granted the seven cities to the knight Fernão Teles. By the 1490s, there were rumors that silver was threaded through the island's sands. But Malcolm made no reference to the symbol of Antillia—the one that they all had tattooed on their arms.

I was scanning the footnotes when someone snatched the book out of my hands.

CHAPTER *Seven*

"What are you doing with my father's thesis?" Griffin demanded. "You told me that you don't even like science."

"I don't. I was looking for a book and when I saw that this one was written by your father, my curiosity was piqued," I blurted out quickly, which was what I always did when I lied. "Then I came across a chapter on mythical islands. Malcolm wrote about Hy-Brasil being mythical, but it's on the map you brought to be fixed."

"Hy-Brasil was often found on maps until the mid-eighteen hundreds."

"I know, I looked it up. I read about Antillia, too, but there was no mention of the symbol."

Griffin threw his hands up in the air, one still holding the thesis. "Here we go again with the questions. Too bad Dad's dead, otherwise you could've asked him about it."

His voice was as sharp as his expression. "This is the only copy we have, and you could have damaged it. It should be in the temperature-controlled case." His eyes flashed to an expanse of paneling. Only then did I notice a small tarnished brass keyhole in one of the grooves.

"So put it there. And you know what? Maybe you could pull off bratty and spoiled when you were an adorable ten-year-old, but now, it just makes you a jerk. So, I guess you were right. You can't stop being an ass."

I whipped around, and with my hands balled into fists at my side, marched outside where I ran right into Richard, who asked me to get some paddles for the canoe.

"One more day," I muttered under my breath as I stomped down the steps. One more day, then it was back to school, my safe haven.

Unlike the main house—a gorgeous combination of stone, shingles, and glass—the boathouse was made of knotty cedar, inside and out, and was somewhat rickety looking. As I crossed the threshold, I shuddered at the thought of all the spiders that probably called this decrepit building home. Inside, an air of neglect clung to each wooden board. Blinking rapidly so my eyes adjusted to the darkness, I leaned against a post and looked around.

Sunlight streamed through gaps in the roof, making a checkerboard pattern on the floor. To the right was a magnificent—albeit grimy—sailboat, and along the perimeter were shelves overflowing with water skis, oars, life jackets, and a large assortment of water toys.

"Clearly, I come from a long line of pack rats."

Whirling around, I found Griffin standing in the doorway, his hands folded behind his back. I banged my head against the post. Why couldn't he just leave me alone?

"You're right. I'm acting like an ass again. I'm sure you're tired of hearing my excuses, but listening to everyone say how sorry they are . . ." Frowning, Griffin raked a hand through his hair. When he continued, his voice was soft and tight. "I couldn't take it anymore, so I went looking for you. Seeing his paper was like a knife in my gut. I didn't read it until after he died. Can you believe it? I always assumed there'd be plenty of time. Now, I have so many questions about the places he visited, his research and theories, and no one to ask."

I shuttered my thoughts, refusing to think about all the things I'd never be able to ask Mom, all the advice she'd never give me. The cluttered boathouse suddenly seemed even smaller and I began to feel claustrophobic.

"Anyway, sorry—once again. Did you have this hard a time coping?"

All I could do was nod. After Mom died, I painted her over and over again. It was always the same: Mom sitting at the bookstore, sipping a cappuccino—our Saturday morning routine. In my paintings, the seat next to her was empty. Until one day I joined her. The next thing I remembered was waking up not in my room but at McLean.

What no one knew was that I still had one of the paintings. It was hidden in my room, wrapped tightly in thick brown paper and taped shut with duct tape, and it had been there for two years. The painting was dangerous—like a smoker's last cigarette, stashed away allegedly as a sign of what she'd overcome, but really it was there just in case.

Just in case.

"Peace offering number two." Griffin held out a handful of pink peonies. "Are they still your favorite?"

"How did you know?"

"You always buried your face in the peonies. I remember when you got stung by a bee on the tip of your nose."

Despite myself, I smiled. "I remember you laughing."

"It was funny, watching you shriek and holler and flap your arms." Griffin twirled around like a drunken ballerina.

Laughing, I smacked his arm. "I did not look like that!"

"Did so."

I leaned toward the flowers that were still in Griffin's hand and then pulled back, wiggling an eyebrow at him.

"What? Don't you trust me?" The corners of his lips tugged up in a sly smile. "I checked each stem for bees, I swear."

As he handed me the bouquet, his fingers brushed against my palm, and a shiver danced across my skin. Blood rushed to my face, so I quickly looked down at the blooms and inhaled the fragrance—rich and rosy, with a hint of citrus. "Thank you."

Griffin took a step closer to me, but I retreated. Being with him was simultaneously too easy and too hard. He was easier to talk to about some things than anyone I knew. Not only had we known each other forever, but he knew what I was going through. He understood how I felt. Yet I didn't want to feel. Numbness had long been my ally, my heart's guard. I cleared my throat. "I need to find some paddles. Do you know where they are?"

"There." Without tearing his eyes from mine, Griffin pointed to a shelf behind me, leaning closer as he did. Swallowing hard, I sidestepped around an oar and reached for the paddles, tripping on an uneven floorboard in the process. I went flying into the post, cutting my arm on a nail. Somehow, Griffin grabbed me by the waist right before I hit the ground. As he pulled me into him, my back to his chest, I was very aware of his bare arms around me.

"You're bleeding, and that nail is pretty rusty," Griffin said as he slowly released me. Rummaging around in a drawer, he produced a dusty first aid kit. With feather-light touches, he wiped my skin with an antiseptic wipe. "Am I hurting you?" he asked without looking up.

"No." My voice was dry and hoarse.

He was quiet as he kept his attention on the cut, gently rubbing antibiotic cream on the scratch, before laying a piece of gauze across it and taping it. "All set."

"Thanks." I looked down at his thumb and finger still encircling my wrist and felt my face burn, which was annoying, as I wasn't someone who easily blushed. The heat of the boathouse had to be the culprit.

"You're welcome. Hopefully, you won't need another tetanus shot. I still feel guilty about the last one."

"You should, but I was ten when you chased after me with that dead fish, so I'm good for another three years."

"In my defense, I was only goofing around. I didn't

think you'd fall off the dock. Then everyone was mad at me. Lucas punched me in the stomach, Dad lectured me, and Mom called me a holy terror."

"Holy terror." I laughed. "That just about sums you up."

Looking at me from beneath dark lashes, he flashed that wicked grin again. As he ran a thumb along the inside of my wrist, I wondered if it was the air—which suddenly seemed stifling—my claustrophobia, or, and I hated to even think it, Griffin himself that was making me feel off-kilter.

A pair of dripping wet, sunburned tweens—dragged here by their parents for the memorial celebration, no doubt—burst through the door, looking for the paddles and bringing me to my senses. It was definitely the heat.

I left Griffin to help the boys and hurried outside, in desperate need of fresh air. Griffin was soon behind me, but thankfully, Richard called him over to say goodbye to some people from the hospital. Griffin groaned, then lightly touched the back of my hand. "I'll come and find you later, okay?"

I nodded, though it would be a lot easier if he didn't. When I was with Griffin, my emotions played hopscotch. It was hard to be the even-keeled, level-headed person I had forced myself to become three years, two months, and eight days ago. I would not let my emotions rule me again—not ever.

"And Annabeth? I am really glad you're here." Griffin's green eyes were wide, his shy smile utterly disarming.

I'd only come to Bradford Manor to support Dad. I didn't want to be here. That's what I kept telling myself. But then why, as Griffin held my gaze, did it feel as if I'd swallowed a dragonfly?

"Griffin!" Richard called again.

"I really need to go," Griffin said, though he didn't move.

I inhaled a deep breath. "Yeah. You should. I'll see you later."

Despite myself, I watched him walk away.

As soon as I was on the patio, Jack pulled me over to meet some people. As usual, he was telling a funny story—this one about how much he couldn't stand Camila when they first met. "We were in bio together, and man, she was an insufferable know-it-all. Always in the library. She made more than a few comments implying I bought my way into the school, which wasn't entirely wrong, but still rude." He paused, and everyone laughed. "Then, she reported me and Paul to the RA for being loud, for having parties, for drinking." He shook his head. "So one night, I bang on her door, all ready to tell her off, and she says, 'Well, finally. I was wondering when I was going to get invited to one of your parties. And I'm Cuban, so there better be rum. Lots of it.'"

"What did you say to that?" a woman asked.

"Nothing. She slammed the door before I could say a word. I did, however, go out and buy copious amounts of rum. I think I might have proposed that night."

Camila came up behind him, her arms around his waist. "You did. I had to turn you down, because at the time, I had a thing for my TA."

Dad joined the group, and soon the conversation shifted to when Mom came to visit Aunt Kathy during their senior year, and Dad made a fool of himself, following after her like a puppy.

And that was my cue to leave. Slipping away, I made a beeline for the library. Oddly, the pocket door was mostly closed. Chalking it up to some of the little hellions who had been running around, I slid it back and stepped inside. It took several seconds for my eyes to adjust. The thick velvet curtains were drawn, casting the room in shadow. I flicked the switch, and by the light of the chandeliers, I saw someone lying on the rug in a fetal position.

Griffin gasped. "Please turn that off."

"Are you all right?" *Stupid question, Annabeth.* I flipped off the light, raced across the rug, and knelt beside him. Even by the dim light that seeped between the drapes, I could see his face contorted in pain. "What is it? What should I do?"

"Bad. Migraine," he choked out. "Get Richard. Now."

"Okay." I tiptoed from the room, then darted outside. I ran around frantically, until I found Richard on the beach with Camila. As I told them about Griffin, Richard clapped a hand over his mouth, while Camila inhaled a sharp breath and clutched Richard's arm. Then they both shot up the steps. From their reaction, I had a feeling that Griffin's condition was a lot worse than he let on.

"Annabeth," Dad called. "We need a fourth for corn hole!"

I hesitated. Physically, Griffin was so strong—I hated to think of the amount of pain he must be in. The muscles in my legs were restless, ready to bolt up the steps. But what could I do? Would Griffin even want me there? If the situation were reversed, I'd just want Dad. With a long look over my shoulder at the house, I crossed the beach and grabbed a beanbag.

Richard and Camila returned for the clambake, but apparently Griffin was still resting. Richard assured me he was doing much better, but worry clouded his blueberry eyes.

"Should I check on him? Or bring him some dinner?" I asked.

He shook his head adamantly. "No. He'll be down soon. I'm sure of it."

He didn't sound all that sure.

Jack was telling me stories about Lucas and Zach's latest escapades when Holly came over with a tray of dessert. "Any luck with the paper?" she said under her breath.

I almost choked on my cannoli. "It's been so busy I haven't had a chance to look yet."

"You can say that again. I think I'll be here until dawn, cleaning."

"I'll help." It seemed a fair penance for lying.

While we boxed the plates and cups, she complained about going to her mom's that night; she far preferred staying with her dad. Not only was Holly a computer whiz, but apparently she had an uncanny ability to get people to talk to her, so she helped the sheriff with his police work, which she loved, and he didn't nag her about homework or curfews or much else for that matter. Her mother expected her to be perfect like her stepsiblings—all four of whom were top of their class and athletic.

"Now that Nik's going to college—Dartmouth, naturally, like the rest of the family—even my stepfather is breathing down my neck about my college apps." She clanged the last plate in the crate and snapped the lid shut. "Is your father bugging you?"

"Not really," I answered, wiping the sweat off my brow with the back of my hand.

"Lucky."

Not really. Dad was careful to avoid stressing me out too much, so he nagged in very small doses, which I found even more annoying.

"Thanks so much for helping me."

I wasn't being entirely altruistic. Helping Holly clean up kept me from having Mom conversations, reminiscing, and looking at photos. "Sure. Let's get the rest of the boxes in the truck."

When we finished, Holly yawned. "I better get going or Mom will tack on a day to my grounding. Call me if you find out anything—anything at all. If I break this story, maybe my mother will finally see that college isn't for me."

As I watched her drive away, I made a mental pact

with myself not to tell her anything else. She didn't seem to either care or notice that she was trying to exploit what happened to Malcolm and Sarah for her own benefit, and I was certainly not going to help her with it.

After everyone left, Dad, Richard, Camila, Jack, and I went to the beach for s'mores. Griffin hadn't come down yet, which I told myself was a good thing. When we were talking or joking around, it was pretty easy to forget that he was under investigation. I knew from the detective novels Dad wrote that the sheriff must've had some piece of evidence to get the search warrant in the first place. What could it be? Holly said he wasn't the same kid she'd known, but funnily enough, he was pretty much just as I remembered him— albeit a touch less annoying, far more charming when he wanted to be—and a complication I didn't need.

Yet, just as I was about to say good night to everyone, Griffin scooted into the chair beside me.

"Are you all right?" I asked softly.

He smiled. "Meds kicked in. Thank God. I was worried for a minute I'd"—he paused, a shadow crossing his face— "miss everything."

I was surprised he didn't *want* to miss everything.

"Griffin!" Dad shouted as if he hadn't seen him in years.

"How ya feeling?"

Griffin gave me a knowing smile. "Much better, thanks."

"Another beer, Sam?" Richard asked as he refilled Camila's glass.

"Why not?" Dad slurred.

Camila handed him a water. "Sam, you've always been a lightweight. Drink this. You'll thank me in the morning."

"Yeah, Dad. Drink responsibly."

Dad took a big swig of water. "Why, look at the two of you. Almost all grown up. And my Annabeth, the spitting image of her mother." I prayed he would stop talking, but no such luck. "Like her mother, she's not just beautiful, but smart, too. And strong." He patted my leg.

Dear God, was he ever going to stop?

As I covered my face with my hands, I realized my left wrist was bare. My charm bracelet—it was missing! I swallowed back the panic that burned my throat like bile and forced myself to stay calm. I stood and shook out my dress. Then I ran my trembling fingers along the wooden slats of the Adirondack chair and in between the grooves.

"What are you doing?" Griffin asked.

"My charm bracelet. I lost it." I fell to my knees, my fingers raking through the sand.

"You'll never find it in the dark. I'll help you look for it tomorrow."

"We all will," Richard said.

Turning on my phone's flashlight, I walked around the chair, but my legs felt wobbly, like the inside of a cannoli. This could *not* be happening. I bit the inside of my cheek to keep from screaming. Rubbing my wrist, I said, "I'm just going to look in the library. Maybe it got snagged on something when I was in there earlier." I didn't even care that my voice quavered.

"I'll help." With Griffin by my side, I raced up the steps and into the house. We looked everywhere, but there was no sign of it, so we searched the kitchen, family room, and my room.

"Annabeth, what is it? You're practically hyperventilating," Griffin said.

"It was Mom's," I choked out.

"Oh." Griffin exhaled a long breath. "We should retrace your footsteps."

I knew I'd had it at the campground with Holly, so I listed all the places I'd been since then.

"Let's check the patio."

Griffin grabbed a pair of flashlights from under the kitchen sink and turned on all the patio lights. He took one end, I took the other, and when we met in the middle—each empty-handed—my heart sank into my flip-flops.

"Honey," Dad said as he walked over to us, "we'll find the bracelet in the morning, I'm sure of it." He sounded worried—about me, not the bracelet—and more sober at least.

I nodded, fighting back tears. "I'll just check the beach again."

Dad put his arm around my shoulder. "Annabeth—"

"I'm fine, Dad, really. I just want to double-check."

"And I'll look near your car and the fountain," Griffin offered.

Dad sighed in resignation. "I'll give you a hand, Griffin."

The wind moaned through the trees as I walked slowly up and down the beach, my anxiety rising with each step. I remembered how sometimes, instead of reading to me at bedtime, Mom would tell me stories about the charms: the whale from their honeymoon in Nantucket, the lighthouse from our summers in Eastham, the Old English–style letter A with a translucent pink stone that Dad had given her the day I was born.

Camila joined me. "I'm sure we'll find it as soon as the sun's up."

I nodded. Over and over again, I told myself, *It's a big*

bracelet . . . I'd find it tomorrow, just let it go. But I couldn't. I just couldn't.

"You forgot we were in the boathouse," Griffin called from the other end of the beach.

My breath hitched. *Please be there. Please be there. Please be there.* Sand bit my calves as I ran.

Griffin opened the door, and a host of bats swooped in and out of the rafters, like the acrobats Dad had taken me to see once. I didn't exactly love bats, but as we shared an enemy, I was a bit relieved to see them. Still, I inched a bit closer to Griffin, hating myself for it. Why did spiders— even the thought of spiders—always make me behave like a damsel in distress?

Moonlight shone through the gaps in the ceiling, casting the boathouse in light and shadow. It was even eerier at night. We swept our flashlights across each floorboard. Every time I thought we found it, it turned out to be a screw or a hook or a cheap ankle bracelet. My hope deflated like a pricked balloon, leaving me feeling utterly empty. I was about to give up and look again on the beach, when something glowed near the column. Crouching down, I ran my fingers along the seam and there was my bracelet, wedged in a gap between the floor and the post. I clutched the cold metal in my palm and every knotted muscle instantly relaxed. It felt as though a piece of me was back. I tried to fasten it, but my hands were still shaking.

"Let me do it," Griffin said, his voice soft and low. He kept holding my wrist even after he'd clasped the bracelet, his green eyes glittering in the darkness, his chin dipping shyly. Nerves fluttered deep in my abdomen. I needed to tell the others. I needed to go. Instead, I couldn't help but stare back at him. At his strong brow, sharp cheeks, the deep bow of his lips. He was . . . I gave myself a little shake.

Trouble. That's what he was. Two hundred pounds of trouble.

Still, I wouldn't have my bracelet back if it weren't for Griffin. It felt wrong to just ignore that. "Thanks for your help. I'm so glad you're feeling better." I paused, continuing in a softer, more tentative voice: "I didn't know whether I should check on you or not."

Griffin dropped my hand. "Me, too."

His calm voice warred with the tension in his expression. Something I couldn't recognize flickered across his face, something akin to regret, and then it was gone. He folded his arms across his chest. "We should let everyone know we found it."

Had I upset him by bringing up what happened earlier? Or was he embarrassed I had seen him suffering? I had a fleeting impression it was neither. More like my words had somehow snapped him to his senses. Good. We both needed a healthy dose of reality. We were old family friends, and always would be. Sure, joking and flirting kept our minds off other things, but that's all it was.

I forced a smile, squared my shoulders, and walked outside into the starry night. With a deep breath, I inhaled the cool air, letting the perfume from the peonies, lilacs, and roses pool in my lungs. As much as I tried not to, I couldn't stop thinking about the way Griffin had looked at me and the way he smelled—woodsy, like pine trees, and smoke from the fire. I shook my head, as if I could shake all thoughts of him right out. What I really needed was to get back to school. Away from memory lane, away from Griffin—my childhood friend, who was definitely off-limits—and away from all these heightened emotions. Tomorrow couldn't come soon enough. I'd slip right back into my normal routine—classes, meals, painting, reading. At school, I knew what to expect and what was expected of me. It was orderly, not messy, and that's what I needed. That's what I craved.

"Any luck?" Camila called from the steps, startling me.

"Found it. I better tell Dad."

Walking around to the front of the house, I called for Dad, but he didn't answer. I swept the flashlight across the lawn to the marble fountain, and then to where I'd parked, but he wasn't there. I walked back to the patio to find Richard and Griffin talking softly. "Where's Dad?"

"He's not with you?" Richard asked.

I shook my head.

Griffin frowned. "Maybe he went up to bed?"

"He wouldn't just go to bed and not say good night." I pulled my phone out of my pocket and called him. It rang from the patio table.

"I'll check inside," Richard said.

As Griffin and I circled the house, sweeping our flashlights in a wide arc, I asked him where he had last seen Dad.

"I told him I thought the bracelet might be in the boathouse, and he said he'd keep looking near the fountain. I cut through the woods." Griffin shone his flashlight toward the path he'd taken. "Maybe he followed me."

As we climbed down the steep incline, stepping over gnarled tree roots and yelling for Dad, I prayed he hadn't come this way. Dad didn't have a flashlight or his phone, and too little starlight filtered through the lush tree canopy. Soon, I couldn't even see the lights from the house. Dad easily could have gotten turned around.

There was still no sign of Dad when we reached the boathouse. Camila, Jack, and Richard helped us search the lawn and woods near the house. It was a big property and Dad had been drinking—maybe he tripped or something? At least, that's what I kept telling myself. Ten minutes passed . . . thirty . . . When an hour had come and gone, Richard called the police.

The sheriff came, along with half a dozen officers, some firemen from surrounding towns, and search dogs. They fanned out looking for Dad.

But he was gone.

CHAPTER  Eight

The next morning Dad was still missing. As everyone reassured me he would find his way back now that it was daylight, I could do nothing but nod, though the words that I bit back—*what if you're wrong*—burned like vinegar in my throat.

All of us looked for him: Griffin took me out on his ATV to search the woods, Richard went on foot, Camila and Jack drove around in a Jeep, and the police continued to search with trained dogs. Still, there was no sign of Dad.

As the afternoon slipped away, Griffin and I stopped to search a dense area on foot, calling out for Dad until we were both hoarse. Griffin's phone buzzed, filling me with hope. But as he talked to Richard, I could tell from the tense planes of his face that Dad had not been found. Leaning against a rock, I picked up a loose stone and hurled it.

Griffin pulled the map out of his backpack and unfurled it onto the rock. "Okay, we've looked all through this area." He shaded a small section—which Deputy Clarke had divided into quadrants—with a red pencil. "Richard said the police are focusing their search east of the fountain, toward the campground." He shaded that area in green.

I stared at the map, dumbfounded. "There's still *all* this to search?" The wilderness was so vast.

"I'm sure Sam didn't go too far. It hasn't even been twelve hours. We'll find him."

"How do you know?" I asked in a small voice.

Griffin put his hand lightly on my shoulder. "Don't go there, Annabeth."

"What if he's hurt and can't answer us? Or hear us? What if—"

"Don't go to the land of what ifs. Trust me, it's a dark place and it's hard to find your way back."

I knew more than he thought about the land of what ifs. What if I hadn't snuck out that night? What if I had never lost my bracelet? What if I had said okay when Griffin suggested that we look for it in the morning? What if . . . What if . . . What if. My eyes burned as I shut them tightly to cage in my tears. Once I started crying, I wasn't sure I'd be able to stop.

"He couldn't have gone far, Annabeth. We'll find him. Try not to worry."

He might as well have told me not to breathe.

Early the next morning, I woke up thinking I'd just had the worst nightmare, but the scratches on my arms and legs from searching told me otherwise. I hurried downstairs to find Camila and Griffin facing off against the sheriff, while Richard, Jack, and Deputy Clarke stood off to the side.

"I guess you don't mind the police so much when you need us, do you, Griffin?" Sheriff Clayton stood with his hands clasped behind his back, the buttons of his shirt puckering against the strain.

"It's your job to look for missing people. It's not your job to trash private property and break antiques." Griffin's even voice had a fierce edge to it.

"Whatever you're doing isn't enough," Camila said, her hands on her narrow hips. "I want an aerial search, more searchers, more everything, goddamn it! And I'll happily pay for it myself!"

"We're doing all we can, ma'am," the sheriff said. "We're expanding the search area today."

As I looked at the map laid out on the kitchen table, I was once again struck by the miles and miles of woods surrounding Bradford Manor. I pointed at the tiny black *x* marking the fountain. "He was so close to the house. I just don't understand."

Deputy Clarke crossed the room and stood next to me. "The security cameras show him walking this way"—he pointed—"into this dense section of the forest. The darkness can be impenetrable in the woods at night and spatial disorientation is common. We will find your father. I'll call you as soon as I have any news. You don't want to get in the way of the searchers, so stay put."

There was no way I'd be sitting around doing nothing, but I suspected Deputy Clarke would argue with me on that point, so I kept quiet.

"Are you ready?" I asked Griffin after the police had left.

"You heard Deputy Clarke. No searching," Richard said.

"Nothing and no one is keeping me from looking for my father. Please, Richard."

Richard put his arm around my shoulder. "Annabeth, I think it's best if you go back to school. I know how hard you worked to be accepted into the summer program. Your father was so proud. I'm sure he'll be home today. I'll call you the second there's news."

"I can drive you anytime," Griffin said gently.

I felt like smacking the sympathetic, pitying look right off Griffin's face. Pushing Richard's arm away, I turned and faced them both. "I'm not leaving here without Dad. And I *am* searching for him. I can drive into town and rent an ATV if I need to."

Richard shook his head furiously. "That is out of the question. It isn't safe."

"I've driven an ATV before," I snapped. "And I'm pretty good at directions." I could read a map, find a trail, and figure out which way to go without anyone's help. "I'm not asking for your permission."

Shaking her head, Camila said, "Honey, why don't you stay put, right here. That way, you'll be the first to know when Sam's found. But let the searchers do their jobs. They're trained in this sort of thing."

"No. If I stay here doing nothing, I'll drive myself crazy."

There was a pregnant pause while Richard, Jack, and Camila all looked at me, then at each other, then down at their feet.

Jack sighed. "Well, you sure as hell aren't going alone. I'll—"

"I'll take her," Griffin offered. "I know these woods better than anyone."

Frowning, Richard muttered to himself as he stuffed the backpack with water, granola bars, sandwiches, and sunscreen.

Jack pulled me into one of his patented bear hugs. "Listen here, darlin', I can't tell you the number of times Sam got all turned around when we were traveling. We used to call it Sam patrol, when we went looking for him. We always found him then, and he'll be found now."

Leaning against his chest, I inhaled his reassuring smell—whiskey, maple, and the cigars he snuck when Camila wasn't looking. He'd always smelled like that, for as long as I could remember.

"No reason to cry." He wiped away my tears with his thumbs. "Sam will be back before you know it. And when he is, we'll all go to Tulane and surprise the boys. How about that?"

I drew in a shaky breath. "I've always wanted to see New Orleans."

"We'll go in style. Riverboat cruise along the Mississippi, late night jazz on Frenchmen Street, fried oysters, beignets, eating out at the best restaurants, and darlin', you ain't had coffee until you've had coffee in New Orleans. Leave it to me. I'll plan the whole thing."

"Oh no. How much is this going to cost?" Camila said, laughing.

Jack winked at me. "Perks of being a trophy husband."

Camila swatted him with a dish towel and then made me a thermos of iced coffee. "Be careful. Both of you."

Richard handed Griffin the backpack, along with the map. "Stay clear of the searchers and stick together. Check in. Frequently. And listen to Camila. Both of you, be careful."

We headed out into the hazy early morning sunshine. It was already hot, and the sky was marred with a few wisps of clouds intertwined like lace above the mountains. "Are the mountains part of the state-owned land?" I asked.

Griffin unfurled the map and spread it out on the patio table. "Yeah. The state owns the property all around the first ring of mountains." He traced it with his index finger, which looked very long next to his amputated ones.

"What's this?" I pointed to a cabin and barn drawn in pen.

"A guesthouse we haven't used in years. Richard and the

police have already checked the entire area and Richard left a cell phone in the cabin just in case. There's also an old stable."

"You have horses?" I grimaced.

"Two. Why, don't you like horses?"

I pointed to the scar above my eyebrow. "I got thrown from a mare at camp. So yeah, I'm not a fan." Being a King Arthur nut, I had begged to go to Knights and Knaves Camp, which was basically a knight-themed summer camp with fencing, archery, quests—capture the flag with banners—and tournaments. I had medaled in everything except for horseback riding, which was hardly my fault; the horse threw me, not the other way around. I argued with my counselor, but she said to get the medal I only had to mount the horse one time. So it could buck and fling me onto a rock again? Not a chance.

"What's behind the guesthouse?"

"Undeveloped land that's been in my family for a long time."

"So, other than this house, your guesthouse, and the campground over there, there's nothing but woods. No place that Dad could go for help or shelter."

"All the more reason to search."

We rode through the dense forest, the ATV careening around massive trunks and bumping over tree roots that erupted from the soil like claws, all the while calling out for Dad. As the sun melted behind the mountains, my cell phone vibrated in my pocket. I held it in my hand as if I were holding a ticking bomb, one that could explode at any second and shatter my world to pieces. Again. My hand shook so hard I almost missed the call.

"Sheriff Clayton here. We found a pen, a nice one. Gold, engraved with the initials SBW. Is that your father's?"

"YES! Mom gave it to him when he got an offer on his first book!" Tears streamed down my dirty face. "It's his lucky pen!" The sheriff explained exactly where he found it and my heart swelled with hope as I wrote the word "pen" in quadrant 4. Dad had been right there. Not far from the house.

Griffin and I sped back to Bradford Manor, eager to tell everyone the good news, but the house was empty. I paced back and forth in front of the expansive windows in the living room, my eyes trained on the driveway, expecting the police to come barreling down it any second. Dusk softened the outline of the trees and still I paced, yet with each minute that passed, my heart dropped lower and lower, so that by the time the blanket of night was pulled across the sky, it sat like a stone in my stomach.

I picked up my phone—ignoring the many texts and voicemails from Holly and Dr. Harrington—called Deputy Clarke, who confirmed what I feared—the search had been called off for the night. "Is there any news at all? Any other sign of Dad?"

"Not yet. But the pen is a great lead because now we know which direction he was headed. We do about five hundred searches a year in Maine and almost all end happily. The weather's been mild, not too hot or cold, and there's plenty of fresh water in the area. We'll find him."

I clung to that hope like a life raft keeping me from drowning.

I went into the kitchen and found Griffin at the table; he was banging on his laptop. "Richard, Camila, and Jack are at the station giving the sheriff hell and demanding an aerial search and I'm looking up private search and rescue companies. Dinner's on the stove. You should eat."

"I'm not—"

"Hungry or not, you should eat." Griffin jumped up, ladled chili into bowls, and put them on the counter along with a bag of shredded cheese and a container of sour cream.

I slid the bowl away. "I don't need food; I need some air." My chest was so tight, it felt as if I couldn't breathe.

After unlocking the doors, I stepped onto the patio, with Griffin right behind me. It was a beautiful night: The full moon hung over the mountain like a giant crystal ball and I wondered what my future held. What would happen if Dad wasn't found? How long could I stay here and look for him, before I was sent—sent where? After Mom had died, Dad made Aunt Kathy and Uncle Paul my legal guardians in the event that he died before I turned eighteen. It seemed so unimaginable at the time. I couldn't fathom losing both of my parents as a teenager, and now here I was, with a dead mother and a missing father. I had no family left, nowhere to go. I looked up at the star-pricked sky and the pain that was knotted in my chest expanded, twining up my throat and into my abdomen.

"What are you thinking?" Griffin asked tentatively.

I kept my eyes trained on the night sky. "I'm being selfish. I'm wondering what happens to me if we don't find Dad."

"We'll find Sam, so don't torture yourself. But if it makes you feel any better, you could always stay here." He put his arm around my shoulder. "For as long as you needed to or wanted to."

I slapped away the stupid, useless tears slipping down my cheeks. "Wouldn't Richard love that: two teenagers to look after."

Griffin squeezed my shoulder and gave me a small smile. "I'm sure you're not as big a pain in the ass as I am."

If he only knew. "Trouble comes in all different packages. Believe me, I put my father through hell. I vowed I would make it up to him. I never got the chance."

Lifting my chin with his thumb, Griffin forced me to look at him. "Stop talking like that, Annabeth. The pen was only a few miles from the house. He'll be home soon."

Griffin, Richard, the police—everyone said that to me with such certainty. I kept telling myself that the police wouldn't say it if they didn't believe it. "Do you think Dad dropped the pen on purpose, knowing we'd be looking for him?"

Griffin nodded. "I'm sure he did."

I didn't dare surrender to the hope that was once again swelling inside of me. I knew all too well that hope was usually nothing more than a trick played by fate. Although it was a warm night, I wrapped my arms around my chest, shuddering.

"We can go in, if you're cold."

"I'd rather stay outside." I didn't want to say why, it sounded so ridiculous, but I felt closer to my father out here. Both of us beneath the same sky, listening to the same night music—the cicadas, tree frogs, and of course, the loons. Mom loved the solitary call of the loon. She said it was both the saddest and most beautiful sound she'd ever heard. I never understood what she meant.

"Annabeth, you don't have to be so brave. I'm here, if you want to talk."

Brave? Clearly, he didn't know me well. And talking about things was not my strong suit. Besides, what could I say? That I was worried we'd never find Dad and it would be just me, alone? If that happened, I'd likely end up back in the hospital. Without him, what would be the point?

"I'm tired," I lied. Retreating to my room with the pair of binoculars I found in the sunroom, I sat on the window seat, scanning the woods and beach.

The next day went almost exactly the same, except instead of finding a pen, they found a note, *schedule tour of RISD*, about a mile from the pen. From the two clues, the police mapped out several trajectories which considerably improved everyone's mood but mine.

The fourth, fifth, and sixth days were each another repeat: Griffin and I searching on an ATV, Camila and Jack driving around in a Jeep and looking on foot, Richard pacing at home in case Dad came back, and the police conducting an official search—except with no new clue. My life was beginning to feel like the movie *Groundhog Day*. I only wished I could have a do-over.

Saturday came, the one week mark. From the moment I climbed out of bed, dread wrapped around my solar plexus, tightening with each passing hour. Initially, it was in minutes that I had measured the time Dad was gone. Then hours. Days. Now, it was weeks.

How many weeks could he survive?

When Griffin and I returned from searching, I sat on the patio. As the last long fingers of sunlight stretched through the veil of thin, wispy clouds, all at once the lake glowed like honey in the golden light. I wished Dad were here to see it.

Remembering my promise, I darted to the car and grabbed my watercolors. My fingers moved furiously, knowing the magical light was fleeting. I was almost done when the sun slipped behind the mountains and the lake was dark and deep again. I tried to finish but could no longer see the vibrant colors in my mind.

Ripping the painting in half, I went inside and tossed it in the garbage. I turned on the faucet with my elbow, letting the scalding water prickle my skin as I scraped "burnt orange" off my palm with my nail.

"Want to talk?" Griffin said haltingly from behind me.

"No."

He turned off the faucet. "You're going to scrub off your skin."

I ran my wet hands through my tangled hair. "The waiting is driving me near mad."

"Let's do something to keep your mind off it, even for a little while. We could go to a movie? Get ice cream? Miniature golf?"

I shook my head. "I'm not leaving. If—*when*—he comes back, I need to be here."

Nodding, Griffin caught his bottom lip in his teeth, the dimple in his chin smoothing out. "Scrabble?"

I let out a laugh that sounded more like a sigh. "Yeah, because waiting for you to form a word will be so riveting."

"You look exhausted. Why don't you try to get some sleep?"

"I wish. Nighttime is the worst. Either I lie awake, worrying, or I wake up, then I remember, and then I can't fall back asleep, or if I do, I fall into a nightmare."

Griffin grabbed my hand. "Come on, I have just the thing."

He held my hand as if he'd done so a thousand times. His rough and calloused skin felt oddly comforting, so I resisted my initial impulse to pull away.

We walked up the kitchen staircase, down the hall, then up another set of narrow stairs. I had never been on the third floor. Malcolm's and Sarah's offices were located up here, which is why it was off-limits during hide-and-seek. Not that I hadn't been tempted. But I was still the undisputed champion, as no one had ever discovered my hiding spot—a hidden compartment beneath the window seat in the library that Malcolm had shown me.

The stairs led to an open sitting room with three windows overlooking the fountain and gardens. "Suzette's rooms are over there," Griffin said, pointing to a door.

"Dad's office is down that hall, but I want to show you Mom's study." Griffin led me through an archway, opened the last door at the end of the hall, and flicked on the lights.

Stepping over the threshold, I gasped.

If I could have a room all to myself, this would be it. Part gallery, part library, part cozy retreat—with a private balcony overlooking the lake, no less—it was absolutely perfect. Above the white wainscoting, the walls were painted the softest yellow, like pale morning sunlight. Two overstuffed chairs upholstered in an oatmeal linen decorated with rose branches and red and gold birds sat on either side of a stone fireplace, each with an ottoman. Flanking the fireplace was a pair of bookcases crammed full of books, pictures, boxes, and knickknacks—seashells, petrified wood, a hunk of red rock—things, I supposed, from their travels.

On one wall was a grouping of works by the Hudson River School artists. Each of the paintings had a dreamlike quality, but one by Bierstadt—a waterfall spilling into a glassy pool of water—drew me in.

"My mother loved that one, too. She said it was like stepping inside her favorite poem.

On the ocean that hollows the rocks where ye dwell,
A shadowy land has appear'd, as they tell;
Men thought it a region of sunshine and rest,
And they call'd it 'O Brasail—the Isle of the Blest.'
From year unto year, on the ocean's blue rim,
The beautiful spectre show'd lovely and dim;
The golden clouds curtain'd the deep where it lay,
And look'd like an Eden, away, far away."

His smile was sad and happy at the same time, as I suspected was the one I returned. "That's lovely. Who wrote it?"

Griffin pulled a well-used book from the shelf and handed it to me. In faded gold letters, I read: *Fairy and Folk Tales of the Irish Peasantry*, edited by W. B. Yeats.

"The Irish love their myths and legends. Maybe that's why Mom fell in love with the country," Griffin said, his voice forlorn.

I shifted my gaze to a watercolor by Hopper, which was so breathtaking I had no words. I could almost feel the ocean sway and smell the air, thick and heavy with salt and moisture from the impending storm. And yet, like the others, it was surreal—as if a mystical film had been applied, making the real place feel like a fantasy world.

"This Monet is a print, obviously. I bought it for her for Mother's Day," Griffin said and then pointed, "and I think you'll recognize this artist."

There was my Avalon-inspired painting, framed and hung. Taking a step back, seeing it on the wall with the others, I shook my head. "That was so thoughtful of you, but it doesn't belong there."

"It wasn't thoughtful at all. I had it framed for *me*, not you. I find it peaceful, sitting in here, surrounded by the things she loved, and I think your painting is every bit as beautiful and dreamy as the others. Mom would have loved it, and I intend to keep adding to her collection. Since she died, I sit here a lot and talk to her. I'm sure you think that's weird, but I feel close to her here. For some reason, that makes me less sad."

"It doesn't sound strange at all." I understood, all too well, the hypnotic lure of memory. "It's almost as if all the paintings are of the same magical place."

Griffin nodded. "I know. They reminded Mom of an island we visited."

Staring again at the Bierstadt, I sighed. "Next time you go, take me with you."

Griffin laughed, and I found that I quite liked the sound of it.

"When I was younger, sometimes Mom and I would both come up here. I had my own secret spot." Griffin pulled open a door that had been cut into the paneling, crouched down, and went inside.

I followed after him, into a room about the dimensions of a car with no wheels. Pillows and fuzzy blankets were scattered across the fluffy blue rug, while brightly colored plastic bins lined two shelves on one wall. The constellations were painted in glow-in-the-dark paint on the low ceiling, which Griffin's head almost scraped against even though he was sitting down.

"Welcome to my fort."

I sat in front of him, cross-legged. "Very cool. Strange architecture, but cool."

"Not so strange. The house was built by my great-grandparents, who smuggled in liquor from Canada during prohibition."

I laughed. "Here I assumed you came from old, respectable money."

"Nope. Not that old money was usually earned in anything close to a respectable way," Griffin said, fiddling with a LEGO Millennium Falcon.

"That's true." Yawning, I leaned back against a pillow.

Griffin shook the dust off a Bruins blanket, tucked it around me, and slid over a box of books. "Pick one."

"What?"

"Pick a book and I'll read to you. I've reread all three *Lord of the Rings* books since they died. When I'm reading, I forget."

I nodded. "For me, it only works with fantasy. My mind wanders too much with most other books."

Griffin pulled out *The Magician's Nephew*. "Will this do? I remember you loved the Narnia books."

As Griffin read about Digory and Polly exploring the attic, I closed my eyes, soon caught up in the adventure.

When I woke again, it was dawn and Griffin was asleep, his long body curled around me. Leaning up on my elbow, I couldn't help but stare at him. Other than his cleft chin and the dark stubble dotting his jaw, his skin was smooth. I peered closer at his injured fingers, looking for some indication of an incision, but there weren't any scars. Rubbing my own scar above my eyebrow, I wondered how the plastic surgeon managed that. When I fell, the ER doctor told us I could see a plastic surgeon if the scar really bothered me, but it would never be completely gone.

Sitting up, I yawned and checked my cell phone, but

it was dead. I left Griffin asleep, hurried to my room, and looked around frantically for my charger—searching through pockets, dumping the contents of my purse and duffel on the floor, looking under the bed, pulling up the cushions of the chair and the window seat—until I finally remembered leaving it in the kitchen. *Someone would wake me if there was news,* I said over and over in my head as I practically flew down the stairs, coming to an abrupt stop at the landing when I heard Camila say, "How much should we tell the police?"

"Nothing. We can't tell them anything. For everyone's sake," Richard said firmly. "Most likely, Sam is lost in the woods and will be found anytime now. He was always getting lost on our travels, you know that, Camila."

"Who are you trying to convince, me or yourself?"

Richard breathed out loudly through his nose. "Both of us, I guess. Look, if he'd gone with us on the expedition, I'd be worried. He didn't."

"I still can't wrap my head around it. Seven of us went. Three are left. Do you think it's possible that whoever is following me is the—"

"Stop it, Camila," Richard said, interrupting her. "You're letting your imagination run ahead of the facts. We know what happened to Malcolm and Sarah and *why*. The police investigated Kathy's and Paul's deaths; it was a tragic accident. And we have no reason to believe that Sam is anything but lost."

"I pray to God that Sam is lost, Richard, but we have plenty of reasons to think he isn't."

"I disagree, as does the Council. Even if we told the police, assuming they took us seriously, what could they possibly do?"

Camila sighed deeply.

"Be careful around Annabeth and keep your suspicions to yourself. She's just like her mother; she doesn't miss a thing."

"I hired a private search and rescue team. We need to find out once and for all if Sam's in these woods," Camila said.

"The sheriff's convinced Sam was disoriented due to the alcohol and that he'll be found near the pen, but he did bring in the Maine Warden Service—one of the best search organizations in New England."

"If Sam isn't found in the next couple of days—"

"We'll cross that bridge when—and *if*—we have to."

Camila sighed again, then walked toward the stairwell. I retreated a few steps, pretending I was just coming down.

Keeping my face unreadable, I asked if there was any news as I grabbed my charger. It took all my self-control not to demand they tell me what happened on that expedition, who the hell the Council was, and what they knew about the circumstances of Malcolm and Sarah's deaths, but I knew they'd only lie.

And I was done with being lied to.

CHAPTER Nine

I sat at the window seat, wondering if Dad really was out there somewhere, lost. If not, where was he?

I waited impatiently, watching my phone. At precisely seven o'clock I called Deputy Clarke and told him what I'd overheard, answering his questions about the expedition. "Here's what's strange, though. Malcolm and Sarah weren't the only Magellans to die young in a fluke accident. My aunt and uncle died two years ago of carbon monoxide poisoning—a blocked flue in their fireplace. Now Camila is sure she's being followed. Maybe all of it is connected somehow. What if that's why Dad was taken?"

"Annabeth, there's no evidence your father was taken by anyone. I studied the security footage myself and saw him wander off into the woods. However, Camila and Richard should have told us about the other deaths and any suspicions they may have. We need to be the ones to decide what's relevant. I'll come over later and talk to them."

"Don't tell them you heard it from me."

"I'll say it's background information. We need to keep the focus on the search, because all the facts point to your father being lost in the woods, but I'll call the investigators who oversaw your aunt and uncle's case and see what I can find out."

"What about your investigation into Malcolm and Sarah's deaths?"

"As I already told you, I can't discuss an ongoing investigation. I'm sorry. But please know, I'm on your side. Call me anytime about anything—even if it doesn't seem important." Deputy Clarke cleared his throat. "One more thing. With everything that's going on, maybe it's best you leave Bradford Manor. Do you have any family you could stay with until we find your father?"

"No. But I'm not leaving here until I leave with Dad." I hung up, expecting to feel better, but I only felt worse. At least when I thought Dad was lost in the woods, I knew where to look.

Holly called again and this time I picked up.

"Finally you answer. How are you? I've been worried."

"The one you should be worried about is my father. Have you found out anything about the Bradford investigation?"

"No. I think it's on the back burner while they focus on finding your father. Dad's under a ton of scrutiny, since your father's a well-known author. Even the governor's breathing down his neck. I'm surprised you care about the investigation with everything going on. Unless"—her voice became higher pitched—"you know something?"

I hesitated. Holly would do almost anything to crack this story—no matter who she took down in the process. Just about the last thing I wanted was to see Richard or Griffin hurt, but I needed to find out what was going on with the Magellans. "Look, I did overhear a conversation between Camila and Richard. But I can't tell you if you're going to print it or use it against them."

For a long minute, all I could hear was Holly tapping something—her pencil, I assumed. "Ugh. Okay, as much as it will kill me, I'll keep anything you tell me private until—unless—you say otherwise. A friend is more important than a story."

Friend? I liked Holly, I really did, but was she anything more than a casual acquaintance? I didn't want a friend who expected me to spill my secrets, and I didn't want to know anyone else's, either. As it was, my cup runneth over when it came to secrets.

"Tell me anything. I'll do whatever I can to help."

I smiled into the phone. Maybe I didn't want a friend, but I sure as hell needed one. I told her about Camila and Richard's conversation and Holly promised to search through her father's notes while he walked the dogs.

Hurrying downstairs, I found Richard alone in the kitchen. With a tense smile, he told me that a private search team Camila hired was looking for Dad on the far side of the lake and the police were conducting an aerial search. "Oh, and Camila and Jack had to leave for an important board meeting and didn't want to wake you to say goodbye, but they'll be back soon."

How dare he smile and sound hopeful about the expanded search when he was keeping secrets from me? Maybe whatever he and Camila were hiding had nothing to do with Dad being missing, but maybe it did. Either way, I had a right to know. I clenched my teeth around my bottom lip to keep in the words I longed to say. Hard as it was, I needed to hear what Deputy Clarke and Holly found out first. I wasn't going to give Richard a chance to evade my questions.

"Listen, Annabeth, I called your art program. They're holding your spot. Why don't I bring you back today? I don't think this stress is good for you. Your father would want—"

"Don't, Richard. Don't. I'm not going to have a relapse, if that's what you're worried about." At least, as long as Dad was found. "I'm not leaving without my father."

Richard's expression was conflicted, as if he were having an argument with himself inside his head. I wish I could read his mind. But his face told me plenty—he was worried, a lot more worried than he let on.

Griffin came into the kitchen, his hair sticking up on the side. He gave me a sheepish grin. "Sorry, I overslept. I'll just grab a granola bar and we can go."

Between Richard walking us out to the patio and the noise from the helicopter, Griffin and I didn't have a chance to talk privately until we stopped for a break. He pulled over along a rocky inlet and immediately checked in with Richard. While I waited for him to get off the phone, I splashed water on my legs and arms, longing for a cool breeze to refresh me. But it was so muggy that even the breeze was stifling, like sticking your face behind a car's exhaust pipe. I sat down on a long, flat rock and stretched my legs, watching as the droplets evaporated like miniature pricked balloons.

"No news." Griffin slid his cell into his pocket and sat beside me. "You look less tired today. Did you get some sleep?"

I nodded. "More than I have been, at least. Thanks for last night."

"Anytime."

"Griffin, what do you know about the expedition the Magellans went on?"

He opened the backpack and handed me a water and a sandwich. "Probably the same as you. They talk about it often enough. Why?"

I filled him in on Camila and Richard's conversation.

Griffin rubbed his creased forehead. "I don't know what to make of that, Annabeth. Did you ask them about it?"

"Not yet." I looked away, feeling a twinge of guilt about calling Deputy Clarke before I confronted Camila and Richard. "I hate to ask you this, but after what I heard, I need to know why Camila's worried that Dad isn't lost. What were your parents really doing on the lake at one in the morning?"

Griffin's shoulders tensed. "My parents were doing

research, research that no one can find out about. I'm sure your father told you that. It has absolutely nothing to do with Sam being lost."

"But Richard's words were, 'We know what happened to Malcolm and Sarah and why.'"

His lips formed a long straight line and he tossed his half-eaten sandwich into the woods. "That's true. We know they were doing an experiment and we know why they were doing it."

I took a bite of my turkey and avocado sandwich while I replayed the conversation I had overheard in my head. Griffin liked talking about his parents' deaths about as much as I liked talking about Mom's, but I had no choice. I had to figure this out. "If that's all there is to it, why would Camila include your parents and my aunt and uncle in a conversation about my father maybe not being lost?"

It took a long minute for Griffin to answer: "They also said they weren't worried because he didn't go with them on the expedition. Why didn't you just ask them about it?"

I blew out a frustrated sigh. "Because I didn't think either of them would tell me the truth. Richard even warned Camila to be careful around me so I wouldn't suspect anything."

Griffin rested his chin on his fist. "Then I'll try to find

out what happened on the expedition that has them so worried."

"Thanks."

We were packing up as a low grumble of thunder rippled through the air. Griffin slung the backpack over his shoulder. "We should get back."

Was my father listening to the thunder, too—wishing he had shelter—or was he someplace worse? While I watched the clouds tumble above me, tinging the sky a menacing shade of dark green, the air became thick and heavy and an unnatural darkness descended. My head was still tipped toward the sky when the clouds gaped open and rain pelted to the ground.

As I hurried over to the ATV, long bony fingers of lightning reached out to the lake and thunder roared through the woods like a drum solo. Another bolt zigzagged behind us, soon followed by another. The hair on my arms stood on end as the air became charged. Panic, sharp and hot, filled my lungs—it seemed as if the ATV was a mile away. I was never going to make it.

Before I knew what was happening, Griffin roughly grabbed either side of my waist and tossed me into some scrubby bushes as if I were a Chihuahua. Then, it seemed as if time slowed for an instant as an ear-splitting boom reverberated through my body and a blinding flash of lightning struck the tree next to Griffin. I watched in horror as he flew up in the air—his sandals sailing off his feet—his body crashing down on the other side of the tree. He writhed on the ground for several long seconds as I raced over to him, my heart in my throat.

Be alive, be alive, be alive, I said over and over in my head, willing it to be true as I knelt beside him. I dug my fingers into his neck and was about to start CPR when I felt a faint pulse. I splayed my hand across his soaking wet T-shirt and could feel his chest rising and falling beneath my palm. Griffin's breathing was shallow, but he was alive. He was alive.

Letting out the breath I'd been holding, I fumbled with my cell until I finally plucked it out of my pocket to call for help. I hit Deputy Clarke's number . . . waiting for it to ring . . . and then saw I had no service.

"Damn it!" I yelled into the howling wind.

Griffin's eyes slowly opened.

"Are you okay?" I choked out.

Leaning up on his elbows, he nodded. "Yeah. Let's get the hell out of here."

I stared at him, dumbfounded. "You were just hit by lightning! We need help!"

Griffin shook his head as he slowly stood up, leaning on a rock for support. "I wasn't. It was close, though, and I'd rather not tempt fate. Let's go."

I grabbed his hand and helped him over to the ATV. Despite his protests, I insisted on driving since I was worried he was going to faint. When we pulled up to Bradford Manor, I put my arm around Griffin and led him across the patio.

"Annabeth, don't take this as a complaint—you can keep your arm around me anytime." He flashed a roguish smile. "But I'm more than capable of walking on my own."

"Well, I don't understand how."

I pushed open the door then made Griffin lie down on the leather sofa. "Richard!" I yelled, my voice frantic.

He darted into the kitchen, his face ashen. "What is it? What's wrong?"

"Griffin was hit by lightning. I think it was ground lightning that went up into his feet. We should call an ambulance."

Richard expelled a long breath, seeming relieved.

"Did you hear me? He needs to get to the hospital!"

"I wasn't hit by lightning," Griffin said.

Ignoring him, I explained what happened to Richard, who was oddly unconcerned about the whole thing as he felt Griffin's pulse and examined his feet. "Annabeth, I'm sure it was terrifying for both of you, but Griffin could not have been struck by lightning, not even ground lightning. First of all, I'm sure he would know it. Secondly, his skin is fine—not even a blemish, see?"

I peered at the soles of his feet and was shocked to find there wasn't even a mark.

"I saw it hit the tree next to him, Richard. The jolt sent Griffin flying—he had a seizure! Look at him, he's white as a ghost!"

Griffin sat up. "Annabeth, you're not remembering it right. We both tripped over that fallen log—you sailed in one direction and I went in the other. Which was probably about the luckiest thing that could have happened."

I shook my head. "No. You threw me into those bushes."

"Those bushes were at least fifteen feet away. No one could have thrown you that far. Certainly not me." Griffin held up his injured hand.

"It sounds like you had quite a fall, Annabeth." Richard drew his eyebrows together as he peered closer at me, running his fingers along the back of my skull. "Did you hit your head? Are you dizzy?"

I pushed his hand away. "No! I'm fine. It's Griffin you should be worried about."

"I appreciate your concern, really, I do, but I'm fine. Although I could use a shower. I feel a headache coming on." Rubbing his temples, Griffin gave Richard a pointed look before disappearing down the hall.

"You should take a shower, too, Annabeth. You're soaking. You'll catch your death of cold. But promise me, the next time you hear thunder, you'll get home right away. You are both damned lucky to be alive."

"Richard, you need to at least call a doctor. I'm positive Griffin was hit by lightning. Maybe he doesn't remember it clearly, due to the shock or something."

He nodded. "I will. About you both. Now upstairs with you."

I showered, but I couldn't get the image of Griffin being thrown in the air and shaking on the ground out of my mind. Wrapping myself in a towel, I sat on my bed and looked up "lightning strikes" on my laptop. I was certain that Griffin had been hit by either side flash lightning, which is when lightning strikes a taller object near someone and a portion of the current jumps from the taller object to the person, or a ground current, which is when lightning strikes an object like a tree and then travels along the ground and up into someone. Although the current often would leave skin burns called Lichtenberg figures or lightning flowers, it didn't always, and it was possible—although unlikely—for a person to be struck by lightning and still walk away unscathed.

Even stranger than Griffin being hit by lightning and then seeming fine was how both Griffin and Richard reacted. Why would Griffin downplay it—insisting he wasn't struck—and why was Richard—who was usually a worrier—not concerned at all?

As I paced back and forth in my room, my head felt like it was going to explode. Did Griffin throw me, or did we trip? I was sure I felt his hands on my waist—he grabbed me so tightly it hurt. I lifted up my T-shirt, and sure enough, there was a faint pair of handprints just below my rib cage—and three of the fingers on one hand were missing.

How did he throw me so far? And why was he lying about it?

My phone buzzed, startling me. As I lunged for it, my heart thudded. I was both relieved and disappointed when

I saw that it was Holly.

"Hey, Annabeth, good news. Deputy Clarke hurt his back again—an old hockey injury, according to Dad—and he's in a lot of pain, so he's working from home."

I cringed at Holly's gleeful tone. "Why is that good?"

"Because he calls Dad all the time, and Dad was working from home this morning."

"And you eavesdropped."

"Yup, and read Dad's notes. An officer took those boxes of documents from Bradford Manor to Deputy Clarke's house for him to go through, and he found references to a subject that isn't named or labeled. He can tell it's a mammal—but there's something weird going on with the DNA."

"Weird how?"

"I wish I knew. Do you know anything about it?"

"Dad said something about Malcolm, Sarah, Richard, and Griffin conducting groundbreaking experiments with mutations they didn't want anyone to know about. I asked Griffin about it, but he won't tell me anything." I banged my head against the turret window. "I'll never figure it out."

"Hmmm." There was a long pause, followed by tapping. "I have an idea. The newsroom will be pretty much empty now, so I'll be able to sneak you in. We can search the paper's databases. Maybe we'll come up with something."

It felt like a long shot—how could information about top secret experiments possibly be found in a newspaper database? On the other hand, Griffin and Richard weren't going to tell me anything, and pacing was sure as hell a waste of time. "Okay, thanks."

I couldn't find Richard, so I went to tell Griffin I was going out, but he wasn't in his room. I called for him on every floor—no answer. Figuring he went somewhere with Richard, I left a note on the counter that I was meeting Holly for dinner, unlocked the front door, and headed down the driveway in Dad's car. I stopped at the gate to enter the security code, waiting impatiently for the iron doors to slowly open.

It was strange leaving Bradford Manor. Dad went missing eight days ago, but it felt like it had been a month. If I had said yes when he offered to bring me back to school, would he still be missing? If I hadn't lost my bracelet, would I be at school, and Dad safe and sound at home? Once again, was I the catalyst?

My entire body shook. I had forced myself to come to Maine with Dad, to be there for him as he was always there for me, and instead . . . I couldn't even finish my thought. Instead, what? Dad got lost? Dad got snatched by someone? Who? Why? How could I fix it? How could I make it right? I had to find a way.

I pulled off the road near the Laketown Daily News building, as Holly had instructed, and hopped into her car. I laid down in the back seat and she threw a blanket covered in dog hair over me. Then she drove through the security gate and around to the back door.

"Aren't there security cameras inside?" I asked as she ushered me down a long, wide hallway, with speckled linoleum floors, harsh overhead lighting, and dull gray walls. It reminded me vaguely of my middle school.

"Yeah, but I doubt anyone will go through them without a reason. And there are no cameras in here—I checked." She unlocked a door with her card, and we entered a windowless room. It was probably big—huge, even—but it was cluttered with row after row of metal shelves, cubbies, computers, and file cabinets.

"Welcome to 1972," Holly moaned. "I swear, other than the computers and printers, nothing's been updated."

Dust floated everywhere as we wove around beat-up bookcases, stacks of boxes far taller than me, and a series of long desks—scattered across were notebooks and crumpled pages, piles of old newspapers, and a few mugs of stale coffee, one with a cloud of something green floating on the top. Holly navigated to the back wall, where a row of six desk cubbies was wedged in between two metal file cabinets. Holly slid a chair over to the farthest one and motioned for me to sit. It felt as if the walls were angled toward me, closing in. Looking up at the ceiling, I took deep breaths and focused on the vast open space above me.

"You okay? You're as green as the cinder-block walls."

I nodded.

"Claustrophobic?"

I nodded. "A little bit."

"My boss has it bad. Which is why I know this place like the back of my hand. He always sends me down here. I don't mind it. I've even named a few of the bigger spiders," she said with a laugh.

Great. Just great.

"Here's what I've got so far. Nothing I haven't told you already," she said as she opened a drawer and slapped a tattered manila folder in front of me.

Holly got to work, her fingers flying over the keyboard, while I read through the pages on Malcolm and Sarah—resumes, positions, papers they presented at various conferences. I couldn't help but think about what was missing. There was nothing about how Malcolm ruled the fire pit, mesmerizing us with his stories, or leading us in old camp songs as he strummed his guitar . . . there was nothing about his passion for sailing, his amazing grilled cheese sandwiches, his deep laugh and love of practical jokes, or what a terrible cook Sarah had been, how she woke us kids up in the middle of the night to watch meteor showers, how much she loved animals, or how much Monty Python made her laugh. How they both adored Griffin. I could picture the pair of them, belting out Grateful Dead tunes while we boated around the lake. Blinking rapidly, I shut the folder.

"Hey. This is interesting." Without looking up, Holly twisted her wild curls into a makeshift bun, securing it with two pencils. "I'd focused my research on Mr. Bradford's papers and presentations at cryptozoology conferences, so I missed this before. He was a visiting professor at Trinity for a year—"

"Yeah, I know."

"But did you know he also went to Ireland as an expert—to identify a weird animal that washed up on the Aran Islands that same year?"

I shook my head. "No. But that was . . ." I paused, doing the math in my head. I was thirteen when they left. "Four years ago. What could that have to do with the experiments?"

Holly shrugged. "Maybe nothing. But this was in a local newspaper . . ."

Leaning over Holly's shoulder, I listened as she read from an article about a strange discovery on the shore of Inis Oírr: a winged horse, and a man who appeared middle-aged, but who scientists believed was one hundred and fifty years old.

"Why haven't I ever heard about this?" I asked. "I mean, it's incredible on both counts."

Frowning, Holly read a follow-up article. "Because come to find out, the dead guy was closer to one hundred and five—old, but not record-breaking—and Malcolm Bradford proved it wasn't a winged horse, but a genetically and surgically modified horse. They traced the dead guy to a shoddy circus. Sick. People are sick."

"That's awful."

"Whoa. Wait a minute." Whipping out her notebook, Holly started scribbling under a page titled, THEORIES.

"What? What is it?"

She dropped her pencil and looked at me. "Remember? Deputy Clarke found info on a mammal with weird DNA. According to your father, the Bradfords were doing secret experiments involving mutations. According to the paper, Mr. Bradford examined a horse that had been genetically and surgically modified. They're connected somehow. I'm sure of it. Maybe the horse gave him an idea—or a road map. Maybe he created his own new species? A creature?"

A shiver of fear scuttled down my spine. Maybe the creature was dangerous.

Maybe the creature had Dad.

CHAPTER

My mind was whirling, desperately trying to prove Holly's theory wrong, but panic kept me from concentrating. From thinking. From breathing.

"Annabeth, are you all right? You're shaking."

Rubbing my arms, I took in a gasp of air and stared at her notebook until something jumped out at me: *EXPEDITION*.

I exhaled loudly several times, until my heart stopped racing. "That can't be it. Richard's sure that whatever's going on with the Magellans has to do with the expedition—which they went on twenty-five years ago, long before Malcolm went to Ireland as a professor. Besides, I would have noticed a strange animal lurking around Bradford Manor. And Richard is keeping secrets, sure, but he'd never invite us all if he was worried about some dangerous creature on the loose. Never. This is interesting, but what could it possibly have to do with Dad being missing?"

Chewing on a pencil, Holly shook her head. "That, I don't know."

"This"—I tapped her notebook—"has nothing to do with Dad's disappearance. We need to focus on the expedition. That's the key." Still, the ominous feeling rooted in my stomach wouldn't go away.

Holly adjusted her glasses. "Okay. Let's keep researching."

A couple of hours later, all we had was another stack of papers from speeches and conferences and a few articles that were never published—Holly wouldn't tell me how she found them—but we were no closer to an answer.

"Annabeth, do you have any other family that you could stay with?" Holly asked as she drove me to my car.

"No. It's just me and Dad." And I was getting tired of answering that question.

Holly shot me a slightly nervous look before quickly continuing: "I also overhead Dad talking to a doctor—I'm pretty sure he was your psychiatrist. He's having a fit that he can't reach you."

My chest tightened and I squirmed against the leather seat. "Look, after Mom died, Dad made me see him." That was partly true, at least. "Now I just call in once in a while."

"I would need to talk to someone, too, if I'd been through what you have, but that's not what I mean. If your father doesn't turn up soon, Dad's going to call family services."

There was no way I was leaving Bradford Manor without Dad. If he was lost, I needed to search for him. If he wasn't, I needed to search for answers. "Holly, if you're really my friend, you have to help me. Please. Convince your father not to call them. Besides, Richard's my godfather, wouldn't that make him my guardian?"

"I'm not sure. But honestly, getting away from Bradford Manor isn't such a bad idea." Holly held up her hand, ticking off reasons I should leave on her fingers: "Griffin and Richard are definitely hiding something—and that something could be dangerous. Griffin had to be isolated for some reason—and that reason could be that *he's* dangerous. Someone's experimenting on a strange animal—and guess what? The creature could be dangerous. Not to mention that half of the Magellans died in freak accidents—the husband and wife at the same time—within a few years of each other. If you don't have anywhere else to go, you could come and stay with me. I'm sure Dad wouldn't mind. He doesn't like you mixed up in whatever is going on."

I shook my head furiously.

"What if *you're* in danger? I don't understand why you won't leave."

"You're right. You *don't* understand. It's my fault my mother is dead." I opened my mouth to tell her, but all that came out was five strangled words: "I. Snuck. Out. She. Died." That's all I could manage. "It's my fault my father's missing. I'm not going to lose him, too."

Holly's face softened and she leaned across the seat and gave me a hug. My body stiffened at first, but then I found myself hugging her back and sobbing, wiping away the tears that streamed down my face with the back of my hand.

"Every single day I think about the night my mom died and I wish, more than anything, that I could go back and change things. But I can't. Now, I'm doing the same thing with Dad. I won't spend the rest of my life wondering if I could have done something more to help my father. I'd rather put myself in danger than live with the constant what ifs. They eat away at you until you look in the mirror and you don't even know who you are anymore. So don't ask me to leave. I can't. I won't."

"Annabeth, I am so, so sorry. But please, if you're going to insist on staying there, be careful."

"Of course I will."

"If you change your mind, just let me know. I'll try to convince Dad that you're fine"—she cast a wary glance at the manila folder on the back seat—"on one condition. You need to answer my calls."

I made an X over my heart. "Promise. And Holly? Thanks."

Watching her drive away, I replayed the conversation between Camila and Richard in my head and knew I had made the right decision. Richard had doubted the police would even believe whatever it was they were hiding, so it was up to me to discover their secret. Before it was too late.

After answering the many texts I missed from Richard, I headed back to Bradford Manor. Suzette buzzed me through the gate and then lectured me for five minutes straight on how I shouldn't be out alone at night—as if I were a kid. Ignoring her, I went into the kitchen, bracing myself for another lecture, but found the kitchen and family room empty.

My legs felt like they were made of concrete, I was so damned tired, but my mind was in overdrive. I knew what would be in store for me if I went to bed: another night of staring out the window, wondering where Dad was. Been there, done that. So I might as well get to work while no one was around.

I brought the photo albums of the expedition into the library. Most of the pictures were dated on the back, so I worked on making a timeline. It was strange—someone, either Malcolm or Sarah, had meticulously documented where they were, taking shots of possible finds, clues, and fossils. Yet for seven months there were no photos taken. Not one.

Where the hell were they? And what were they doing? Did it have something to do with the secret experiments?

Standing, I arched my back and rubbed the kink in my neck.

What was the matter with me? I was in Malcolm's library. It was filled with his books. If "Myth, Legend, or Fact" formed the basis for his work—and he finished it right before the Magellans left for the expedition—it must have clues as to what he was hoping to find during their trip. I climbed the ladder and searched the top shelf, but the thesis was gone. Griffin had said it belonged in the temperature-controlled case, so maybe he moved it. I felt around the paneling, but it was locked. Dad was constantly losing his house keys, borrowing mine, and then losing those, too. So I had learned years ago how to pick a lock. Unbending a paper clip from the tray, I got to work on the tarnished brass keyhole, until it finally opened with a satisfying *click*.

I slipped on a pair of gloves from the basket on the table, then pulled open the hidden door. The case was about twice the size of a broom closet, and the shelves were stacked with dozens of old books, journals, and diaries. As I inhaled the smell of old parchment and ancient secrets, I felt a rush of exhilaration. I was certain the police never found this. And if Malcolm wanted to safely hide something special to him, what better place could there be?

I scanned the many volumes but didn't see "Myth, Legend, or Fact"—although there were several sealed containers it could be in. The first box I opened contained half a dozen old journals dealing with the Nazca Lines, but I couldn't read them as none were written in English. Below that was a box filled with papers and documents referencing Antillia—or Antilha—but all were in Latin or Spanish, so I could pick out only a few words.

Frustrated, I pulled down a long container from the top shelf and plucked out a worn leather diary, dated 1845. My fingers tingled when I turned the page and found that it was written in English. I sat on the floor and started reading. It was a heartbreaking account of a boy named William, whose parents and six siblings starved to death during the Irish Potato Famine. Wondering why Malcolm included it in this case, I scanned the pages until I read:

I found work on a ship setting sail for Scotland. All aboard were gaunt and weak, and many huddled together for warmth in the morning chill. A fierce wind came, blowing us off course, and then the fog rose up like a serpent. We could not see our feet below us, let alone the labyrinth of rocks surrounding the ship like the teeth of a great beast, until it was too late. The ship went down in three fathoms of water. Only two of us survived.

Clinging to a piece of the hull, Mary and I were tossed and turned in the waves until, by the grace of our Lord, we came upon an island. There we were greeted by a man who led us through a cave and into a city, the likes of which I'd never seen.

On either side of a channel of the clearest blue water stood limestone buildings, creamy white, topped with golden domes. Wide paths curved around them, lined with gardens and flowering trees. The citizens of ███████ surrounded us. Visitors were rare, as apparently the fog surrounding the island only thinned once every seven years.

We were brought inside a chamber lit without candles and given food and drink. Oh, the things Mary and I witnessed! Instead of horses, the people rode ████████, and ████ around the island. None on the island had ever been ill and lived for ████████ █████. We stayed for a fortnight and were nourished back to health. When we left this magical city, we were given a ship and enough gold to start our lives together in Scotland, in exchange for our vow of secrecy.

We intend to return someday and have drawn this map to guide us.

My heart racing, I turned the thick parchment—but an entire section of the journal had been ripped out. The next passage was about the birth of their son.

Why did William blot out some words and rip out a few pages? Or did someone else do it? More importantly, what island did William visit? Could it have been Elizabeth's island—the one whose location she died to protect?

Beneath the diary was a thin metal-edged box—which I knew was used for storing old illustrations. I opened it and pulled out a dozen large envelopes. Inside the first was a protective polyethylene bag. It held a drawing of a perfectly circular island with a channel dissecting it. Mountains, or perhaps volcanoes, bordered the channel. Surrounding the island was a series of rocks, which had been lightly shaded in gold and green. The right edge of the paper had been torn.

As I opened each folder in turn, I peered at many other drawings—some of islands, others of gold-domed buildings, strange beasts, vehicles that looked like convertibles without wheels hovering above winding streets, a lake with fish that glowed . . . each one was more fantastical than the last.

"Annabeth?" Griffin called from the kitchen.

Shit.

Panic fed adrenaline right to my muscles. In record speed, I returned everything to the box, locked the case, tossed my gloves in the basket, and grabbed a book. "In here! Just reading. Be right there."

Griffin was sitting at the kitchen island, practically inhaling a bowl of spaghetti and meatballs. "Where'd you go for dinner?"

My stomach grumbled. "Umm. Some pizza place Holly likes. I don't remember the name. How are you feeling?"

He smiled. "Much better."

"That's good. Where were you earlier?"

Griffin tapped his forehead. "In my bed all day with a migraine."

I quirked an eyebrow at him. "I looked for you before I left but couldn't find you anywhere."

He caught his bottom lip in his teeth. "Huh. Maybe I was in the bathroom? Often the headaches make me puke. It's great being me."

"Oddly, I read that most people who are hit by lightning get migraines."

Griffin snorted. "Maybe it will have the opposite effect on me. I wasn't really hit, though," he quickly added.

"You were on the ground, shaking."

Griffin jabbed his fork into a meatball. "Nope. Just like you, I fell as the lightning hit the tree—I felt more of a vibration. Did you feel anything?"

"No. But you threw me to safety." I lifted up my shirt. "Are you going to deny that's your handprint?"

Griffin inhaled a sharp breath. "Jesus, Annabeth. I'm sorry. I had no idea."

I dropped the hem. "No need to apologize. I'm pretty sure you saved me. If you would admit it, I'd even thank you."

Griffin frowned, his forehead creased, as if he was trying to work something out. "It's all a bit hazy, but I must have fallen on you without even knowing it." He looked up at me. "I really am sorry."

I hated seeing him look so stricken, especially when I was *almost* positive he had only been trying to protect me. Maybe it was all hazy to Griffin. In one lightning strike case I had read about, the guy didn't even remember being struck. "Calm down. I'm fine."

Griffin's shoulders, which had been pushed up to his ears, relaxed. "Good." He ruffled a hand through his hair before the corners of his mouth turned up. "Well then, I guess I can accept being your knight in shining armor."

I gave him a withering look. "Hardly." Still thinking about the strange island, I opened the freezer and looked through the dozen pints of gourmet ice cream left over from the memorial, until I found coconut almond chip. "Want some?"

"Grab me a coffee toffee crunch."

"Huh. Strange. It's mostly these two flavors left." I grabbed two spoons and sat beside him.

"I ordered extra of our favorites. I guessed yours was the same as it used to be."

As I shoved a large spoonful into my mouth, I wondered how I could have changed so much and yet so little at the same time. "Griffin . . ." I began, wondering how to ask him about what I'd seen without letting him know I'd picked the lock to the case.

"Oh no, what now?" Both his eyes and his tone were teasing. "Whenever you get that line between your eyebrows, I know you're up to something."

The front door banged open. "Griffin? Annabeth? Where are you?"

The panic in Richard's voice made my heart thud against my ribs and bounce up into my throat.

"What's wrong?" Griffin called.

Richard came into the room on wobbly legs and leaned against the wall to steady himself. "I have horrible news."

I felt like an abyss had opened up before me and was going to swallow me whole.

"You're freaking us out. What is it?" Griffin sounded almost as frantic as I felt.

Richard opened his mouth to speak, but all that came out was a low, guttural sob.

I jumped to my feet, the spoon slipping from my fingers and clanging loudly on the floor. "Richard! What happened?"

"It's Jack." He exhaled a long, shuddering breath. "He's dead, and Camila is missing."

CHAPTER

A cross between a cry and a moan escaped my lips as my knees gave out. Griffin caught my elbow as I swayed and guided me over to the family room sofa. My body shook so hard, my leg kept knocking into Griffin's thigh. Jack. Dead? The same Jack who gave me a hug yesterday? It didn't seem real. It couldn't be real.

Richard lowered himself into the chair across from us. "They never made it to their board meeting and neither answered their phones, so Camila's assistant went to their house. He found Jack." Richard grimaced as if he were spitting out nails instead of words. "There was no sign of Camila."

I clutched my stomach, certain I was going to vomit.

"Was he murdered?" Griffin whispered.

Richard flinched. "The police aren't saying much, but

at this time they are not calling it a homicide. It appears to be heart failure."

They exchanged a dark look, and Griffin clapped a hand over his mouth, his eyes wide.

Once the trembling subsided, my mind slowly started working again. "We were all together eight days ago. Eight. Now Dad's missing, Camila's missing, and Jack's dead. It's connected somehow, it has to be."

Richard ran a hand through his thinning hair, the vein in his forehead throbbing. "We shouldn't jump to conclusions."

"Jump to conclusions?" I said incredulously. "I heard you and Camila talking. She was worried that Dad wasn't lost. She thought that it might be connected to whoever was following her. What's the big secret that the police won't believe? What's the Council?"

"Annabeth!" Richard snapped his head back. "If you overheard our conversation, you'd have heard me say that I'd be worried if Sam went on the expedition. He didn't. For God's sake, I just lost one of my best friends. This is hardly the time."

I laughed. Even to my own ears I sounded a bit unhinged. "I think it's the perfect time. Before you either die or go missing. You're the only Magellan left."

The air seemed to be sucked out of the room as I said the words. Each one of us felt it. Richard's breath rattled in the back of his throat. Griffin leaned forward, his elbows on his knees, his head bowed, as if he felt faint.

"You need to tell me what's going on, Richard. Jack thought the break-in involved corporate espionage. Do you all know something that's putting you in danger?"

Richard shook his head furiously. "No. I swear to you, Annabeth, nothing happened in those jungles that could explain any of this other than someone wanting Camila's discoveries."

"Then what happened on that expedition? Why are seven months undocumented—where were you?"

Fear flittered across his face for just an instant before Richard said emphatically, "Nothing happened on that trip that involved your father."

"Do you think Dad's lost in the woods? And I want the truth, damn it!"

Standing, Richard stared at me, his eyebrows knitted together. "Here's the truth. I don't know what happened to Jack or where Camila is. But I'm not giving up hope that we're going to find both Sam and Camila, and neither should you. I don't have anything else to say on the subject." Richard checked the locks on the windows and doors and double-checked the alarm. "I'm going to the study. I have calls to make. And neither of you is to leave this house without checking with me first. If you do, I'll change all the codes."

I jumped to my feet. "Why's that? Because you're worried we might be next? You may not know what happened, but you certainly have theories!"

Richard kept walking, his stride lengthening.

"What about Zach and Lucas?" I called after him. That, at least, got Richard to freeze. "Are they in danger? Are they okay?" My voice broke. What a stupid question. Of course they weren't. They'd lost their father. Just like I'd lost Mom and Griffin lost his parents. Damn, maybe we were all cursed.

Richard turned, his shoulders stooped, his face pinched—he looked like he was seventy instead of fifty. "They're staying with Jack's parents in Texas. Their house has a state-of-the-art security system, but they've hired bodyguards just to be on the safe side. They'll be there until we know what happened." He blew out a long, weary breath. "Annabeth, Griffin . . . I'm sorry. I'm so sorry you're going through this. I love you both, very much."

As I stared at Richard's harrowed expression and his bloodshot eyes, I wanted to hug him. To comfort him. To let him comfort me. To make him promise nothing bad would happen to him. Yet I also wanted to shake him until he told me what was going on. Too many conflicting emotions quaked through me—and I collapsed on the sofa. My mind shattered into memories of Jack: the time he rented out an amusement park one night for Camila's birthday, the pair of us going on the roller coaster again and again . . . how he used to dress up as Santa on Christmas Eve . . . the way his eyes twinkled when he winked . . . I could almost feel his arms around me in one of his bear hugs.

A sob caught in my mouth, soon followed by another. Before I knew it, my face was wet with tears. Griffin pulled me against his chest. It made me feel better, knowing I had someone to mourn with.

I looked up at Griffin, whose tears clung to his dark lashes. "Why does this keep happening? How many more times do we have to go through this? I can't . . ." I caught my lip, trying to contain yet another sob. "I can't keep doing this. I can't keep losing people I love."

"I know." His voice was soft and gravelly.

I touched Griffin's wet cheek. Staring at him was like

looking into a mirror; I saw my own pain reflected in his face. Another lump rose in my throat. "Then help me find Dad, before it's too late."

Confusion clouded his eyes. "I have been."

"Not just by searching. Dad told me your parents were worried the information from the experiments might fall into the wrong hands. Maybe it did and somehow Dad got caught up in it? Why were your parents really on the lake in the middle of the night? Why couldn't the experiment wait until morning? It doesn't make sense."

Wearing the look of someone trying very hard to keep their composure, Griffin folded his shaking hands around his shoulders.

I didn't want to make Griffin think about their deaths. I wished I didn't have to. I stared into his eyes, bright and teasing only minutes ago, now dark and tormented. "I deserve the truth, Griffin. If the situation were reversed, I'd tell you."

The kitchen clock ticked rhythmically . . . a floor creaked . . . the faint call of a loon sounded mournfully from across the lake. Still, Griffin was quiet.

He stood, his back rigid, and I expected he'd walk away like Richard had. He didn't. He stopped before the French doors and stared into the darkness. How awful it must be to see the site of his parents' watery graves every single day. I never drove again on the street where Mom died, or past the park. If I could, I'd bulldoze it.

Griffin's muscles alternately tensed and twitched, as if he was struggling between staying and leaving. Finally, with his palms splayed against the French doors in a gesture of surrender, he said, "They were on the lake because of me. They're dead because of me." The ensuing silence was heavy, and Griffin looked utterly exhausted, as if the weight of what happened that night was pressing down on him. Smothering him. "The headaches I get are intense. Sometimes I black out. Other times I sleepwalk. That night, I had a terrible migraine. Apparently I woke up and went outside through this door, setting off the alarm. My parents, Richard, and even Suzette searched for me. When they couldn't find me, my parents were worried I'd gone into the lake and took off in the boat. It was pouring and foggy. They missed the marker and hit a rock." His voice—raw and choked—was barely a whisper. "They drowned and I don't even remember it. I don't know where I was or what I did. Richard found me in the woods."

Crossing the room, I put my arm around his shoulder.

"Oh, Griffin. I'm so sorry. But it was an accident. Why not just tell the police? It would put an end to the entire investigation."

He pulled away. "Believe me, I wanted to. Maybe the guilt"—he let out a single sob—"the shame, wouldn't be so all-consuming if I confessed. But Richard doesn't want the police to know what really happened. He made Suzette and me both vow to never tell anyone. With my memory loss, he's worried the sheriff will charge me with their deaths. But make no mistake about it, accident or not, it was my fault."

I wanted to tell him that it wasn't, but there would be no point. I knew that all too well. My guilt was buried deep inside of me, like a tumor. No one could see it, but I knew it was there. Yet Griffin couldn't hide the pain that came from sharing this secret. He stood completely still, his face unreadable, his eyes filled with sorrow. The knots of my own secret started to unravel, bringing with it the familiar sharp ache that radiated out from my chest. I wrapped my arms around my waist, and with a deep breath, I told Griffin what really happened the night Mom died.

He looked at me as if my pain were his pain and reached for my hand. It felt as if a net had been drawn over us, binding us together with guilt and secrets and grief and loss. I feared we would never be free of it.

"I know what living with guilt is like. I couldn't save Mom, but I need to do everything I can to save Dad. I need to know what happened on that expedition."

Griffin stared at me with a ferocious intensity. "Obviously, I wasn't on the expedition, but I'll try to find out what—if anything—it has to do with Sam being missing. That's a promise. I swear to you, Annabeth, I'll do whatever I can to find your father and bring him back."

From the set of his jaw and the determination in his eyes, I knew he was telling me the truth. I squeezed Griffin's palm, hoping it conveyed how much his help meant to me, how I felt a little less alone knowing I could count on him.

"I'll look through their studies tonight and pull out everything related to the expedition. We can go through it together."

"Can we look in that temperature-controlled case, too?" I asked. "I'd like to read 'Myth, Legend, or Fact' since it was the road map of the expedition."

Tilting his head to the side, Griffin asked, "Who told you that?"

"Ummm . . . Dad, I think."

"I've read it, and I don't think it will help."

"I need to read it for myself."

"Sure. No matter what it takes, we will figure out what's going on."

"Thank you." The words I said so many times each day without thinking—when someone handed me a napkin or opened a door—seemed so, so inadequate.

Sometime in the middle of the night, I woke up drenched in sweat, the sheets twisted around my legs. This was the third time I'd had the same nightmare: I was lost in a dark forest, with huge, menacing trees that almost seemed alive, their wiry branches leaning toward me. I was trying to reach Dad, and I could hear him, but I couldn't find him. No matter how fast I ran, his voice grew fainter and fainter. Shadowy figures loomed all around me, watching me, and slowly moved closer and closer.

Turning on the light, I ran to the bathroom and vomited—again and again, until my stomach was empty and my throat burned. I must have dragged myself back to bed at some point, because that's where I woke up—hours later, exhausted and bleary-eyed—to the sound of the phone ringing. Lunging for it, I hoped it was good news, but it was just Dr. Harrington—*again*. I hit Decline. If I told him I was fine, he'd either know I was lying or think I'd retreated into a fantasy world again. If I admitted how I couldn't even bear to consider a life without Dad in it, how the knot in my stomach twisted tighter and tighter with each hour that he was gone, he'd insist on seeing me and maybe even sending me back to McLean.

After dressing quickly and heading downstairs, I was surprised to find two strangers in the kitchen. "Annabeth, I'd like you to meet Galena Swift," Richard said. "She's the head of a private search and rescue firm that I hired."

Galena would have been quite pretty if she weren't so angular—her cheeks, jaw, chin, and even her shoulders were all hard edges—and her dark red hair was pulled back in a severe braid. It was a bit out of style for a woman of her age, which I'd guess to be around forty. She had few wrinkles, but something about her eyes, or perhaps her expression, gave the impression that she was not as young as she appeared.

Ms. Swift introduced the man standing next to her as Mac. Mac was tall and lanky, with dark skin and hair that skimmed his shoulders. He gave me a warm, sympathetic smile as he shook my hand. If I never saw another warm, sympathetic smile again, it would be too soon.

"We'll see to it that everyone stays safe as long as we establish some ground rules," Mac said. "You can walk down to the beach and around the perimeter of the house during the day only. Other than that, you can't go anywhere without telling us first."

My eyes slid from him to Richard. "Are you worried we'll be kidnapped—like Camila? Like Dad?"

Richard exhaled a weary breath. "Annabeth, as I've told you, I don't know what happened to Jack or where Camila is. I'm taking every precaution I can until I do know."

Ms. Swift nodded. "I also have several teams looking for Camila in New York. Here, we're scouring areas of the property that the police, the Warden Service, and the private search team Camila hired have not yet covered. We are doing everything we can to find your father."

I'd be relieved if I thought he was just lost. "Wait a sec, these new security rules—are you trying to tell me I can't search for my father? Because no one is going to stop me from doing that. I'll leave here and stay with Holly if I need to, but I *will* search for Dad."

Richard looked at Ms. Swift as if to say, *I told you so.*

"I'd strongly advise against it. You'll only get in the way."

Ms. Swift's imperious tone left no room for discussion. It was as if the matter was settled and she was simply waiting for me to come to terms with it.

Like hell.

"I didn't ask for your opinion," I said with more confidence than I felt.

Clearing his throat, Richard shifted his feet from side to side.

"Very well." Her voice was curt, her expression annoyed. Clearly, Ms. Swift was used to calling the shots. "You may go with Griffin on one of our vehicles. They are equipped with a navigation system and a tracking device. If you find your father, you'll be able to notify us. As Richard suspected you would be insistent on searching, Griffin is out now, getting used to it."

The buzzer at the gate rang, breaking the tension. Richard sent Deputy Clarke up, and I waited at the door, asking him for news, half terrified of what he'd say.

"I have a few questions for Richard and then I'll speak to you," he said kindly.

After a courteous but cold greeting, Richard ushered Deputy Clarke into the study, shutting the door behind them.

Needing a very large cup of coffee, I returned to the

kitchen, relieved to find Ms. Swift gone. I was on my second cup when Griffin walked through the French doors. I took one look at him and gasped. His face was smeared with blood from a deep gash across his forehead, his cheeks and arms were all scratched up, and his T-shirt was ripped open. "Oh my God, what happened? You need to get to the hospital—you need stitches!"

"I figured I'd look for Sam while getting used to the new ATV. Bad idea. I hit a branch and fell. But I'll be fine." He held my gaze in that completely disarming way of his. I had to force myself to look away.

"Sit." I jerked my head toward the stools. "Those cuts need to be cleaned at the very least."

"Honestly, I'll just take a shower."

"Sit," I ordered again, staring at Griffin until he complied. "Did you find out anything about the expedition last night?"

"Not yet, but I pulled out a bunch of my father's old research notebooks for us to go through."

"Thank God the police didn't take them," I said as I ran a clean dish towel underneath the faucet.

Griffin gave me a wry smile. "His office has a secret closet, just like Mom's."

"Why did your father hide his notebooks?" I asked as I gently wiped the blood off his face.

Griffin tugged at the dark waves curling around his neck. "He was more than a little paranoid that someone might steal his research."

I snapped my head back. "You have a room full of valuable paintings from famous artists and your father was worried about his research?"

"The bootlegging business was good to my great-grand-parents. Paintings can easily be replaced. Dad's research couldn't be. I'm not sure it will be helpful, but maybe there's something in there that will tell us what Camila and Richard are hiding. Although, I've been thinking about it, and I know they both would do anything to get Sam back."

I did, too. That's the part that didn't make sense. So why the secrecy? What could possibly be more important than my father? More important than Jack's life? "Still, there's something strange going on with the Magellans, and I'm going to get to the bottom of it. I have to, if there's even a chance it has something to do with Dad being missing. It means a lot to me that you're helping."

Griffin nodded.

When I was done with the cloth, I grabbed a first aid kit

and ripped open an alcohol wipe. "This is going to sting." I gently dabbed at his forehead.

He didn't even flinch. "I don't feel a thing," he whispered.

"You have a much higher tolerance for pain than me." I ripped open another wipe as Griffin yanked off his torn T-shirt, revealing more cuts and bruises and a tarnished silver medallion hanging from a leather rope.

I ran my finger over the cold metal. "Uncle Paul had the same necklace. I miss him, and Aunt Kathy."

"This was my father's. They got them during the expedition."

"So, the men all wore the same necklaces and the women, the same lockets. All the time. That's strange."

Griffin shrugged. "All gifts from a good friend they met, at least according to Mom and Dad."

"Weird no one takes them off."

Griffin clutched the orb in his palm. "Mine reminds me of Dad, so I never will."

I looked down at my charm bracelet and understood.

"This cut throbs." Griffin pointed to his shoulder.

It felt strangely intimate, cleaning his cuts and spreading antibiotic cream on his arms, chest, and face. So intimate that I kept my eyes trained on his injuries while trying to ignore the heat radiating off his skin, or the way his corded arm muscles felt beneath my palm. After bandaging the gash on his forehead, I dabbed cream on my fingers and lightly traced a cut that ran diagonally from his collarbone to just above his heart. His warm breath stirred a strand of hair that had come free of my ponytail, and it tingled against my neck. Despite myself, my heart beat wildly. Taking a step back, I handed him the tube. "You can do the rest."

I wrapped my arms around myself and turned away to pour another cup of coffee. Hopefully, a jolt of caffeine would bring me back to my senses. Griffin was a distraction, nothing more. A distraction I didn't need.

Richard came into the kitchen. "What happened to you, Griffin?"

"I fell off the ATV."

"Be more careful," was all Richard said. That was the second time Richard seemed pretty unconcerned about Griffin's injuries. In both cases, Dad would have insisted on bringing me to the hospital.

Turning to me, Richard said grimly, "Deputy Clarke is waiting for you in the library."

I practically sprinted down the hall. Scanning the

empty room, I thought perhaps I'd heard Richard wrong, but then I spotted Deputy Clarke in the back corner. He was casually perusing the reference books, as if he were at the public library on his day off.

"Deputy Clarke?"

He crossed the room. "Annabeth, how are you holding up?"

Shrugging, I folded myself into an armchair. "What did you find out?"

He sat in the chair beside me. "I spoke with the detective who investigated the deaths of your aunt and uncle. He faxed me the medical examiner's report, the police investigation, everything. We went over the file page by page. The fireplace wasn't venting properly, which caused a build-up of carbon monoxide, pure and simple."

I didn't know whether to be relieved or disappointed. "What about the Magellan Club? Why is everyone except for Richard dead or missing?"

He leaned forward, his elbows on his knees. "That's what I'd like to know. Not surprisingly, Richard has not been forthcoming about what happened on that expedition or the scientific work he performs. If I bring him in for questioning, he'll just call his lawyer and that will be a dead end. Is there anything you've seen or overheard that you want to tell me about? Any reason why the Magellans could be targeted? Anything at all?"

I told him about the experiments and showed him my timeline of the expedition. "Do you think they could have uncovered something that put them in danger?"

"I don't know." He rubbed his chin, his wide face serious—as usual. "If you do hear or see anything, I want you to call me right away, day or night. We'll keep searching the woods and keep trying to get to the bottom of whatever is going on here." Standing, Deputy Clarke put his hand on my shoulder. "I'm afraid I'm also here to deliver some bad news: Your house was burglarized. The police investigated, of course, but I need you to make a list of anything that was taken—when you're up to it. The television is there and some artwork, so we think it was probably a bunch of kids who thought it would be fun to trash the place, knowing that your father is"—he paused—"not home."

A cold ache spread from my heart to my abdomen. Aunt Kathy and Uncle Paul's house was broken into right before they died, as was Camila and Jack's. Now it was my house. More than ever, I was certain someone was after the Magellans. How long would it be until they robbed

Bradford Manor? How long until someone else died in an "accident"?

Maybe the Magellans really were cursed.

I decided it was time to take Holly up on her offer. I could search for Dad from her house. I couldn't search for him if I was dead.

CHAPTER *Twelve*

My legs shook beneath me as I told Deputy Clarke about the other break-ins. From under a furrowed brow, he took notes, promising to call both police departments. "Nothing was stolen from your aunt and uncle?" he asked yet again.

I shook my head.

"I need you to come with me to your house as soon as you're ready."

Closing my eyes, I imagined my house, trashed. Were Mom's paintings still hanging on the walls? What about her studio? It hadn't been touched since the day she died, her oil painting in progress still on the easel. What about our family photos? The jar of sea glass we had collected—was it still on a shelf on the bookcase? Had the intruders broken Mom's collection of music boxes?

I understood now why Griffin had reacted the way he did during the search warrant. He flipped out when he was upset, while I flipped in. Rubbing my temples, I felt the indentation above my eyebrow. The memory of the horse throwing me played out in my mind—Dad had climbed through the slats in the fence in the middle of the competition, dodging the galloping riders as he raced to my side. He didn't care about himself; he had to make sure I was safe. Now it was my turn to make sure he was. I *would* make sure that he was. If the break-ins were all connected, as I suspected was the case, maybe I'd find a clue.

"I'll go whenever you can take me."

"I'll check with the sheriff and let you know." Deputy Clarke paused in the doorway, his hand massaging the small of his back, his lips drawn together. "Think about what I said earlier, about staying someplace else. I don't know what's going on here, but I don't like the thought of you being in the middle of it. I'm worried you're not safe at Bradford Manor."

"I was thinking the same thing," I admitted. "How's your back? Holly said you hurt it?"

A shadow crossed his face. "A long time ago. One minute you're flying around the ice and talking to a bunch of pro teams, the next an illegal check against the boards sends you down for the count."

"Life has a way of screwing with our dreams." For the millionth time, I wondered what my life would have been like if I hadn't snuck out that night. What would have become of Annabeth-*before*? Would she still be dating Bobby? Would she still be in public school, with the same group of friends? I couldn't help but compare us.

"You're right about that. But then you need to find new goals and new dreams." He gave me a sad smile. "Take care of yourself, Annabeth, and stay safe. The sooner you leave here, the better."

I saw him to the door and watched from the window as he talked to Suzette, who was watering the flower pots, before walking purposefully toward his cruiser.

As I was tossing ice cubes in my coffee, Suzette came into the kitchen and reiterated Deputy Clarke's words, warning me that I should leave Bradford Manor, that my father wouldn't want me here. I slammed the glass on the counter. "You don't know my father, so don't tell me what he would or wouldn't want." Spinning on my heels, I marched outside to find Griffin talking to Ms. Swift and a group of searchers.

Ms. Swift acknowledged me with a curt nod. "We're

focusing today on the area around the guesthouse. It's too steep for ATVs, so my team will search on foot. Don't go anywhere near there. I don't want you disturbing any markers." She gave Griffin a pointed look. "In fact, you can search the area around the boathouse, but don't go anywhere else without checking with me first. The sheriff is mad as hell we're involved. I don't need to give him a reason to limit our area more than he already has."

With a roar of engines, her team zoomed off, and Ms. Swift went inside.

I jammed on my helmet and climbed on the unfamiliar ATV. It was sleek and curved, and very high-tech. There was a row of colored buttons above a row of screens. "What's this for?" I asked, pointing to the red button.

"That sends a distress call." Griffin wagged his finger to the next one. "This sends our location, the blue one monitors speed, and I honestly can't remember the rest of the buttons."

"What about the screens?"

"This is for navigation, then there's topography, weather, and I think this is like a walkie-talkie to the other ATVs in the team. Any more questions?"

I shook my head. "Are you sure you're up for this? I'm

perfectly capable of going alone."

Griffin looked at me curiously. "What do you mean? Why wouldn't I be up for searching?"

I pointed to his bandage. "Because of your fall."

"I'm fine," he said dismissively. "Let's go."

We searched and searched until dusk seeped between the trees, cloaking the forest in an early nightfall. Griffin turned around and I leaned back against his chest, defeated. Before long, the expanse of lawn spread out before us and we picked up speed as Griffin tried to outrun the setting sun. We pulled onto the patio just as the last bands of magenta and orange slipped behind the mountains.

"Annabeth, what's wrong? You've barely said two words since we left this morning," Griffin said as we got off the bike.

I removed the helmet and dragged my fingers through my matted hair as I told Griffin about the break-ins. "Someone is after something, something relating to the Magellans."

"God, I'm sorry about your house." His mouth flattened to a grimace. "Why didn't you tell me?"

"I didn't want to think about, let alone talk about it— not when we're searching."

The unsaid words hung in the air. *Because I don't think Dad's lost.*

Griffin drew his eyebrows together. "Maybe the robbery has nothing to do with the Magellans—my house wasn't broken into."

I threw up my hands. "Griffin, there are banks that probably have less security. Maybe something happened on the expedition and someone is tracking all the Magellans, even though Dad only met up with them for a couple of weeks. The break-ins, the travel journals being stolen, it must be connected somehow. Did your parents' experiments involve stuff they discovered on the expedition?"

Griffin stiffened and craned his neck from side to side. "I can't tell you about their work—it's pretty groundbreaking stuff—but I guarantee you that the experiments are not related to the expedition or Sam being missing."

I threw the helmet to the ground. "I'm so tired of hearing that! Dad said that they were worried about their research falling into the wrong hands." I put "wrong hands" in air quotes. "Maybe the people with the wrong hands are involved, have you ever thought of that?"

Griffin set his hand on my shoulder, but I shrugged it off. "Tell me."

He rubbed his brow, his face tense, his eyes darting in every direction. "They were studying mutations," he said so softly I could barely hear him. "Some of the results were surprising and could have *very* dangerous consequences. That's all I will say about it, and please, keep your voice down."

I crossed my arms. "Does the research have anything to do with the winged horse that washed up in Ireland?"

Griffin flinched. "How do you even know about that?"

"Why, is that a secret, too?"

He rolled his eyes. "No. And no, the experiments have nothing to do with that poor, mutilated horse. I swear it." Once again, his voice was low, and he cast his eyes around furtively before he continued: "Look, Annabeth, you need to let this go. No matter what you do or say, I won't tell you any more about the experiments for one reason and one reason only. If I told you, I'd be putting you in danger and I won't do that." There was no guile in Griffin's expression, only a ferocious intensity laced with both fear and guilt.

What was Griffin so afraid of? "In danger from who? Who knows about the experiments?"

"No one but Richard and me. I gave my parents my word that I wouldn't tell anyone else and I won't. Not even you. But trust me—it has nothing to do with your father. *Nothing.* I wouldn't lie to you about that. Let's focus on figuring out what happened on the expedition that Camila and Richard are hiding. We can go through the travel logs tonight. But first I need to eat. I'm starving."

I couldn't help but notice that Griffin didn't answer my first question. I decided to leave it for later, *after* we went through his father's journals.

We found the kitchen empty. Richard left a note on the counter, letting us know he was at the police station and telling us to text when we returned. While I texted him, Griffin scooped chicken pesto pasta into two bowls from a pot on the stove. I picked at mine and waited impatiently while Griffin inhaled two helpings.

"Let's work in the library. I left the notebooks there," he said as he cleared our plates and put them in the dishwasher. "Oh, and Richard took Dad's thesis to a friend of his to make another copy, since he was worried the police would come back and trash it. Hopefully, it will be ready in a couple of days."

I blew out a frustrated sigh. It made sense that they should have more than one copy. Yet I couldn't shake the feeling that Richard purposefully hid it from me. Dad had already been gone nine days. How many more days did he have? Swallowing back the panic that bubbled up in my throat, I rubbed my charms and forced myself to focus.

The only way to help Dad was to search the area and search for clues, and I intended to do both.

Griffin and I sat side by side on the floor in the alcove, out of view in case Richard came in. Griffin pulled out a couple of notebooks and handed me one. We took turns reading aloud to each other while I scribbled down notes. Just like with the photo albums, everything was documented meticulously—except for that same seven-month period.

Which meant that after three hours, what we had amounted to a whole lot of nothing.

"Where the hell were they and what the hell were they doing?" I slammed the notebook down on the hardwood floor.

Griffin slumped back against the wall. "I am so sorry, Annabeth. I wish you guys never came here."

The hopelessness in Griffin's voice seeped into my heart and tears pricked my eyes.

Griffin put his arm around my shoulder. "It's going to be okay."

"You don't know that."

"We'll do everything we can to make sure it is," Griffin said fiercely. "We'll search the woods, hire more people, and find out what happened on that expedition. I won't stop helping you find your father until he's back."

Griffin pulled me against his chest as I sobbed, stroking my hair and whispering soft, soothing noises in my ear until I had no more tears left to cry. He kissed my forehead, and as his warm, slightly chapped lips brushed against my skin, all the thoughts went out of my head. I looked up at him, my pulse racing.

His lips crashed into mine, stealing my breath and making my heart ricochet against my ribs. It felt wonderful not to think, to only feel, and I surrendered to it, pulling him against me. Griffin ran his hands along the back of my thin T-shirt, and I raked my fingers through his hair. My thumb brushed against his forehead, accidentally yanking off one end of his bandage.

As I pulled back to fix it, a cold wave of realization hit me square in the chest. What was wrong with me? Dad was missing out there in the woods somewhere, maybe hurt, or maybe someplace far worse. The list of questions I didn't have answers to was growing longer by the day. And here I was kissing Griffin?

Griffin stroked my cheek with the back of his injured hand. "You okay?"

"No. I'm not."

"I'm sorry. I shouldn't have kissed you when you were upset. It's just—"

I put my finger to his swollen lips. "It's okay. I just . . . feel like . . . like I'm free falling, and I wanted to think about something—anything—else, other than the fact that . . ." I swallowed back another sob. "And for a few moments, it worked. But that's not fair to either one of us. We're both going through hell right now. We can't let our frayed emotions make us do something we'll regret later."

A shadow crossed Griffin's face. "Regret?"

I nodded. "We've always been friends, Griffin. We always will be. Let's not jeopardize that because we're both hurting."

Confusion, along with something else, something I couldn't quite identify, flickered across Griffin's face before he rearranged his features into a neutral expression. "Of course."

He gave me a small smile, his bandage sliding further down his forehead.

The tension in my shoulders gone, I smiled back, happy the kiss wouldn't change things or make things awkward. I pushed back Griffin's hair so that I could realign the bandage, and my breath caught in my throat.

The gash above his eyebrow had completely disappeared.

I looked closer—the scratches on his face and arms were gone, too. "What happened to your cut? It's fully healed."

He inhaled a sharp breath and pulled his hair over his forehead. "That's good."

I snorted. "No, it's strange. You had a deep cut *this morning.* There's no way it could've healed that fast."

Griffin straightened the stack of notebooks he must have kicked when we kissed, and without looking at me, said, "I'm a fast healer."

I yanked down the collar of his ratty Neil Young tee, and the long cut that had bisected his chest had vanished, too. "No one heals that fast."

"I also applied a salve Camila was testing that accelerates the healing process. She said it worked quickly. I guess she was right." He gave me a lopsided smile that accentuated his dimpled chin.

I fought the urge to slap him. "Show me this miracle salve."

"She only gave us a small tube and I used it all."

"I figured you'd say something like that. How about you tell me the truth for a change?"

Scowling, Griffin curled his hands into fists. "Annabeth, stop. This is ridiculous." His voice was strong and commanding, but I could see the desperation in his eyes.

"No. *You* stop. Stop keeping things from me, Griffin. Because one way or another, I will get to the bottom of it."

In one quick movement he was on his feet, dashing out of the library.

CHAPTER

I raced after him, screaming his name, but he was long gone. I banged on his locked door. "Griffin Bradford, you open up right now! You can't avoid me for long!" Giving it a swift kick for good measure, I waited and waited, knowing—even if he was on the other side of that door— he wasn't going to answer. Damn him.

My stomach churning, I returned to my room. While I paced back and forth along the area rug, I went over every strange thing I'd seen since I'd been here. Grabbing my sketchpad, I wrote a list of questions I needed answers to:

1. *Dad lost?*
2. *Dad kidnapped by whoever kidnapped Camila? Why? Something during expedition? Corporate espionage? Secret experiments?*

3. *Deaths—Jack, Kathy, Paul, Malcolm, Sarah—*
   accidents or murder? Cover up?
4. *Griffin—heals fast—how? Salve?*

I stared at the list until my head throbbed; it felt like I was losing my mind. I wished I had someone I could talk to, someone who might be able to help me find answers. Then it occurred to me, I did.

I pulled out my phone but hesitated. If I told Holly about Griffin, could I trust her to keep the secret? Would she even believe me—or would she think I had lost it?

My finger hovered for a minute before I pressed Holly's number. After she promised once more to keep anything I told her to herself, I told her about Griffin's miraculous recovery.

Staring at the silent phone, I tried to imagine what she was thinking. What any normal person would think. "You think I'm imagining things, don't you?"

"What? Of course not. I'm just adding to my list of working theories."

I wanted to reach into the phone and hug her.

"Theory number one. Maybe they found one of those creatures Mr. Bradford was searching for, like Bigfoot or something, and brought it back with them from the expedition. If it got loose, it could have killed the Bradfords."

"But that doesn't explain everything else," I pointed out.

"Yeah, I know. Theory number two. Corporate espionage—what if Camila found more than just those plants she used to develop medicine, and they're testing whatever it is at Bradford Manor because she doesn't trust her own scientists not to steal the information? If it's a salve that can completely heal a gash in a couple of hours, leaving no scar, imagine how much it would be worth."

Shaking my head, I told her again what Griffin had said about his parents' experiments.

"Maybe he lied," Holly said matter-of-factly.

My stomach twisted uncomfortably. Maybe he did. The betrayal hurt more than I wanted to admit. "If Griffin was telling the truth about the salve, maybe it does even more than heal? Griffin didn't seem to feel pain while I cleaned his cuts. And since Dad was with them during part of that trip, maybe he knows where the plants or whatever are from. Someone could have found out about it and is kidnapping the Magellans for information." I strained to connect all the pieces. "But then there's the conversation I overheard—something must have happened on that expedition when Dad *wasn't* with them, some secret the police may not even believe."

"Hmmm."

I could almost hear the gears in Holly's mind turning.

"Maybe whoever is after the Magellans thinks your dad knows more than he does? Or, it could be that after your father left, they found out even more—or discovered something truly amazing—game-changing." She paused. "Annabeth, whatever it is, you're in danger just being near Richard. Come stay with me and we can work on this with Dad. You need to get out of that house of horrors."

Much as I wanted to, I realized I couldn't leave Bradford Manor. From Holly's house, I could still search the woods, but the odds that Dad was lost were small. I needed to stay here, try to get answers from Richard and Griffin, and search the library. I intended to read every book in the temperature-controlled case for clues. "Believe me, I really wish I could stay with you. But I can't. I have access here—" A floorboard in the hall creaked. Peeking my head out the door, I saw Griffin's broad back as he descended the staircase that led to the kitchen. "Holly, I gotta go," I whispered. "I'll call you later."

"Annabeth, wait! I'm worried about you. Please listen—"

"I'll call you back." I hung up and quickly hurried after Griffin. As I crouched on the landing, melting into the shadows, I watched him remove something from a cabinet cut into the kitchen wainscoting and put it in his mouth before going out through the French doors.

I crept down the stairs, opened the secret cabinet, and found it empty save for four prescription bottles. None came from a pharmacy and all were oddly labeled in pen:

1x daily an hour before breakfast
1x daily with food for three days following an episode
take 4 when you feel episode coming on
take daily before bed

What the hell?

I positioned myself behind the family room curtain, the soft linen brushing against my face, and peered out the window. When Mac disappeared behind the sunroom, I punched in the alarm code, unlocked the French doors, and slipped outside. I looked around for Griffin until I finally spotted him swimming back and forth in the same small area. I hurried down the steps, my bare feet not making a sound, and stood in the dark forest, watching him. After several minutes, he climbed out of the water, his wet skin glittering in the moonlight. As he rubbed a towel over his long limbs, I stepped onto the beach.

He clutched either side of his head. "What are you doing out here, alone?"

"You're alone."

His jaw tightened. "Mac and Richard know I'm here. Exercising before bed helps with my migraines and Mac walks by every five minutes. If you want to go outside, you need to tell someone."

"That's right. There's a security protocol now to make sure none of us are kidnapped, right?"

Griffin hung his head. "You heard Richard. He's just being careful."

A breeze blew across the lake, spreading waves of white ripples along the surface like dominoes. Each piece of information was also like a domino, one leading to the next, and whatever lay at the end terrified me.

"I'm going in," Griffin said in a deadened tone.

I grabbed his arm as he walked past. "Not so fast. What episodes do you have and who made all those medications in the hidden kitchen cabinet? Do they have something to do with how you can heal so quickly, or is there really a salve?"

Griffin's body froze, his muscles tight beneath my palm. After a long pause, he answered: "The medicine is for my migraines. Episodes are when I black out. Not that it's any of your business, but my mother and Richard developed the drugs, with help from Camila's company." His voice sounded robotic, as if he'd rehearsed it a thousand times.

"You have an answer for everything, don't you? Too bad I don't believe one word out of your mouth. Tell me what happened on that expedition. I know that you know. Nice ruse, though. Keeping me busy with journals, making me think you were on my side. The kiss, that was a nice touch."

Griffin snapped his head back. "Do you really think that kiss was part of some game? Didn't you feel what I did?"

I turned away from his probing gaze. At this point, I had no idea what to think. "I know you're keeping things from me, Griffin. That's what I know. I thought you were my friend. Well, friends don't do this to each other. They don't watch the other person suffer and do nothing to help."

"Oh, Annabeth." His deep voice was gravelly with pain. "It kills me to watch you suffer, you have to believe that. I can't add to it. I won't."

I tugged at my hair. "What does that even mean?"

Griffin inched closer to me, his green eyes flashing in

warning. "It means that what you don't know won't help you find Sam. Richard knows, and it isn't helping him a damn bit. Have you noticed how exhausted he looks? Or that he's even thinner?"

"And what about my father? How do you think he looks right now? Not knowing is worse than knowing, believe me."

Griffin shook his head wearily. "Believe *me*, it isn't. I swear to you, Richard's doing everything he can. You couldn't do more."

"You don't know that! I need to know what Dad's up against. That's the only way I can help him. Whether you tell me or not, I *will* find out whatever the hell this secret is."

"Annabeth," he whispered, tucking my hair behind my ear, his palm resting on my cheek. "Listen to me. Please. I care about you. You must know that. You must *feel* that. I would do anything in the world to bring Sam home. I'd do anything in the world for you. Tell me you believe that."

I couldn't bring myself to lie to him, not when he looked at me the way he did. I nodded.

"Then trust me and let this go."

"I can't."

The inches between us felt like the ocean, too vast and tumultuous to cross.

His hand flinched against my skin. "If you keep pushing, you'll set things in motion I won't be able to protect you from. That, I couldn't bear." His eyes were tormented. "You need to stop trying to figure this out. For your own sake. *Please.*"

Both his tone and his expression—a strange combination of desperation and dread—frightened me, but I refused to give in to it. I tipped my chin and matched the intensity of his stare. "I don't need protection. I need answers."

"You both should go inside now," Mac called from the patio. It was a demand, not a request.

Griffin closed his eyes and shook his head slowly. "I'm sorry. I can't give you what you want." He whirled around and darted up the stone steps.

Alone, I replayed Griffin's cryptic words in my head. I cast my eyes around the forest and wondered what the darkness concealed. A cold finger of fear scraped down my spine. Shuddering, I wrapped my arms around myself and hurried up the steps to the patio.

Mac kept his eyes trained on me, but I saw Griffin standing in the shadows of the trees near the sunroom. I was certain he was watching to make sure I made it safely back inside the house and away from the danger that surrounded Bradford Manor. A danger everyone here knew about.

Everyone that is, but me.

I pretended to go to bed, but instead I tiptoed back down the front staircase, through the butler's pantry, and slipped into the library. I wiggled my fingers into gloves, picked the lock on the case, pulled out a long box containing maps, and was cloistered in the alcove studying a drawing of Antillia when I heard raised voices coming from the kitchen. Gathering the maps and my notepad in my arms, I looked around frantically for a place to stash everything. My gaze fell upon the compartment beneath the window seat where I used to hide. I pushed the recessed button that opened it, only to discover that it wasn't empty. Inside was the map I had fixed, along with a few others—and "Myth, Legend, or Fact."

Why had Griffin lied about bringing the maps to be repaired? And why had he lied about his father's thesis? If I confronted him, I'm sure he'd have a plausible explanation.

And it would be just another lie.

Griffin was leaving me no choice. I would go through Dad's cell tonight and make a list of all his law enforcement contacts. As soon as it was morning, I'd start calling them.

Someone had to believe me. But as I imagined what I would say, how ridiculous it sounded even to me, I wasn't so sure. I needed concrete evidence, not strange coincidences and things Richard and Griffin could lie about—like the lightning strike. Because with my history, who would the police believe?

After I stashed everything in the compartment, I stood in the corner, to the right of the pocket door, straining to listen to the voices—but I could only hear every few words. I stole down the hall to the butler's pantry, peered around the corner, and spied Griffin, Richard, and Galena huddled together. Griffin stood pencil-straight while Galena met his hostile stare. Richard's anxious eyes darted from one to the other.

"Annabeth shouldn't be here. It's my house and I want her to go. Tomorrow."

"Let's get something straight, Griffin. The Council has allowed you to remain at Bradford Manor. For the time being. If you do not cooperate, that can, *and will,* change. While I'm here, I'm in charge of this operation, not you. Annabeth stays." Both her tone and her expression were cold and hard.

Griffin crossed his arms. "No. She's in danger here."

"Right now, there is no place safer for her than Bradford Manor. Make sure Annabeth follows the rules and remains in the dark. Otherwise there will be no place on earth where she is safe."

"As if I didn't know that." Griffin's voice was quiet, but it was so harsh he might as well have been yelling.

"You'd be wise to remember it." There was an unmistakable warning in Galena's words. "I need to speak to Richard about a few things. Privately."

Griffin opened his mouth, but Richard silenced him with a hand on his shoulder. "You look exhausted. Try to get some rest."

With one final glare at Galena, Griffin stormed off.

"College, of course, is now out of the question," Galena said softly.

Richard sighed. "I know. Breaks my heart, all that he's had to give up."

"Give up? He should be dead. I need to report to the Council, and I'm sure they'd like to hear from you, as well."

Richard unlocked the French doors and they stepped out onto the patio.

I counted to ten and then crossed the hall and peered out the mudroom window—but they were gone.

My head spinning and my thoughts scattered, I leaned against the wall to steady myself. Why should Griffin be dead? Who the hell was the Council—and *where* were they? What was this secret that Griffin was protecting me from? Each new piece of information confused me more. It was like trying to figure out a puzzle with half the pieces missing.

Then it occurred to me that half the pieces might be missing, but I still had half to work with. In Dad's books, Doctor Dan always figured out the crime by examining each piece of evidence as if it were a smoking gun. Starting at the funerals, I turned over each clue in my mind, replaying my conversation with Holly, what Griffin said that first night on the beach, and how volatile Griffin acted during the search warrant. I sat down on the edge of a bench and examined that day again. Something wasn't adding up. Griffin had freaked out when Deputy Clarke said he was going to search the basement lab, almost getting himself arrested, yet afterward—after Richard told him not to worry—he was completely indifferent, not even mentioning the search warrant again. This house was built by bootleggers. It had plenty of hiding places.

There could be only one reason why Griffin had been frantic about the police searching the basement and then unfazed by it. Deputy Clarke never found what Griffin and Richard were hiding.

It was well past midnight when, equipped with the flashlight on my phone and a paper clip, I picked both locks and opened the door to the basement. Creeping down the stairs as quietly as possible, I opened the first door on the right and found myself in a huge dusty game room with both a ping-pong and a pool table, pinball machines, and arcade games. Despite everything, my heart ached for Griffin as I surveyed the room. On a table stood a wooden chess set—an unfinished game still hanging in the balance. I wondered if it was a match Griffin was playing with Sarah, who had loved chess.

Running my fingers along the mahogany bar, I looked at the framed family photos: a preteen Griffin staring back at me, skinny and lanky, and even then, wearing his signature impish grin; Griffin and his mother both laughing while she looked up at him adoringly; Griffin playing lacrosse; Griffin, Zach, Lucas, and me playing hockey on the lake; Griffin and Malcolm sailing; Richard, Sarah, and Griffin on the dock; Griffin and his parents at a Bruins game . . . I could see why this room wasn't used anymore.

Shutting the door behind me, I crossed the hall and entered a state-of-the-art gym that reeked of sweat. Clearly, this room was used. Frequently. I weaved around free weights, a treadmill, and an elliptical machine, before stopping in front of a pair of doors. After opening the first, I stepped inside a large all-white bathroom with a cedar steam room tucked into the corner. Three towels hung from hooks—one was still damp.

I turned my attention to the second door. With an ominous feeling blooming in the pit of my stomach, I ran a finger over the cold metal lock. The lock that bolted the door shut from the *outside*. Which begged the question: Who, or what, was being locked *inside*?

Heart hammering, I leaned my ear against the door but heard nothing. My fingers hesitated on the deadbolt. *Come on, Annabeth, you can do this. For Dad.* Slowly, I slid back the lock. Half expecting some creature to burst through the door, I paused, my muscles clenched, ready to run.

Then, with a deep breath for courage, I yanked open the door.

Nothing charged out. I looked inside at what appeared to be a small bedroom, empty save for a mattress on the floor and a blanket. Hardly the lair of a monster. So who, or what, was this door designed to keep in? And even more worrisome, where was that creature now?

I wanted nothing more than to run upstairs to my

room, but I was certain of only one thing: Wherever Dad was, he was running out of time.

Exiting the gym, I moved on to the next door in the hallway, which was locked with a high-tech security pad. I touched the screen, hoping the code for the upstairs alarms would work, but there was no way to input numbers. Or letters, for that matter. Instead, the screen displayed a constellation map that quickly faded, only to be replaced by the words:

FAILURE. 3 MINUTES TO ALARM

Alarm? How would I explain this? Richard and Griffin I could handle, but Galena was another story. What would she do if she found me down here—lock me in my room? The sinking sensation in the pit of my stomach answered for me. That's exactly what she'd do. With a guard stationed outside, most likely. And there would go any chance I had of saving Dad.

My anxiety rising and my heart racing, I pressed the pad again. Which constellation was the password? Picturing the stars and symbols in my mind, I quickly considered each in turn until I came to Capricorn. That must be it—a cryptozoologist would definitely choose a Sea Goat! I traced it with my fingers.

FAILURE. 2 MINUTES TO ALARM

I wiped my sweaty palms on my jean shorts. If it wasn't a constellation, then what? Frantic, I searched for some pattern in the shapes.

FAILURE. 1 MINUTE TO ALARM

Staring bleary-eyed at the screen reminded me of the "Seeing is Deceiving" exhibit Dad had loved at the Museum of Science. The paintings and posters featured images that were not what they appeared to be at first glance—curved lines that were really straight, shapes that seemed to be different sizes but were really all the same size, pictures within pictures, that kind of thing. It was worth a try. I closed my eyes and reopened them, focusing beyond what was in plain sight—and there it was: a replica of Dad's tattoo. I traced the circle, line, and the arrow with my finger and held my breath.

The door opened with a soft *hiss.*

Unbidden, Galena's warning rang in my ears: *Make sure Annabeth follows the rules and remains in the dark. Otherwise there will be no place on earth where she is safe.* I only hesitated for a moment. If I didn't find Dad, there really would be no place safe for me. Losing Mom was almost too much to bear. Losing Dad would be . . .

As I crossed the threshold and turned on the overhead lights, I was hit by a strong smell—bleach, formaldehyde, and antiseptic commingling in a bitter perfume. Scrunching my nose, I looked around the pristine lab: The wall paneling had been painted a high-gloss white, and along two sides of the square room stood a series of white lacquered cabinets with stainless-steel countertops. Three long tables stood perpendicular to the cabinets, also topped with sheets of stainless steel, stools tucked beneath them. There was a multitude of very high-tech looking microscopes, computers, and machines, along with a commercial-sized refrigerator.

I pulled open a file cabinet and flipped through a series of folders labeled only with a date, each containing charts and graphs labeled in some sort of strange shorthand that was impossible to decipher. In the refrigerator, I found a whole case of test tubes labeled with dates, but there was no indication of what was in them. It was as if someone had painstakingly made certain that if anyone stumbled across this lab, the person would be none the wiser as to what was being studied.

Why? Was Richard studying whatever he kept locked in the bedroom next door: a mutated creature with strange DNA? Could they have snuck it out before Deputy Clarke searched the basement? Is that where Griffin and Jack ran off to?

As I crossed the tiled floor, searching each cupboard for a secret cabinet like I found in the kitchen, I realized the room was quite a bit shorter than the rectangular gym next door. Running my hands along the back wall, I came upon dirt smudges on one board of paneling that led me to a hidden door. With my fingernails in the groove, I pushed it open and entered what appeared to be a storage room with shelves lining the concrete walls. I pulled out a box of files, sat on the cold cement floor, and started reading.

The first file contained notebooks relating to bone marrow transplants. It was way beyond my knowledge or understanding. There were pages and pages of notes about immunosuppressant drugs, anti-inflammatory drugs, and anti-rejection drugs. I really wished I had paid more attention in biology. Exchanging this file for a folder that contained notes about a chimera, I slid my phone out of my pocket—ignoring the many texts from Holly and missed calls from Dr. Harrington—and looked up chimera on my phone. It was basically an artificially produced organism generated by mixing the cells of two or more species. *Like a labradoodle?* I wondered as I scanned page after page of charts and diagrams of variant strands of DNA. Then I read something that made my stomach flip:

> *Unexpected and potentially dangerous results from mixing cells from two different species. Subject experiences periods of rapid cell regeneration that causes negative and painful side effects.*

Beneath it was a note written in a different handwriting:

> *During these periods subject must be monitored and confined.*

I dropped the box on the ground. Did Malcolm combine two species of animals and accidentally unleash a monster? Were they keeping it in that locked room? Was that why Griffin's parents were out on the lake—did the monster escape? Worse still, did the monster have Dad?

My body trembled, suddenly as cold as the floor beneath me. Maybe Malcolm had gone too far. Maybe he had been seduced by his own brilliance, his own power, and had transformed into a real-life Doctor Frankenstein, testing the limits of science and playing God. And just like Doctor Frankenstein's fiancée, maybe Dad was paying the price.

I read through every page for some clue as to where I could find this creature, but there was nothing to help me in my search.

Back in the kitchen, I unfurled the map and studied it. Griffin and I had traversed the forest all around the house except for one area—the woods surrounding the guest-house, the one place Galena insisted that I *not* go.

With the linen family room curtains shrouding my face, I peered out the window and waited until Mac rounded the corner of the house. Then I hurried outside into the inky black night, desperate to find answers, yet terrified of what I might discover. I didn't dare use a flashlight for fear of being spotted, so it was slow going in the dark. I couldn't help but think about my recurrent nightmare as I wove around tree trunks, tripping more than once over gnarled roots.

From directly above me, an owl screeched in indignation,

and my heart hammered even faster. *Aaaauuuu!* A coyote—
or could it have been a wolf?—howled in the distance,
soon answered by an even closer call. I glanced over my
shoulder, but the house had been swallowed by the night.
Fear—of losing my bearings, of what else was lurking in
these dense woods—quaked through me, but I rubbed my
charm bracelet like a talisman, conjured an image of Dad,
and kept going.

As the sun climbed over the mountain, its long fingers
reaching into the forest to chase away the darkness with a
soft golden light, I picked up my pace. Griffin had said the
guesthouse was rarely used, yet the path told a different
story. I followed the meandering trail until I came upon
a pond surrounded by a multitude of trees. They arched
toward the center of the pond—the only sunny spot—and
their thick limbs and swooping branches cast macabre
shadows on the murky water.

Shrugging off the feeling of doom that clung to me
like spandex, I continued toward the log cabin, stable, and
riding arena on the other side of the pond. As I walked
along a short rocky beach, the hair on the back of my
neck prickled. I turned and there, not ten feet away, was a
creamy white horse. The animal stared at me, and despite

the surge of fear that knotted in my throat, I found myself rooted in place.

The horse slowly approached until less than a foot separated us, and continued to watch me with large pale green eyes, like a spring leaf just about to bud. I didn't know horses could have eyes that color.

Then the distant cry of a hawk spooked the animal and it charged past me in such a blur I could have sworn it had wings. I rubbed my eyes and looked again, but the horse that maybe wasn't a horse had disappeared.

A spiral of water swirled in the distance, but other than that, both the pond and the forest were completely still. Dr. Harrington's diagnosis echoed in my head: *Retreats into fantasy at times of great stress.* This certainly was a time of great stress. I sat down on a log, my fingers in my tangled hair. Did I imagine the wings? Did I imagine the animal? Was I thinking about the winged horse that washed up on the shores of the Aran Islands—or was it real?

I wasn't exactly sure what I had just seen, but of one thing I was certain: I was not in a fantasy world.

This was cold hard reality.

With a body count.

Shaking my head as if I could shake every fear and

doubt right out, I got to my feet and walked purposefully toward the guesthouse, my thoughts again on the horse. Could it be the chimera? Was the creature in Ireland Malcolm's first attempt at mixing species, or did it give him the idea—as Holly suggested? The animal I saw certainly didn't seem dangerous. I cast a wary glance around, half expecting to see other strange creatures. Maybe I had it all wrong and Malcolm wasn't a real-life Doctor Frankenstein. Maybe he was a real-life Doctor Moreau.

Instead of opening the cabin door, I decided I'd better know what was on the other side of it first. So, after positioning myself beneath the back window, I lifted my head and peered through the bottom slat of the blind into a small bedroom. A double bed was pushed against the wall, and the comforter was pulled down. But the room was empty.

A woman walked into the room and my breath froze in my throat.

It was Camila.

I ran to the door and banged on the wood. "It's Annabeth. Let me in!"

But it wasn't Camila who opened the door; it was Galena. She quickly stepped outside and shut the door behind her. "Just what the hell do you think you're doing? I specifically told you to stay out of this area. Where's Griffin?"

My nails bit my palms. "What the hell are *you* doing? I thought you guys were looking for Dad and a team was in New York looking for Camila. How long has Camila been here? Why are you hiding her?"

Galena's lips twitched into a hard, thin line. "Annabeth, you're imagining things. Camila isn't here."

I saw her—didn't I?

"New searchers have joined us. One is about Camila's size and has dark hair. Look, you can't be here disturbing markers. It's imperative you leave. I'll have Mac bring you back to Bradford Manor."

I hesitated. I only saw the woman for a second. First a winged horse, now this—maybe the stress was getting to me.

"Wait here." She turned to go inside, and I noticed a leather cord peeking out from the back of her T-shirt—a cord that looked remarkably like the one Griffin wore, but newer.

Without considering the wisdom in it, I pushed past her into a combination living room/kitchen/dining room decorated in a campy nautical theme: blue striped rug, denim sofas with red pillows, and an anchor-shaped lamp. The bookcases had been moved aside, and an electronic map dominated the wall, with different colored points of blinking lights. Three people I had never seen before—all dressed oddly in outfits that looked like they were made from burlap—sat at the kitchen table before square computers that were sort of like tablets, but thinner and larger. Stranger still, for a second, I could have sworn I saw a ghost leaning over a table, talking—but she disappeared in a swish of silver.

It was like I had walked onto a sci-fi set.

"What's going on?" a woman sitting at the table demanded.

I almost laughed. "That's what I intend to find out."

"Call Mac and Griffin," Galena barked at the woman, then sidestepped in front of me, her hands on her hips, as if she could block what I had just seen.

My awe wore off, and I darted down the hall toward the bedroom. "Camila! Are you here? Camila!"

Galena grabbed my arm so tightly it felt as if it would snap in two. "Ouch! Let go of me!"

"Annabeth. Stop this."

"I won't. What the hell is this place?"

"This is our command center, where we oversee the search for your father." Galena's voice was as hard as her face.

I pulled my phone out from my pocket. "Show me this Camila look-alike, or I swear to you I'll call the police and they can get another search warrant. I'm sure the sheriff would find this interesting."

Galena scowled at me. "You will do no such thing."

I smiled. "Try me."

She hesitated for a moment before saying, "What I'm about to tell you cannot leave this room."

"I'm listening."

"You didn't see Camila; you saw her twin sister. Manuela's helping us track down leads. No one can know she's here."

Camila and Manuela were mirror images of each other,

except that Manuela's hair skimmed her shoulders, whereas Camila's snaked halfway down her back. The woman I just saw had her hair in a ponytail. It could have been Manuela, but at this point, I didn't trust a word out of anyone's mouth. "Prove it."

"Manuela," she called, "come on out. I told her."

Wearing a tense expression, the woman walked slowly down the hall, shaking her shoulder-length hair free of the hair tie. My heart dropped like a stone in my stomach. "Hi, Manuela."

"Annabeth? I haven't seen you since Zach and Lucas's graduation. I'm so sorry about Sam." Manuela wrapped her arms around herself.

"If you're helping search for Camila, why aren't you in New York?"

She rubbed her forehead, and I took in the band of white skin where a wedding ring had recently sat. Manuela wasn't married.

"I'm a little freaked out, frankly. We don't know who has Camila or why. I needed a safe haven. The two of us can't give up hope . . . we will find Sam and Cammy." As she hugged me, I carefully pushed the sleeve of her polo shirt up with my elbow, revealing the spot on her upper arm where her tattoo had been removed. This wasn't Manuela; this was Camila.

As I considered why in the world Camila would feed me this elaborate lie, the door sprang open and I found myself face-to-face with Griffin. He stared at me without speaking, but I knew from his eyes that he was terrified—*for me*. His many warnings ringing in my ears, I knew not to say another word.

"So," Camila continued, "I'm in hiding because I don't know who to trust."

"Funny, neither do I," I muttered.

Camila lifted my chin with her thumb. "Trust yourself and don't give up hope."

I nodded, hoping to keep my face expressionless. "Ms. Swift, if it's okay with you, I'm going to look for my dad now. I'll stay out of your way." I kept my voice calm and steady, the exact opposite of how I was feeling. As I walked out the door, I could feel her eyes boring into my back.

"Don't say a word," Griffin whispered angrily into my ear as we climbed on his ATV—not the one Galena had told us to use. "Not one word until we're far from the cabin."

The twenty-minute ride to the far side of the lake felt like hours, the many things I wanted to say—to demand—

boiling up on my tongue.

Bringing the ATV to a screeching halt, Griffin jumped off the bike, tossed his helmet, and then planted his fists on either side of the handlebars, glowering at me. "We aren't supposed to be this far from Bradford Manor. I'm sure I'll pay for it later, but I brought you here on my ATV—without a tracker—because Galena knows I *never* go anywhere near that mermaid statue. I need to talk to you without any risk of being overheard. I understand you have questions, but I can't give you answers. I won't. So don't ask."

Looming above me, his muscles clenched, his eyes flashing darkly, Griffin was simultaneously beautiful and terrifying. If I didn't know him, I'd be frightened. Maybe I'd even do as he demanded. Instead, I moved my face so close to his that I could smell the mint from his toothpaste. "Like hell I won't. Was Camila ever missing?"

"Camila is still missing. That was—"

"Save it. I could see where she'd had the tattoo removed."

Griffin's shoulders drooped, and he took a step backward, tugging at his hair. "Of course you did. Look, Camila was missing, but then she called for help. She's been hiding in the guesthouse."

I threw him a sharp sideways glance. "Did that just slip your mind?"

Griffin shook his head, exasperated. "Don't you get what I've been trying to tell you? Knowing that could cost you your life."

"It's my father's life I'm worried about right now. What happened to Camila—to Jack?"

Griffin shook his head again. "I can't tell you. Don't. Ask."

"Then let's talk about the chimera your father created—did it kill your parents? Did it take Dad? Is that what was locked in the basement?"

Griffin's eyes were wild. "Stop it, Annabeth. Stop trying to figure this out!"

"No! I won't! I told you, I will find out what is going on and what it has to do with my father. Please, Griffin, help me find this monster before it's too late!"

Griffin's face crumpled. He stared at me for a long moment, his eyes holding only regret. When he spoke again, there was neither anger nor frustration in his voice, only pleading. "I promise you the monster that killed my parents did nothing to your father. I swear it. You're going down a dangerous path, a path you can't return from. Don't go down it. Please, Annabeth."

There was no guile in Griffin's face, but if the chimera didn't take Dad, then who did? I ran my fingers through my hair, once again trying to connect the many different puzzle pieces floating around inside of my brain. I conjured a table in my mind, laid each piece down, and the puzzle slowly started to take shape.

At first, I couldn't figure out Griffin and his sudden mood swings. But the times he had snapped at me—when I asked about what the Magellans had discovered, when I saw the message on the map, and when I read his father's thesis—I'd been asking questions he didn't want to answer. After Jack died and Camila disappeared, Griffin and Richard became convinced that it was because of the secret, so they hid the map, along with "Myth, Legend, or Fact," and hired security. The same symbol as the tattoo was on the map, the tattoo that everyone wanted Dad to have removed right away. The tattoo wasn't a symbol of the occult; it was a symbol of the island—but not of Antillia.

I hissed in a breath. "The secret is the location of the island your father wrote about, the one on the map that Elizabeth mailed with the message on the back, isn't it? Did the Magellans find Hy-Brasil on their expedition? Did the Serpent Society track down Camila and Jack and kill Jack when he wouldn't tell them where it was?"

Griffin grabbed my shoulders and pulled me so close I could see the gold flecks in his green eyes. "You shouldn't know that. It's dangerous to know that."

My eyes flashed to the medallion around Griffin's neck. "Wait. They didn't kill Jack, did they? Just like Elizabeth, he killed himself before they could torture him for information." I yanked on the leather and stared at the tarnished silver orb. "There's poison in this, isn't there? And the lockets Camila, Sarah, and Aunt Kathy all wore, they contained poison. Some gift."

Griffin shook me. "Stop it! Do you have any idea who you're dealing with? What they'll do to you if they suspect you know anything?"

"You're hurting me. Let go!"

Griffin pulled away as if I were radioactive. Wearing a look of horror, he stared at his hands for a beat before stuffing them into his pockets.

The last remaining piece of the puzzle snapped into place. "Legend has it that the Fountain of Youth is on Hy-Brasil. You drank from it, didn't you? That's why you heal so fast. That's why you have no surgical scars. A surgeon didn't amputate your fingers. They just healed like that."

Griffin clutched either side of his head, as if to keep it from exploding. "Do you ever listen? It's not just the Serpent Society you have to worry about! If Galena knows what you've figured out, you'll be wearing a locket, too. *If* the Council decides you're trustworthy enough to live."

An ice-cold shiver of fear serpentined down my spine. I wanted to stop. Turn around. Not know. But I couldn't. Dad was still out there somewhere, I had to believe that. "That's the risk I'll take. Tell me."

Griffin stared at me over cheeks as sharp as daggers. "I won't. I care about you, Annabeth. Too much to let you risk your life. To let you live the rest of your life always looking over your shoulder—worried about being tracked like an animal, tortured, or worse. You knowing this secret won't help your father."

"You can't know that." I whipped my phone out of my pocket. "Tell me everything, or I'll call the sheriff and he can get another search warrant for your lab—the hidden one. I'll be sure to call on the main police line. Dispatch logs are public records which anyone can access."

"Annabeth! You don't understand—"

"Then make me! I *will* find out the truth, Griffin. One way or another."

For several long minutes, Griffin paced back and forth on the compact sand. His lips were pursed together, and a muscle in his jaw throbbed as he struggled with my demand. Finally, with a quick nod of his chin, he sat down on the beach, his elbows on his knees, and stared across the lake.

As I sat next to him, waiting for Griffin to find the courage to begin, I realized once again I was in a *before* and *after* moment. By the time the sun reached its zenith, I would know a secret that could change the course of my life.

Forever.

Griffin turned to me. "I don't know how I can protect you." His voice was soft and hesitant.

"I don't want to be protected, Griffin. I want my father back."

Griffin's brows shifted into a pained expression. "The secret is more than just a burden that could cost you your life. If the Serpent Society found out you knew, they'd snatch you and torture you for information until you talked or died from being interrogated. The Council—if they decide to let you live—could do things to make you forget. Horrible things. Are you still absolutely sure that you want to know?"

I didn't hesitate. "Yes."

CHAPTER  Fifteen

Griffin grimaced, looking more defeated than I had ever seen him. It took a long time for him to speak, and when he did, his voice was low and tight. "You can never tell anyone what I'm about to tell you."

"Of course."

"One of the goals of the expedition was to find either Antillia or Hy-Brasil. My father collected maps that referenced the islands, along with journals, papers, even legends. From those, he mapped out where he thought both might be located. As soon as they graduated college, the Magellans took off. They looked for Antillia but never found it. They were exploring some of the remote islands around England and Ireland in search of Hy-Brasil, and hiking in a pretty inaccessible area, when they found an aonbharr."

"Wait a sec. I remember seeing a chapter on aonbharrs

in your father's thesis. Is an aonbharr a winged horse—
creamy white with pale green eyes?"

He arched an eyebrow. "How do you—?"

I hadn't imagined it. "I saw one this morning, near the
guesthouse."

"You did? Usually, Niamh's pretty skittish." Shaking his
head, he gave me a small smile. "But nothing about you
should surprise me."

"What happened when they found the aonbharr?"

"Dad read in one of the journals that the people from
Hy-Brasil flew around on them, so he knew he was close to
finding the island."

I mentally filled in the missing words in William's entry.
It all made sense now.

"What Dad and the others didn't know," Griffin continued, "was that the team of scientists they met on the island
wasn't from England, as they claimed, but Hy-Brasil. They
were there to relocate the aonbharr to Hy-Brasil to try and
save it. While Mom and Richard tried to help the sick aonbharr, Dad and the others told the so-called scientists about
the legend of Hy-Brasil, showing them the maps and journal
entries. The Brasilites forced all seven of them on their boat
and took them, along with the sick aonbharr, to Hy-Brasil."

I inhaled a sharp breath. "Forced? They were kidnapped?"

Griffin nodded. "They were brought before the Council—who rule the island—and told they could never leave."

My insides churned with dread. What had I gotten myself into? "Did they try to escape?"

"There's no escaping Hy-Brasil," Griffin said flatly. "The Magellans made the best of it. Mom helped with the aonbharrs, while Dad and the others tried to learn as much as they could about the island. They became good friends with Galena and her brother, Tristan, who were both on the Council. After several months, Galena and Tristan convinced the other Council members that the Magellans could be trusted. They were each given a necklace and brought back to the island from where they were first taken."

"Galena, Mac, and the others I saw in the guesthouse are all from Hy-Brasil."

"Yup. Camila activated her tracker." He held up his silver medallion. "That's how they found her so quickly. Hopefully, Galena believes you bought her lie about Camila, so no one's tracking me right now."

"Why are you tracked?"

A shadow crossed Griffin's face. "So the Brasilites can find us at any time. They're primarily a peaceful race, but they'll take any means necessary to protect the location of the island. They consider it their sacred duty."

"How can the island be hidden? What about ships and planes and satellites?"

Griffin wrapped his arms around his legs. "Do you remember what you read in my dad's paper?"

I nodded. "That the island is surrounded by a thick fog."

"To get there, you travel through a mist so thick you lose all sense of time and space. It's like . . . a portal to a different place. A different world within our world. I'm sure that makes no sense." Griffin's gaze was unfocused as he stared across the lake.

"What's it like?"

He cocked his head to the side and looked at me, a smile playing at the corner of his lips. "Actually, it's a lot like your painting and the ones Mom collected. She loved them because they reminded her of Hy-Brasil."

"It must be beautiful."

He nodded. "It's like no place I've ever seen. The valley is surrounded on all sides by mountains. There's a lot of gold on the island, so they use it in buildings like the gold-domed towers and in structures lining the channel—the council chamber, the library, school, university, and the astronomy tower. The island is completely self-sufficient and self-contained. It has power, but no fossil fuels are used or needed. Even the air in the valley has a higher concentration of oxygen. There's more to it, stuff I don't know about." His voice was soft and wistful.

"You love it there."

Griffin sifted sand through his closed fist. "It's magical. But magic has a price. Sometimes the price is very high."

I thought of Jack—funny, sweet Jack—and blinked rapidly, hoping to restrain my tears. No island was worth his life. "So what if people found it? What's the big deal?"

"The Brasilites have learned the hard way not to trust outsiders. The Serpent Society was started by people who'd been to the island—people the Brasilites had helped—who wanted to return to Hy-Brasil for their own selfish reasons: information, long lives, and wealth. Hy-Brasil is an advanced civilization, and if anyone stole their technology, it could be bad—some inventions could be weaponized. Even those technologies designed to help the environment could do more harm than good in the wrong hands. Not to mention, if the island was discovered, it would be ruined. Scientists would study it, and the Brasilites would become guinea pigs."

"Why?"

Griffin watched me intently. "Because they're a different species."

I was sure I heard him wrong. "They're not human?"

He shook his head slowly. "Similar, but genetically different."

"Different how?"

"Physically, they're just better than humans. They're stronger, faster, immune to disease and illness. They feel far less pain, they heal fast, and they live a long time."

Drawing in a deep breath, I tried to make sense of it all. I could understand Richard's point—even if he broke his vow, the police never would have believed him. If I hadn't seen Griffin heal in the course of a few hours, I'm not sure I would have. "Why, if you're human, are you like the Brasilites?" I asked softly.

Griffin grimaced, his eyes flashing to his injured hand. I swear I could hear his heart beating in the silence before he explained: "It all started when that aonbharr washed up in the Aran Islands. Since Dad was an expert in cryptozoology, he was asked to study the creature. Dad knew it was a real aonbharr and the hundred-and-fifty-year-old guy was a Brasilite. But he covered it all up. He took a position at

Trinity for a year so he could monitor the situation, and Mom, Richard, and I moved with him. Dad contacted Hy-Brasil so they could come and take both bodies. Galena oversaw the operation and asked Mom to return to Hy-Brasil with her, to help with a herd of sick aonbharrs that had just been relocated."

Holly's instincts were dead-on. The aonbharr and the corpse were related to the secret, just not in the way she thought.

"The night before they were supposed to leave, I was hit by a car." Pausing, Griffin inhaled deeply. "I wasn't going to survive for more than a few days. When Galena heard, she convinced the Council to help me, since they felt like they owed Mom and Dad. I was brought to Hy-Brasil, and Mom performed a bunch of procedures—including a bone marrow transplant, with Galena as the donor. The healing process wasn't instant, but it was fast. It worked. I didn't die. But I never really healed. At least, not the way they hoped."

Griffin gazed at the mermaid statue. As the rays of sunlight filtered through the shredding clouds and danced across the iridescent stone, it seemed like she was swaying in the soft breeze. "Do you know how many times I've thought about slipping into the water, like they did, and not coming back out? Before you came, it was all I could think about. I wanted nothing more than to cease to exist entirely, to be swallowed by the darkness." His voice was barely a whisper.

I'd be a liar if I said I never thought about the same thing. To be free of the what ifs that played over and over in my mind. I threaded my fingers through Griffin's.

"Why did you leave the island if you knew about the Serpent Society? Why not stay?"

"No one was all that worried about the Serpent Society until very recently. In the seventeen and eighteen hundreds, members of the Serpent Society hunted down almost everyone who had ever been to Hy-Brasil. Those who didn't kill themselves were tortured for information, but no one gave up the secret. The Serpent Society hasn't been heard from since then. The Brasilites assumed they'd given up and disbanded or died out. Besides, Mom and Dad eventually wanted me to go to college in the U.S., and they wanted to get back home and continue with their work. We planned on staying for a year. Instead, we cut our trip short, packed up, and took off." Griffin swallowed hard. "Because of me. I started having side effects—the migraines, the blackouts. My parents kept it secret from everyone in Hy-Brasil and brought me home."

"Why keep it a secret? Maybe they could have helped."

Griffin gave me a wry, sidelong look. "They never would have let me leave."

Although the humid air was heavy against my skin, I still shuddered. It seemed that the Council wasn't much better than the Serpent Society.

"We returned to Maine, but now Richard reports to the Council regularly from a communications room in the guesthouse. That's where I went during the search warrant, to hide everything. Jack helped."

I thought back to what I had seen this morning. The strange tablets, a ghost-like person. "How do you communicate with them?"

"There's more than just a poison pill in this medallion. I can use it to send a distress signal or to contact Hy-Brasil." Griffin twisted the orb, which opened like a locket. On one side was a purple pill, and on the other, three clear buttons. "If I press this button, someone from the Council would appear in a hologram." He slid his finger over it. "If I press this one, I'd appear inside the council chamber. Or—a hologram of me would. But it feels as if I'm really there. And before you ask"—his lips curved slightly as he closed it—"I don't know how it works. My parents, Richard, and I were not exactly given the keys to the kingdom. There were plenty of places we couldn't go and a lot that was kept from us."

I reached up and held the silver medallion. It was heavier than I thought it would be, a constant reminder of the overwhelming burden that Griffin had to bear.

Staring again at the statue, Griffin wiped away the tears that clung to his dark lashes. "I have kept secrets from you, but everything I told you about the night they died is true. My parents gave up their lives that night. All because of the side effects from the procedure."

I hooked my arm around his and leaned against his shoulder. "As far as I can tell, sacrifice and love are intertwined."

Silence fell between us while I waited for him to find the words, or perhaps the courage, to continue. I thought about all my parents had sacrificed for me, and how there wasn't anything I wouldn't sacrifice to get Dad back. But I had a terrible feeling that Griffin may be right: Me knowing this secret—even knowing the Serpent Society might have Dad—wasn't going to help in my search.

Griffin looked at me, his face stricken. "At least it will never happen again. I'm locked in the basement during my episodes, so I can't hurt anyone else. I'm the chimera. I'm the monster you were looking for."

I shook my head. "You were taken to Hy-Brasil and experimented on. None of this is your fault, Griffin. You had no say in it."

Griffin's arm twitched beneath my hand and he looked away from me, staring resolutely at the water. "It doesn't make a difference. It doesn't change what I am."

I hated seeing him look so vulnerable, so broken, so lost. I longed to wrap my arms around him and tell him it made all the difference in the world and what he had become didn't matter. But it would be a lie.

"What really happened to Camila and Jack?"

Every muscle in Griffin's body tensed. "As soon as they got home, they were surrounded by four men wearing red masks—the Serpent Society. Jack yelled at them to stay back, or he'd take the poison. While they went for him, Camila got out and signaled for help."

I covered my face with my hands. It hadn't sunk in yet that Jack was gone. Worse, these masked beasts might have Dad at this very moment, and they might be torturing him for information on an island he doesn't know anything about. The others knew the risk and took it. Dad didn't.

"Annabeth, I swear to you, if Richard and I had suspected the Serpent Society was active and looking for the island, looking for us, we never would have invited you to stay," Griffin whispered, as if he could read my mind

I stared at the murky gray clouds gathering on the horizon and at the lake, a brooding shade of green. Both looked as bruised as I felt. Everything was completely still. Even the animals were quiet. The eerie silence was breached by a lone call of a loon echoing across the water. I thought about Mom and wondered what advice she would have for me. Would she want me to tell the police what I knew? They'd never believe me. No one would. But even if I was able to convince one of Dad's contacts to trust me, would it help bring Dad home? I wished, more than anything, that I could talk it through with Mom. Maybe then the knot in my chest wouldn't ache so much. Too many people I cared about were in peril, and I was beginning to care for Griffin more than I wanted to admit. Were my feelings for him clouding my judgment—was I protecting him instead of Dad?

With a desperate expression, Griffin clutched my hand. "Annabeth, can I take you somewhere safe?"

Now that Dad and I were caught up in this, was any place safe? Rubbing my forehead, I heard Dr. Harrington's words: *Focus on what you can control. Not what already happened.* I couldn't control the Brasilites or the Serpent Society.

I couldn't change the fact that Dad was probably kidnapped. But there was a chance—albeit a small one—that he was lost. Continuing to search for Dad was all I could do.

It was twilight when Griffin and I pulled up on the patio. Another day gone. Griffin helped me off the bike, his arm around my waist. "If I found a safe place for you, would you leave? I can't stand the thought of you here. Not with everything we now know."

Mac appeared from around the corner and Griffin quickly dropped his hand. When Mac disappeared from sight again, Griffin took a step toward me, his forehead creased with worry. I retreated. How could I hide out in some safehouse while Dad was in danger? An image of him hurt and in pain filled my head and I couldn't expel it. "I'm going to my room for the night. I need to be alone right now, Griffin. It's just . . . too much. I'll see you in the morning."

I could feel Griffin's eyes on my back as I walked through the French doors, thankful he let me be. Besides, between my rolling stomach and the bitter taste in my throat, dinner was out of the question.

"Dr. Harrington called for you *again*," Suzette said urgently as I walked past her. "He wants you to call back immediately."

I didn't respond.

Suzette grabbed my arm with her bony fingers and pulled me into the butler's pantry. "Listen to me, you need to call him back. And you need to leave this place. For your own good. It's what your father would want." Her voice, although soft, had a fierce edge to it.

I yanked my arm away, but the fear in her eyes unnerved me. Perhaps she had seen something the night the Bradfords died? Or maybe she knew about the Serpent Society? "Why do you want me to leave so badly?" I asked.

She craned her head out the door, looking in one direction, then the other. Turning back to me, she raised an eyebrow. "Why do you think? Don't be a fool, Annabeth. I don't need to tell you that bad things happen at Bradford Manor. You need to get out. Before it's too late."

A cold hand of foreboding pressed against my chest, and I leaned against the marble counter, my legs like rubber bands. It already was too late. I was now a guardian of this secret, just as much as the others. I tugged at the neck of my tee, thankful, at least, I didn't have a medallion. That I wasn't tracked. Maybe I should have listened to Griffin—at least then, if we found Dad, I could have walked away.

"I see the way Griffin looks at you," she whispered. "The way you look at him. It needs to stop. There is something wrong with Griffin. Very wrong. And you know it. Leave, while you can."

I glared at her. She was painting Griffin as the villain, when he was a victim. He didn't ask for any of this. He had to bear the burden of the secret, bear the burden of his guilt, and now worry about me, as well. Everything had been taken from him—his parents, his future . . . he couldn't even go to college as a day student. When we were kids, he wanted to be an explorer; now he couldn't even leave Bradford Manor. "There is *nothing* wrong with Griffin. If you hate it here so much, why don't you go?"

I marched past her and up the stairs to my room. My dark and troubled thoughts were interrupted by the buzzing of my phone. I lunged for it, my heart sinking when I saw it was from Holly. The last dozen or so times she called, it was just to check in on me—she had no information. I wavered for a minute, not really wanting to say I was fine when I wasn't, before answering.

"Finally," she whispered. "I just overheard Dad talking to a social worker. He said he'd been in touch with your doctor and that he thought a temporary guardian should be assigned until your father's found. He doesn't know that I know, so don't tell anyone."

I rubbed my temple, my head already throbbing. What else could possibly go wrong? No way was I staying with some strange family. "Thanks for telling me. I'll call Dr. Harrington now."

"I asked Dad if you could come here for a few days to take your mind off things, and he said, 'Sure.' I can come and get you now. I have a bad feeling about you staying at Bradford Manor and my instincts are usually dead-on."

"I appreciate the offer, Holly. You're a great friend. But I need to stay here. I'll call you in the morning."

"Promise?"

"Promise."

Steeling my emotions, I called Dr. Harrington, but it went straight to voicemail. "Hi, it's Annabeth. Sorry I haven't called; I've been busy looking for Dad. I'll try to call tomorrow during the day. And"—I cleared my throat—"you don't need to worry about me. I'm okay. Really." Truth be told, I was far from okay in many ways, but I was still here, still trying, and that was something. More than something.

Then I called the sheriff and told him I'd called my doctor, so he could back off.

"Listen, Annabeth, some of the things I've *heard* and *seen* have concerned me. I had to call Dr. Harrington myself and let him know there might be an issue. We all want what's best for you. Take care of yourself."

Before I could try to convince him I was fine, he hung up. I tossed the phone on the tufted cushion. What the hell did that mean? Heard and seen what? I clapped a hand over my forehead. Suzette. And recalling the number of times I'd seen her talking with the officers, it was pretty clear *who* the sheriff had heard rumors from. But seen? What did he see? *Oh shit.*

I jumped up and opened my sketchpad, and sure enough, my list of theories was gone. Suzette must have given it to the sheriff—damn her. No wonder Dr. Harrington was worried. Would he attempt to force me back into the hospital? What would Galena do to him if he tried? She told Griffin that I couldn't leave Bradford Manor, and that sounded like an edict.

My phone buzzed, and my relief at seeing that the text was from Dr. Harrington quickly turned to panic. My heart jumped into my throat as I read: *We need to talk privately. I'm at Kendall's Diner, about twenty minutes from you. Please meet me there, or I'll have to come with the police and bring you to be evaluated.*

"No" clearly wasn't an option, but how the heck was I going to get to Kendall's? I was sure, if I could just talk to him, I could convince Dr. Harrington that I was okay. Yet there was no way Galena would let me take off in the car. Pacing around, I tried to jolt my brain into action. *Think, Annabeth, think.* I texted back the address of Bradford Manor and told him to meet me at the entrance. I only hoped I could climb over the fence without being noticed.

Dressed in a black T-shirt, jean shorts, and sneakers, I hurried downstairs and pulled back the living room curtain. When Mac turned the corner, I punched in the code for the front door.

"Where are you going?" Suzette said from behind me.

"Going to meet my doctor—not that it's any of your business."

"Good. Hopefully, he'll talk some sense into you."

"Are you going to report that to the sheriff, too? I know you gave him the sheet from my sketchpad."

She tilted her head to the side, reminding me of a bird.

A bird I'd love to squash. "I cared very much about Malcolm and Sarah and they drowned right in that lake," she said, pointing, as if I didn't know where it was. "Accident or not, it was Griffin's fault. I'd hate to see you have a similar accident."

My nails bit my palms as I glowered at her. Griffin may not remember what happened during his blackouts, but I knew he would never hurt me—or anyone else. "You may think you're helping, but you're only making things worse."

I slipped outside into the dark, dismal night. A thick blanket of fog covered the driveway and crept between the trees like an army of ghosts. Shrugging off my unease, I darted into the woods, melting into the night in my dark clothes. It was eerily quiet as I walked toward the gate, and there was no night music to keep me company. I could just make out the spires of the fence in the distance when it suddenly felt as if mice were running up my spine—I was certain I was being watched. *Damn it!* Mac must have seen me.

Spinning in a circle, I scanned the darkness, but all I could see were twisted branches reaching out as if to grab me. I broke out in a cold sweat. It was as if I were standing inside my nightmare.

And then everything went dark.

CHAPTER *Sixteen*

My eyes fluttered open, but it was black—pitch-black—and my head throbbed. As the fogginess subsided and I assessed my situation, panic, sharp and hot, filled my lungs. I was blindfolded, with my hands bound and strapped to a metal bar, and I was speeding across bumpy terrain, the wind slapping at my face and neck.

I refused to let my mind even consider whose leg was pressed against mine. I couldn't give in to the terror that was rooted in my chest, twining through my body like a weed. I couldn't give in to the voice in my head telling me that my situation was hopeless. I couldn't allow my limbs to just freeze in resignation.

I wouldn't. I had to find a way to escape.

Clawing at my wrists, I tried to free my hands, but the rope was tied too tight. When my fingers found my bracelet, I clutched the cold charms tightly, the edges digging into my skin, and prayed that Mom would watch over me. We slowed, and when I heard water gurgle past, I unclasped it and let it fall. I only hoped Griffin, Galena, or the police would find it.

We zoomed straight up a hill, twisted through the woods, and then came to an abrupt stop. It felt like ice water coursed through my veins as my captor released my wrists from the handlebar and slung me over his shoulder.

Could I surprise him and elbow him in the face or try to choke him with my clasped hands? The ease with which he carried me told me that he was strong. Fear had its tenterhooks in me, digging deeper with each step my captor took.

I froze.

As we descended a steep staircase, the strong tangy smell of blood mixed with rot snapped me to my senses. Gathering up my courage around me like a shield, I waited for an opportunity. The instant my captor placed me on a stiff board of some type, I rolled to the side and made a run for it, pushing up the blindfold just in time to see a hand come down hard across my face, splitting my lip and caus-ing me to stumble to the ground. My captor crouched over me—his thickly muscled arms stood like tree trunks on either side of my shoulders, and his legs squeezed around my hips. But it was his eyes that petrified me, flashing black beneath a red mask.

My body shook uncontrollably. I tried not to think about how long the Serpent Society would torture me in a vain attempt to discover the location of the island.

He yanked me to my feet, holding me roughly by my hair. "Take a good look around, Annabeth."

I wished I hadn't followed his command. The floor beneath me was uneven stone, as were the walls. A half-rotted wooden staircase led to a trap door. I was five foot six, but the ceiling was so low that I could have easily touched it. My captor had to stoop. The only light in the room came from a single bulb hanging from a wooden beam above a cot. Behind the cot stood shelves of medical instruments—needles, vials, rubber gloves—along with weapons, including knives, daggers, swords, and an axe.

"Welcome to your new home, Annabeth. The stone cellar of a burned-out cabin, long since forgotten about. We've reinforced it to make sure no one will hear your screams." His voice was as sharp and cold as a dark winter's night.

My shield cracked and splintered; my body went still and I surrendered to my fate. I only hoped it would be over quickly, but I doubted that would be the case.

Through the still-open trap door, the cry of an owl—or could it have been a loon?—breached the silence. It sang out again and again, the tone and tenor changing with each iteration until it became my mother's voice: *Run, Annabeth, run.*

I slammed my foot into my captor's instep. He let out a low howl of pain, releasing me, and I made a dash for the stairs. Before I got two feet, he shoved me, hard, in the small of my back. My body slammed onto the stone floor. He grabbed me by my ponytail, twisting it back as he pulled my head up, my stomach still pressed against the cold ground, my eyes stinging.

"You will tell me everything I want to know. Where's Hy-Brasil?"

I swallowed back the lump of fear knotted in my throat. "I don't know what you're talking about."

"Wrong answer." He let go of my hair and my face crashed into the rough and ragged stones. Before I could even gasp, he kicked me in the stomach. Involuntarily, my body curled into a ball. I opened my mouth to scream, but no noise came out—I was mute from the pain, unable to take anything but a shallow breath.

Dragging me to my feet, he held my arm behind my back—both my shoulder and stomach screaming in protest—and marched me across the dark cellar toward another cot, but this one wasn't empty. The room tilted beneath me as I looked upon the bloodied and bruised body of my father lying unconscious, a wet gurgling sound coming from his lips.

"I'm shocked he's still alive after what we've done to him. Broken both hands. His ribs. Burned his flesh. Deprived him of food. Water." My legs gave out, but my captor held me firmly. "Whether he lives or dies is now up to you. Tell me everything you know about the island."

Tears streamed down my face—not due to the searing pain in my arm as he pulled it tighter, but because I fully realized the hopelessness of our situation. I couldn't save Dad. Even if I told him everything I knew, it would only hasten our deaths and endanger Griffin, Richard, and Camila. I promised Griffin I wouldn't tell anyone what he told me, and I would be true to my word. No matter what it cost me.

"I don't know anything about an island."

He threw me as if I were a rag doll. When my head hit

the cellar wall, the room spun around me until everything went dark again.

I slipped in and out of consciousness, summoning every bit of strength I had to stay awake. Opening my eyes—as much as I could, since one was almost swollen completely shut—I found myself on the cot, my wrist attached to a metal cuff chained to the bed. Of course, my phone was no longer in my back pocket. Sitting up as far as the shackle would allow and finding no sign of my captor, I called for Dad repeatedly until he finally answered, his voice dry and splintered. "No. Oh no," he cried. "Not you, Annabeth? You need to escape from here."

The door creaked open. Strange how such a small noise could be the most terrifying sound in the world.

"Pretend you're still unconscious," Dad whispered.

I forced myself to stay still, to feign sleep, even though my heart was racing. When the footsteps stopped directly in front of me, my muscles clenched so tightly that my pinky finger twitched.

"Python, what the hell did you do? You were ordered to

wait to interrogate her until I arrived!" This man's voice—
although angry—was oddly muffled.

"Save your lecture, Cobra. She tried to escape. I did
what I had to," Python answered without apology.

Rough fingers gripped my chin, tilting my head from
side to side. The man cursed under his breath in the same
stifled voice. "I've warned you before that we follow the
ancient code. We torture them for information, not because
we enjoy it."

"As I said, I did what I had to." There was a note of
contempt in Python's voice. "We no longer have the luxury
of time. Unlike her father, we can't just pass her off as lost;
the search will start immediately. While she was awake, I
took the opportunity to ask her about the island. Although
she denied knowing anything, the fear in her eyes told a
different story. Regardless, we'll find out what she knows
soon enough. Even if she won't talk under torture, she will
when I take a saw to her father's arm."

I held my breath to stop myself from screaming. *Focus,
Annabeth, focus.* What would Doctor Dan do? He'd pay
attention to every little detail and find some obscure way
to save himself. I opened my eyes ever so slightly, and the
lightbulb swinging above revealed three men surrounding

me: the large, burly one was Python; another was wide and solid; and the last one was tall and thin. All were dressed in black T-shirts and camo-style jackets and pants. They would have passed for hunters if not for the red masks.

Beneath the masks they were men. *Just men.* I repeated this in my head, as if it were an incantation to keep fear at bay.

While they calmly debated the best way to make me crack—torturing me, beating Dad, giving me a truth serum, finally deciding on a combination of the three—staying still became a harder task than I had ever imagined.

"If we've agreed, we'll start with the truth serum. It should be in effect by the time she comes to, at which time the interrogation can begin," the tall man said. His speech was refined, and he had a hint of an accent—English, maybe?

The one called Cobra looked at his watch, his arm twisting above my head. I noticed a tear in the dark brown leather strap right above the gold buckle.

Great, one rolled his *rrrs*, and one had a torn watch. That was really helpful.

"I'll administer it now," Cobra said. As he removed a syringe from his pocket, my heart punched through my chest. As long as they thought I was unconscious, I had time to try to come up with a plan. Thanks to my trypano-phobia, once that needle pierced my skin, I wouldn't be able to fake it anymore.

Working methodically, Cobra placed the needle on a silver hospital-style cart adjacent to the cot and secured leather straps across my chest and legs, fastening them tightly. The memory of another time I was restrained came back to me for the first time. I knew all about my treatment from Dr. Harrington and Dad but couldn't remember much of my time at McLean. Now, it was almost as if I were watching a movie of myself but not really reliving it, as I viewed a younger version of me on a bed with a nurse and an anesthesiologist standing to the side as Dr. Harrington gently explained that I'd be receiving anesthesia, followed by electroconvulsive therapy to treat my catatonic depression. It wasn't scary; it was peaceful. I didn't know if it was due to the sedation or my condition, but I was surprised to find that I didn't seem to be panicked by the needle, or even bothered by it for that matter.

I had to find a way to channel that feeling and remain calm. *You can do this*, I told myself, as I ran through the English monarchs, starting with Egbert.

But still I flinched as the sharp, cold needle pinched my skin.

Cobra placed a cap on the syringe and returned it to his pocket before jabbing his fingers into my neck, feeling my racing pulse. "She's awake," he said, his voice excited but still muffled. "Good. The truth serum will reach maximum potency in one hour. I'll question her then."

I had one hour to get us out of here, or I would tell them everything.

The needle. Maybe, just maybe, I could reach it without him noticing. Cobra was leaning over my body, returning a vial to the table and blocking my view of the other men and hopefully theirs of me, his pocket inches from my hand. It was a chance I had to take. If he caught me, what would it matter? I'd be tortured and killed regardless. Still, my hand trembled as I slipped it inside his jacket. After sliding the needle out slowly, I laid it under my palm.

"I don't see any reason why we can't start the questioning sooner." Python's voice was thick with anticipation. "Time is of the essence."

"I agree," the Englishman said.

With his hands on either side of my head, Python leaned toward me. "As long as you cooperate, we won't hurt your father. I'd suggest that you cooperate."

Fear clawed its way up my throat. If they tortured Dad,

I probably would tell them everything. There was only one way I could think of to buy us some time.

I needed to return to my fantasy world.

I summoned the painting in my mind; it was easier than I had hoped it would be. It spread out like an alternate dimension I just needed to enter, as I had so many times.

For a moment, I hesitated, worried I'd be trapped inside it once more.

Then I thought of Dad. If I told the Serpent Society he knew nothing about Hy-Brasil, why would they bother keeping him alive? When I told them what I did know, they would hunt Richard and Camila. They'd know about the guesthouse, the alarm codes, everything.

And then there was Griffin. Broken, beautiful Griffin. They could harvest his cells, as his mother had harvested Galena's.

I had to protect everyone.

The darkness receded as I stepped into the dappled sunlight of the bookstore, the reassuring aroma of Chanel No. 5 perfume and freshly roasted coffee beans swirling around me. There was Mom, sitting by the window. Her hair tumbled in waves over her shoulder, almost the same mahogany color as her sweater. I wondered if my hair would become redder as I got older—*if,* I got older. Taking a sip of her cappuccino, Mom tilted her head in my direction. Her mouth split into a wide smile as she opened her arms. I threw myself into them.

As she stroked my hair, I felt safe, as I always did in this world. But something was bothering me, tugging at me, like an itch I couldn't scratch. Slowly, I turned my head. I could still see Dad, chained to a cot in the cellar, like a dog tethered to a tree. The real world had not disappeared as it usually did.

And Dad needed me. I wasn't sure what I could do to help him, but I wouldn't let him suffer and die alone.

Mom cupped my cheeks with her hands. "Always remember, 'You're braver than you believe, and stronger than you seem, and smarter than you think.'"

For the first time in years, I believed her. I promised myself I would be there for Dad, and I would keep my promise. I would free him from whatever terrors awaited us in that basement.

As I kissed her goodbye, the warmth disappeared from her skin and was replaced by a bone-chilling cold.

Opening my eyes a fraction of an inch, I saw Cobra still hunched over me.

"What the bloody hell happened?" the tall man asked.

"She's out cold. The serum, combined with the drug I administered, must have knocked her out again. Who knows what's in her system; she's under the care of a psychiatrist. I have calls to make. Python, have the team on standby. If she wakes, get me."

"Give her a shot of adrenaline," Python suggested.

Cobra shook his head. "Too risky. Like I said, we don't know what's in her system. It could send her into cardiac arrest. She's the key, and she's no good to us dead. We need to make our preparations. Within a few hours we should know far more. Viper, do what must be done. No loose ends."

No sooner had Python and Cobra left than Viper stooped toward Dad. "Time to wake up, Mr. Winters. This is your last chance to tell us what you know."

As the man tried to rouse Dad, I pushed the point of the needle into the bottom of the keyhole, rotating it to the right and then to the left. It wouldn't budge. Drops of perspiration dotted my forehead as I focused on the lock and tried again and again. I wiggled my fingers. *Come on, Annabeth, you've picked dozens of locks. Now is not the time to choke.* When my hands were finally steady, I inserted the needle into the hole and turned it very slowly until I heard the softest click.

"This should wake you," Viper said.

Dad moaned.

"If you tell us what you know, we'll spare your daughter. If not, we will do what we have to in order to make her talk."

"You won't touch her, you bastard!"

"Tell us what you know."

"Nothing! I don't know anything about the island other than what I've already told you!"

"You know what, Mr. Winters? I believe you. No one could withstand the pain you have and not talk. Your suffering will end soon. Unfortunately, your daughter's will soon begin."

Dad let out a bloodcurdling scream.

As noiselessly as possible, I slid my wrist out of the cuff and quickly unfastened the restraints. Jumping off the cot, I saw Viper—a dagger in his hand—approach Dad, who was still screaming to muffle any sounds I made—at least, I told myself that was why he was screaming. I grabbed a short sword from the wall, pulled my arm back, and smashed the heavy pommel against the back of Viper's skull.

He fell to the ground.

My hand trembling, I felt for a pulse. It was faint. I tried to remove the mask, but it was attached with some kind of adhesive and wouldn't budge. Then I searched his pockets, retrieving a keyring holding two keys.

I exchanged the sword for the dagger he dropped, slipped it in the belt loop of my jean shorts, and hugged Dad gently—he was bruised and bloodied and his hands were swollen to twice their normal size.

"Go and get help. Don't worry about me."

"I'm not leaving you." Once Dad's cuff was off, I helped him to his feet and up the stairs. After unlocking the trap door, I pushed aside the branches and vines that concealed it and let out the breath I'd been holding—we appeared to be alone. I climbed out and hoisted Dad through the opening.

I looked in every direction, but the night was as black as tar; I couldn't tell where the trees stopped and the sky began. Then a sliver of a moon broke free from the clouds that imprisoned it, illuminating the mist as it snaked along the forest floor. Remembering the ride here, I half-dragged Dad down a slope.

"Annabeth, listen," Dad said, panting. "I can't go any further. I haven't had anything to drink or eat . . . my ribs . . . even breathing is painful, let alone walking. Leave me in the woods and run and get help."

I was certain that if I left him, I'd never see him alive

again. "If I leave, you won't make it. You're not athletic, and you get lost using a GPS—and that's when you're healthy."

"I see the truth serum is working," Dad muttered.

"Besides, you're probably dehydrated. You need water." I circled my arm around his waist. "We'll do this together, or not at all. I'm not losing you."

Dad sighed and we kept going—excruciatingly slowly, as he kept having to stop to catch his breath. The trees thinned, easing our way, until we came to a field. With a surge of hope, I realized that it wasn't a field but a ski trail—which meant we weren't far from the stream I had heard. As I dragged Dad down the hill, my foot caught on an old toboggan, giving me an idea. I heaved Dad onto it, grabbed the torn rope looped to the front of the sled, picked up one end, and pulled.

With each bump, Dad gasped and moaned, but I knew it was nothing compared to the pain he'd be in if they found us. That thought kept me going, despite the throbbing ache in my back and hands from both my beating and the rope burn.

As the sky lightened to a lapis blue, a soft gurgling noise sang in my ears—it was the sweetest sound I had ever heard. I pulled Dad off the sled and led him toward the water. He could barely move his hands, so I cupped mine and eased several handfuls of cool mountain water into his mouth. Then I drank thirstily, ignoring the pain in my split lip.

While Dad rested, propped against a large oak, in my mind's eye I brought up the map of the forest surrounding Bradford Manor that I had stared at countless times. One of the streams ran between two trails, eventually emptying into the pond near the guesthouse. If this was *that* stream, all we had to do was follow it. I trudged through the dense woods, but there was no sign of another trail, and the idea of leaving Dad for too long worried me. I paused, deciding whether to go forward or back, when the sound of a motor breached the silence.

Fear fed adrenaline directly to my legs as I raced back to Dad, helped him onto the sled, and pulled, weaving around trunks as fast as I could in the opposite direction from the ATV.

But not fast enough. An engine revved behind me, growing louder and louder.

The trees gave way to a meadow bordered by the forest on three sides and a cliff on the other. Squinting into the darkness, I spied several narrow openings cut into the imposing rock, and my exhaustion melted away as if I'd just drunk a double espresso. The sled felt almost light as I pulled Dad across the long grass and slipped inside the farthest cave, while trying not to think about the huge hairy spiders that probably called this place home. Even though I knew they were the least of my worries, my shoulders still wiggled.

A strange noise—like heavy breathing—sounded from the depths of the cave. Dagger in hand, I crept farther into the cavern but couldn't see anything—it was absolutely dark, like being inside a black hole. Dad's rattling cough was quickly followed by a moan, and I decided whatever was making that noise couldn't be as dangerous as Python. At this point, I'd actually prefer a wolf or a bear. Leaving Dad on the sled, I went outside to gather brush and branches to camouflage the opening. The first rays of sunlight tore through the darkness, illuminating the hillside—and the track the sled had left in the damp ground.

How could I have been so stupid?

Dropping the twigs and leaves I had gathered, I bolted inside the cave and gently shook Dad. "Wake up!"

He didn't respond, forcing me to shake him harder. "Dad, I need you to do this, or we're both going to die."

His eyes flew open.

"They're close. We need to go. Now," I said with as

much authority as I could muster. I helped Dad up, but the sound of crunching pine needles stopped me dead in my tracks. We melted into the shadows against the cave wall, the bone-white handle of the dagger clutched tightly in my palm.

My heart leaped into my throat when a man stepped into the cave, his red mask gleaming in the darkness. As the light of his flashlight shone all around, I hid the dagger behind my back and stepped in front of Dad.

"You're a resourceful girl, Annabeth, I'll give you that," Cobra said in his muffled voice. "But the serum I injected you with is still affecting your system. Where is Hy-Brasil?"

"I don't know."

"That is disappointing. Who has been to the island?"

A sharp jolt split my brain in two. One half commanded me not to answer, while the other half willed me to. Gritting my teeth, I clutched my pounding head.

"Who has been to Hy-Brasil?" Cobra demanded once more.

I tried to fight it, tried to hold on to the secret, but my resolve ebbed like a wave buckling beneath itself as it is reluctantly dragged from the shore. My voice was pinched as I answered: "Aunt Kathy . . . Uncle Paul . . . Malcolm

. . . Sarah . . ." Each face floated ghost-like in my peripheral vision as I uttered the corresponding name.

"Your father?"

"No."

"Camila?"

"Yes."

"Jack?"

"Yes."

"Griffin?"

As I closed my eyes tightly, I was flooded with images of Griffin: his wicked grin . . . the heart-wrenching sadness in his eyes when he talked about his parents . . . his tormented face as he told me his secrets, trusting me to keep them . . . the look in his eyes when he kissed me . . . My body trembled violently as the opposing forces went to war in my head: *Answer him, don't . . .*

"Did Griffin go to Hy-Brasil and drink from the Fountain of Youth? Or did someone bring the water back for him?" Cobra watched me expectantly, his eyes shining with anticipation as I opened my mouth.

Balling my hands, I could almost feel the way Griffin's large palm and short fingers felt against my skin as he led me to his secret fort, reading to me so that I could fall asleep. I fastened my lips together tightly, my bottom teeth holding my split upper lip shut, blood pooling on my lips from the effort.

"Tell me!"

Each heartbeat seemed to shake my entire body as he slowly approached, a long blade in his outstretched hand. "Answer me or I'll cut your father into pieces. Limb. By. Limb."

Rage coursed through my veins, bringing with it a sudden clarity, and I drew my arm back and charged. He slashed at me again and again, aiming for my arms, thighs, legs—but his desperation to take me alive terrified me more than anything else, and I dodged each blow. Backing me into a recess cut into the jagged rock, Cobra swept his blade toward my shoulder. As I twisted away, he sliced my arm right above the wrist just as I thrust my dagger into his stomach, beneath the rib cage, angling it upward.

Cobra let out a loud groan that reverberated against the stone walls, and then he fell to the ground.

My breath came fast. In equal parts, I hoped Cobra was dead—he would never be able to hurt me or anyone I loved again—and I hoped I was not a killer. On wobbly legs, I stepped closer to him, peering at his chest still rising and falling, and expelled a long breath. I had enough blood on my hands.

Dad coughed again, a horribly raspy sound, snapping me into action. With my arm around him, we raced outside.

Yet my hope for escape vanished as quickly as it appeared, for before us stood two men silhouetted against the dawn, staring at us from behind their blood-red masks. One wielded a dagger, the other a gun.

There was no chance of escape.

CHAPTER *Seventeen*

I knew what I'd have to do, if it came to it, as much as I hated to even think it. I'd use the dagger to kill Dad and then turn it on myself. A quick death was far preferable to the torture we'd endure otherwise and the result would be the same, regardless.

No, that wasn't exactly true. Death by my hands would save Griffin, Richard, and Camila. I had no choice.

Drawing in a deep breath to steel my nerves, I clutched the handle tighter with my left hand—hoping I had the strength to do it—while trying to ignore the searing pain that burned up my right arm. Already, I felt light-headed, and the smell of my own blood was making me sick to my stomach.

The large man stepped slowly toward me. "Annabeth, you need to stop this and come with us. We don't want to hurt anyone. Our goal is to find the island. If you tell us what you know, it ends here. You both will be free to go."

I recognized the voice—Python's. The man who enjoyed swatting me around the way a cat plays with a mouse before finishing it off. I stared again at the blade in my hand glinting in the cold pale light of dawn, and my resolve strengthened. I would not return to that cellar. "Do you really think I'm stupid enough to believe you?"

"If you don't get on that ATV, I'll shoot your father. He has outlived his usefulness," the smaller man said.

I had one advantage—they wanted me alive. I stood in front of Dad, the dagger in my outstretched hand. "No."

"What happens now is up to you." Python fired, the bullet echoing against the rocky hillside above my head. "Next time, I won't miss. I'll shoot you in the leg and then kill your father. As long as you're breathing, you'll tell us what we need to know."

I swallowed hard, my legs swaying beneath me and blood dripping from my fingers onto the carpet of wild-flowers beneath my feet. "I won't."

He fired off another shot so close, I felt the bullet as it whizzed by my leg and into the cave. "Last chance."

He cocked his gun again. I pulled Dad against me to explain what I was about to do—what I *had* to do.

And then the aonbharr tore out of the cave snorting loudly, her side streaked with blood.

Before Python could get off another shot, Niamh reeled on her back legs and let out a high-pitched screech, shrill and loud, making my teeth chatter and sending my shoulders up to my ears. The two men hunched over, hands covering their ears, as she lowered her head, pawing her hoof like a bull. Without considering the wisdom in it, I hoisted Dad onto her back and slid in front of him, twisting his arms around me. The aonbharr didn't seem to either notice or care.

As both men lunged for me, she reared up again. Dad and I almost slid off her back before she charged at them, knocking one to the ground as she galloped down the hillside. Shots rang out behind us, but Niamh was too fast—the trees whizzed by in a blur. I felt like I was on a roller coaster that was flying at breakneck speed and I'd left my stomach behind.

Dad clung to me as I grasped the aonbharr's mane, as soft as silk between my fingers, placed my throbbing arm on her back, and lay against her neck. I was so dizzy, I closed my eyes. A clammy warmth spread through my body.

"Annabeth? Stay with me, honey."

Dad sounded far away.

As Niamh's pace slowed, so did my pounding heart. I opened my eyes and saw that we were riding through a stream that snaked through the forest. We followed it for miles until the water became deep and dark. Before Niamh slipped beneath the surface, Dad and I jumped off, making our way to the bank. We continued on foot, until at long last we reached Griffin's lake. I could just make out the mermaid statue glowing in the golden sunrise.

"Annabeth, it's Griffin. Wake up. Please." His voice was soft but urgent.

My eyelids fluttered open. His face was just inches from mine. He had deep purple circles underneath his bloodshot eyes, but he had never looked so beautiful to me.

In the distance, a loon called out and another sang back. For the first time, I understood what Mom had meant when she said a loon's call was both the most beautiful and the saddest sound she'd ever heard. Maybe we can't appreciate the beauty without the sadness; maybe we can't love without suffering loss.

Maybe I was ready to feel again.

Something cold pressed against my face. Nice—refreshing, like a popsicle on a hot summer day. Mmmm, a popsicle would taste so good. My throat was parched. Opening my eyes—or rather, opening one eye, since the other stayed stubbornly shut—I saw Griffin holding a compress to my forehead. I was lying on a hospital bed, but I wasn't in a hospital room—it was more like a fancy, antiseptic-smelling hotel, with a door leading out to a small balcony, a beige fake-leather sofa and chairs, and a big flat-screen television perched on top of a dresser.

Griffin's furrowed brow smoothed. "Annabeth? How do you feel?"

I lifted my head off the pillow. "Where's Dad?"

"He just came out of surgery. He had some internal bleeding, and the orthopedic surgeon set his bones. Don't worry, he's going to be fine. As soon as he's in his room, you can see him."

"Where am I?"

"You're at Bradford Memorial Hospital. Your father will be in the room next door. There are guards outside both of your rooms and Richard had the floor sealed off—no one is allowed up here without authorization. Annabeth, you're safe."

"Niamh?"

He brushed my hair off my forehead. "Just fine. The bullet only grazed her hide and trust me, aonbharrs have tough hides."

As I lay back into the soft pillows, I saw that my right hand was in a mammoth splint from my elbow to my fingers, and my left hand was hooked up to an IV. My stomach churned. "Griffin, I need that needle taken out."

Grinning, he shook his head. "You escaped from the Serpent Society, but you're freaked out by a needle? I'll ask, but I'm guessing the answer will be no. You have an infection."

Placing a pillow over the IV needle so I wouldn't have to see it, I took in my strange surroundings. "I've been in this hospital before, thanks to you." I smiled. "This isn't how I remember it."

"This is the private floor."

I rolled my eyes.

"Don't give me attitude. The private floor pays for most of the hardship cases and the Bradford Foundation covers the rest." He tucked my hair behind my ear and rested his hand on my cheek. "Are you in any pain?"

"No. Just tired and thirsty." I held up my mummy

hand. "Is this really necessary? It was just a cut."

"Yeah, it is. The bastard who stabbed you tore your flexor tendon and your wrist is broken, along with your cheek." Griffin's voice was calm and low for my benefit, but as much as he tried, he couldn't disguise his rage; his eyes always gave him away. "The doctors don't think you'll need surgery, but they aren't positive yet, which is why you can only have ice chips."

I sighed. "I'd kill for an iced coffee."

He smiled, but his face was still clouded with anger as he dropped a few ice chips into my mouth. My cracked and swollen lips stung at first, but nothing had ever tasted as good as the ice, and as I rolled it around with my tongue, it slowly dissolved, touching every parched spot until it melted away all too soon.

"Do you know who kidnapped me?"

Griffin shook his head. "Not yet."

I had little faith in *yet*. Would I spend the rest of my life looking over my shoulder? Wondering when they'd attack? I hoped, at least, they wouldn't bother anymore with Dad.

Griffin knitted his eyebrows together. "When you didn't come down in the morning, I went to your room and panicked. Suzette admitted she saw you run out to meet Dr. Harrington. Richard called him—he never contacted you about a meeting; his cell had been stolen. Someone impersonated him to lure you out of the house. Who knows about him?"

"Up here? Holly, Suzette, Deputy Clarke, and the sheriff. At home—the staff at McLean, my headmistress and counselor at school, some neighbors, some of my old classmates—maybe all of them . . . I'm sure word spread— all the Magellans know . . . I guess a lot of people."

"Why did you leave without telling anyone?" Griffin's voice was soft, but his eyes betrayed him once more; he wasn't just confused, he was hurt.

Griffin had trusted me with all his secrets, even knowing that doing so could cost him his life. I owed him the truth. With a deep, shuddering breath, I told him about what happened *after* Mom died: the painting, McLean— everything. "I was worried Dr. Harrington would send me back to the hospital. And"—it was time to admit the truth, even to myself—"I didn't want you to know."

"Annabeth—"

I looked down at the lumpy white blankets covering my legs. "People treated me differently for a long time after my hospitalization. Even Dad."

Griffin lifted my chin, forcing me to look at him. He gently wiped away my tears with his thumbs. "I wouldn't have treated you differently. I understand what it's like to be broken. To have the people you love watching you anxiously. To feel as if"—he paused, choosing his words carefully—"you've let everyone down. But you have nothing to be ashamed of. You are a fighter. A survivor. You fought back then, just as you fought for Sam. You saved yourself and your father from the Serpent Society. You're the only one who's ever escaped. You're the heroine of your own story, Annabeth."

I stared into Griffin's eyes and wished I could see what he saw: That I could believe in myself the way he believed in me. I pushed back the lurking shadows of my mind that kept reminding me of all the mistakes I had made, and I focused instead on what I'd done right, letting that swell and fill all the empty places within me.

"I feel like such an ass, Griffin said, his face stricken. "After all you've been through, to lie about the lightning strike, to make you question what you saw, I gaslighted you. I'm so sorry."

I looked up at the ceiling grids—arranged like a giant tic-tac-toe board—and once again, words failed me. A painting always showed how I felt; I was able to convey my complex emotions and feelings in a way that language couldn't. But truth had its own power, both healing and destructive.

"I forgive you. Besides, I need to come clean about a few things, too. A lot of things." Drawing in a deep breath, I told him everything—the searches, the sketchpad, my many conversations with Holly and Deputy Clarke. I couldn't look at him as I catalogued it all, afraid of what I'd see in his eyes.

"Annabeth, you did what you did to save your father. Not to hurt me." His voice was soft and laced with pain. "If I had told you the truth, you wouldn't have needed to. It's my fault. All of it. From now on, no more secrets. No more lies. But I need you to promise me something." His tone became as serious as his expression. "I need you to promise you'll stay far away from the Serpent Society, the Brasilites—all of it—from now on."

In the silence that ensued, the ambient background noise—the faint beeps, drips, and hisses of the machines surrounding me—practically screamed. From the set of Griffin's face, his furrowed brows angled over his piercing eyes, I understood what he was asking.

But I couldn't give it to him.

"I'm sorry, Griffin. I can't promise you that."

"But you could have died!"

"If I hadn't snuck out, Dad would be dead." I knew that with every fiber of my being. He couldn't have survived much longer in that godforsaken cellar. "I will never make a promise to you I can't keep."

Griffin tugged at the hair curling around his neck. "Why do you make everything so much harder than it needs to be?"

"If life is easy, you're not living it." For years, I had been an observer in my own life, but no more. "I'm not fragile and I won't be treated like I am."

Griffin stared at me in that completely absorbing way of his. "You may not be fragile, but that doesn't mean you can't break."

After Mom died I had broken. Dad and Dr. Harrington had helped put me back together, but I never fully recovered. In science, we learned that when you break a bone, your body makes a hard callus around it to protect it, and the bone actually becomes stronger while it heals. Maybe the mind works the same way? I had done something I never imagined I'd be able to do: I faced the painting again. It no longer had a hold over me. And I wouldn't let fear rule me again. "Everyone can break, Griffin. But we can't live our lives trying to avoid it—believe me, I tried."

Shaking his head, Griffin opened his mouth, but just then my nurse came in. Despite my protests, she changed my IV, and I soon surrendered to sleep.

When I woke again, Richard and Griffin were sitting by my bed. The dark circles under Richard's eyes had blossomed, looking bruised, and his face was gaunt, but his mouth split into a wide smile. "Thank God you're all right." He kissed my forehead.

Guilt hit me like a blow to the chest. I couldn't stand seeing Richard look at me with so much love and concern, not when I had betrayed him and Camila. My confession tumbled out of me in one long quaky breath—if I stopped, I'd lose my courage.

Richard squeezed my uninjured hand. "The Serpent Society had already figured out the connection to the Magellans. You could have told them so much more. About the guesthouse, the codes"—his eyes slid over, softening when they reached his nephew—"and about Griffin.

Somehow, you didn't. We will forever be grateful to you."

The regret that had been sitting like a stone on my chest lessened.

"Is there anything else? Any detail that could help us find who did this to you?" Richard gently prodded.

My throat went dry and blood pounded behind my ears as I forced myself to return to that cellar. Even though I knew in my head I was safe, adrenaline surged through my body, and I fought the impulse to throw off the covers and run and run and run. Griffin sat beside me on the bed and put his arms around my trembling body. "You don't have to do this right now. Rest."

"I do have to, while the memories are fresh." Dad's alter ego—Doctor Dan Danger—had taught me that. Fear, pain, and dread all could alter recall. Hard as it was to believe, a day might come when my mind softened the shards of this memory. I hoped so.

With Richard squeezing my hand and Griffin holding me tightly, I closed my eyes and forced myself to relive my kidnapping, sifting through the memories for clues. I told them about my captors' builds, hair color, accents, code names, the mention of cells . . . and then my heart gave a horrible lurch. "Oh my God! Cobra—the leader, I think—asked me if you'd drunk from the Fountain of Youth, Griffin. Even though I didn't tell him, he's connected the pieces somehow."

Richard's mouth gaped open. "Why would he think that? Did he say anything else?"

I shook my head.

"I don't know how you didn't tell him everything, Annabeth. I'm sure I would have." Griffin stared at me, his face fierce. "All that matters to me is that you're safe and you stay safe—I'll do anything to make sure of that."

He said it with such conviction I almost believed him. But a part of me knew that I'd never be safe—that was the price I paid for Dad's life.

Richard and Griffin waited outside when my doctor came in. He told me I was doing well, but the cut near my eye would scar, and he left a list of plastic surgeons he recommended. After he left, I went into the bathroom to see how bad I looked. Even though I braced myself for the worst, I still gasped. My eye was swollen shut and was a gruesome shade of dark bluish-green, like a stormy sea. Black sutures zigzagged from my eyebrow down past the corner of my eye. My cheek was even worse—a bruised violet bleeding into a cadmium green border. My lip, at least, looked better than I expected: crimson red and inflamed.

Running my finger lightly over the thin red fissure, I smiled back at the unfamiliar face—the face of a warrior.

As soon as Dad woke up, Griffin helped me push the IV pole across the fake marble floor while Richard checked with security—again—finally ushering us into Dad's room. Even though Dad looked terrible—both hands were in casts, and in the fluorescent light he was even more bruised than I thought—days of worry, torment, and fear visibly slipped from his body like a snake shedding his skin. I rushed to his side and gently kissed his cheek, the one spot that wasn't bruised or bandaged.

Dad beamed at me, the fine lines around his bright blue eyes wrinkling. "My darling girl, look at you. You have your battle scars, don't you? Your mother would be so proud."

I thought about Mom. Was she really talking to me in that cellar, or was it my mind's attempt to cope with the stress—had it splintered into my imaginary world again? Remembering her words to me, I smiled.

"I guess fencing club wasn't such a bad thing after all."

I laughed. "Yeah, I guess I owe Headmistress Reynolds for making it a requirement that all students join clubs." Even thinking about school was strange, as if it was from another lifetime.

"Deputy Clarke has been pushing to get in here to talk to both of you," Richard said. "Of course, the truth is out of the question, so let's go over the story I worked out with the Council."

We discussed the lie, with Dad adding details here and there to make it more believable. It was the most plotting he'd done since Mom died. While we waited for Deputy Clarke, I turned on the television—certain I'd made the local news. Sure enough, images of Bradford Memorial Hospital filled the screen while a reporter said:

"*New York Times* bestselling author Sam Winters was found yesterday by none other than his daughter, Annabeth Winters. Sources close to the family have expressed concern about Miss Winters's mental state since she has a history of instability."

I hissed in a breath, for the hospital photo was replaced with a terrible picture of me at a fencing match. As bad as that was, I forgot all about it as I read the breaking news scrolling across the bottom of the screen:

SHERIFF CLAYTON ADMITTED TO
BRADFORD MEMORIAL HOSPITAL DUE TO
INJURIES SUSTAINED BY A KNIFE WOUND.

THERE ARE CURRENTLY NO SUSPECTS IN THIS ATTACK.

I pointed at the television. "The sheriff? Stabbed?"

Richard shook his head. "Terrible. Just terrible. I heard the nurses talking about it. He should pull through just fine, but half an inch either way and he wouldn't have been so lucky."

"Where was he stabbed?"

"Outside of Kendall's. One of the nurses said that he stops there every night to buy scratch tickets."

Kendall's—where I was supposed to meet Dr. Harrington. "Where on his body?"

"In the stomach."

I covered my mouth with my hand. "Oh my God."

"Annabeth, what is it? What's wrong?" Dad said.

"The sheriff is Cobra!"

CHAPTER Eighteen

All eyes were on me, but for a few long moments I couldn't find the words. My brain couldn't accept how wrong I'd been. Not once had I suspected the sheriff. How could I have been so stupid?

Dad was the first to speak. "Honey, what are you talking about?"

"Suzette must've been spying for the sheriff. She gave him the list of questions I'd written down—theories about what could have happened to Dad, including stuff about the expedition and the Magellans. Then there's the search warrant. The sheriff went through all the photos and maps in the library. I'm sure he saw Hy-Brasil on that map and broke the frame to check for clues. The sheriff threatened to have me put in foster care but then said I could stay with him and Holly. Cobra's voice was always muffled, as if he was disguising it. I stabbed Cobra, who was just about the same size as the sheriff, in the stomach. It has to be him."

Griffin's face was all sharp angles. "It was the sheriff who insisted on a search warrant despite the lack of evidence, and he didn't seem overly concerned about Sam's disappearance. Richard, you had to fight with him to get an aerial search."

I nodded, my cheek stinging in complaint. "I wrote about Griffin healing fast and Cobra asked me if Griffin had drunk from the Fountain of Youth. If that's not damning, I don't know what is."

Dad's eyebrows practically arched up into his hairline as he looked at each of us in turn. "Fountain of Youth?"

Damn it.

Richard ran a hand through his hair, which had thinned considerably in the past few weeks. "Listen, Sam, there's a lot about Hy-Brasil that you don't know, and we need to keep it that way."

Dad sat up straighter, grimacing with the effort. "Why does Annabeth know? That puts *her* in danger. Damn it, Richard, she's all I have!" The machines surrounding Dad beeped and hissed in a high-pitched staccato. "We've been friends for a long time. What happened to me"—he paused, his eyes shadowed—"I know wasn't your fault. But you weren't in the cellar with those bastards. You don't know what they're capable of. You didn't have to wake up to your daughter's screams. Annabeth has to stay safe."

Richard flinched, his face the same pasty color as the sheets. "I'm sorry, Sam. The words seem so inadequate, but I truly am. When I invited you to stay, I never suspected we were in danger. But I've kept everyone in the dark about what Annabeth knows."

Griffin tugged at the rope encircling his neck. He wouldn't meet my gaze.

I put my hand on Dad's arm, above his cast. "Don't blame Richard; blame me. I was determined to uncover the secret because I thought it could help me save you. Griffin and Richard tried to protect me. But I wouldn't let it go. And if I had to do it over, I'd do the same thing."

Dad's face softened. "My fearless Annabeth. What am I going to do with you? But it's my job to protect *you*. If I don't, who will?"

"What's done is done. There's no point talking about it anymore. Now we need to focus on proving that the sheriff is Cobra. We should start by questioning Suzette, to figure out why and for how long she's been feeding him information. Maybe he pays her. Maybe she's involved." I thought of all her warnings. "Or, It could be that she really was just worried about me."

"I fired her," Griffin said flatly. "For not telling anyone you left to meet your doctor."

Richard pulled his cell from his pocket. "I'll take care of it as soon as I speak to our attorney. If the sheriff is in the Serpent Society, we need the documents seized during the search warrant back as soon as possible."

"What's in the documents?" I asked, my voice unnaturally high.

"Mostly information about test samples, useless data, but there are some notations that the Serpent Society should not see." His eyes flashed to Griffin.

My stomach dropped into the soles of my white fluffy slippers. "Do they name—"

"The studies do not identify the specimen."

As Richard left to make his calls, Deputy Clarke came in. He told Griffin that Dad and I needed to be interviewed privately, watching Griffin with suspicion until he left.

"My God, Annabeth. How are you feeling?" Deputy Clarke said as he sat in the chair beside me.

"Okay. It looks worse than it is."

"Well, I can't tell you how relieved I am to see the two of you sitting there." He smiled and patted my shoulder. "I'm sure you're both tired, so just tell me what happened and I'll leave you to rest."

Dad and I spewed the lie: Dad got lost following the stream in the wrong direction, fell down a steep embankment, and broke his hands and some ribs. I called for Dad over and over, and when he responded, I stumbled down the same ledge trying to get to him, cutting my arm, hitting my face on a rock, and breaking my phone in the process.

"Anything else to add?"

Dad shook his head and sank back into his pillows. He was soon asleep again.

"How's the sheriff? Is he going to be okay?" I prayed that he would be. As much as I hated him, I didn't want to be responsible for his death. I didn't want to be the person who took Holly's father from her.

"He's in a lot of pain, but he'll make a full recovery. He's lucky to be alive."

I exhaled a sigh of relief.

"Take care of yourself and call me if you need anything. Do you know when you're scheduled to be released?"

"Soon, I hope. If I don't end up needing surgery."

"Between your father and the sheriff, every reporter in the state seems to be camping outside. I can give you a police escort."

"Thanks, but I have plenty of people helping me."

"I'll be spending a lot of time at the hospital with the sheriff—going over old cases, trying to find a motive for his attack—so if you change your mind, or think of anything else, just call me."

Deputy Clarke wasn't out the door five seconds before a nurse bustled in, escorted me back to my room, and changed my IV. Within minutes, my limbs were heavy and I couldn't keep my eyes open.

When I woke up again, my IV was out—thank God—and Richard was reading in the chair beside my bed.

"Where's Griffin?" I asked.

"He was called to report to the Council." Richard forced a smile—which looked more like a grimace.

"Why?"

Richard patted my arm. "I'm not sure. But don't worry." His calm voice contradicted the tension in his face.

What could it mean? Did the Council suspect Griffin had side effects from his procedure? Could they suspect that he told me about Hy-Brasil? Reaching for my phantom bracelet, I went over the presidents in my mind. Arthur, why could I never remember Arthur? I knew there were two cartoon characters in a row, but my mind went from Garfield to Snoopy, every time.

The knot in my stomach twisted tighter and tighter as one hour turned into two, two into three. Richard and I visited Dad. I talked to Holly on the new phone Richard gave me—he wouldn't let me near her until we knew more about her father—and my doctor examined me again. Finally, Richard, who'd been texting Camila, left to see what was going on.

I lay in bed, with only my troubled thoughts for company. What was taking so long? What were Camila and Richard worried about? What did the Council want with Griffin? My mind jumped from one terrible scenario to another. Would the Council demand that Griffin return to Hy-Brasil? If they did, would I even get to say goodbye?

Standing alone on the narrow balcony outside my room, I realized I had a partial view of the parking lot if I craned my neck. As I watched for Griffin's Jeep, I reached once more for my charm bracelet to calm my frayed nerves, but of course it wasn't there. Leaning against the railing, I stared off into the woods. The afternoon sunlight cast a golden glow on the trees, making them appear as if they were statues carved in bronze. The air was so still, not even a whisper of a breeze rustled the branches to break the illusion. I had the urge to paint it, but I had no paints.

The sliding door creaked behind me, causing me to jump. I felt my entire body exhale at the sight of Griffin. "Thank God. You should have called!"

Griffin gave me a tight smile. "Sorry. It took longer than I expected."

"Well? What did they say?"

He stood beside me and leaned his long torso over the balcony, his elbows on the railing and his hands clasped. "They asked me question after question about the night my parents died. They're worried it was the Serpent Society." Griffin's square jaw twitched as he tried to keep his composure. "I don't remember any of it. Of course, now they're suspicious. But I don't know what's worse—thinking it's my fault, or thinking they were murdered. I may never know what really happened."

I bit back the truth. Knowing it's your fault is worse. Far

worse. The rage has nowhere to go but inward. "That was all they said? No threat of making you return to Hy-Brasil? Or worse?"

Griffin shook his head. "They're investigating. My fate depends on what they find out."

A reprieve, that's all it was. "What did your lawyer say about the documents?"

"She's going back to court with an emergency motion today."

"That's great."

Griffin nodded, not meeting my eye.

"Just tell me what else is going on. You know I'll keep bugging you until you do."

"I do know that." A ghost of a smile played at the corners of his mouth for a moment, until his face became all hard angles. "The Council wants to see the documents the police seized, once we get them back."

"What's in those boxes, exactly? They weren't in the hidden room—how bad can they be?"

Griffin blew out a sigh. "Pretty bad. The Council will know about my side effects. As for the sheriff, he knows enough about me that he might be able to piece together what happened."

I swallowed hard. "We need to get them back right away. You're the key. If the Serpent Society hell, if almost anyone—discovered there was a way to make themselves like a Brasilite, like you, life as you know it would be over. The Serpent Society would never stop hunting you. And if they found you . . ." My voice trailed off. I could barely think the words, let alone speak them. Griffin would be a lab rat—tortured, experimented on, cut open—and with his ability to heal, he wouldn't even have hopes of a quick death as an escape.

"It's hard to imagine anyone wanting to be like me." Griffin's voice was raw and choked. "Going over that horrible night again . . ."

He hung his head even lower, and I put my hand on his back, trying to rub away some of the tension between his shoulder blades.

Standing, Griffin ran his hands through his hair. He looked so vulnerable, so tortured, it broke my heart. "The truth is, the Brasilites *should* be worried about me. I'm a risk. A big one. If I was taken by the Serpent Society and blacked out, I'd have no idea what I did or didn't say. I could put Richard, Camila—the entire island—and now you, in jeopardy. During the episodes, I'm not myself, Annabeth."

"But you're getting better. The new meds are helping."

Frowning, Griffin looked down at his hands as if they belonged to someone else. "The procedure changed me. I am so strong, sometimes it scares me." His voice was barely a whisper. "The day of the search warrant, I almost pushed Deputy Clarke so hard I could have killed him."

I entwined my fingers in his injured ones. "But you didn't. You've never hurt anyone. It won't be long until Richard and Camila figure it out and you stop having episodes."

"Regular medicines don't work on me. Not anymore." He looked at me, his face harrowed. "How long until I do something else? Until I put someone else in danger? How could I live with myself? I'm not human. I'm not a Brasilite. I'm a monster."

"Listen to me," I said fiercely. "You're not a monster any more than I am. A monster hurts people on purpose, like the guy who beat me. What we did . . . neither of us could have predicted. When I snuck out, I thought, worst-case scenario, I'd be grounded for a few weeks. When you ran out of the house, you didn't even know what you were doing."

Dropping my hand, Griffin leaned over the railing again, his eyes fixed on a distant spot.

I laid my arm across his back, my head on his shoulder.

"We just need to focus on getting those boxes back."

"Our lawyer is doing everything she can. And even if we get the files back, Galena will just take them." There was a flatness to Griffin's voice, as if there was no hope of changing what he expected to happen.

I spun him around, forcing him to look at me. "Griffin, what will the Council do when they find out about the side effects?"

He put a hand on his chest, covering the silver orb beneath his T-shirt. "Honestly? We don't know. The Brasilites—and in particular, the Council—are ruthless when it comes to protecting the island. While I lived on Hy-Brasil, I met this old guy, Pierce Piedmont, who was being kept there against his will because he knew too much. His grandfather had been to Hy-Brasil and had told him all about it. When my father was at Trinity, the Council asked him to keep tabs on Pierce since he lived near the college. Dad reported back that he was a fixture at the local pub, where he tended to drink too much and share stories of his grandfather's adventures on the island—which, of course, no one believed. Dad thought the Council would lecture him, but they didn't. They kidnapped Pierce and took him to Hy-Brasil, where he's been a prisoner ever since. He had to leave his kids and grandkids without a word. He'll never be able to see them again. All because he knew too much and couldn't be trusted to keep his mouth shut."

Wrapping my arms around myself, I leaned against the brick wall of the hospital. Would they do that to Griffin? And if they did, would I ever see him again? What if the Council found out about me? The Brasilites might kidnap me, just like the Serpent Society had. I wouldn't be tortured physically, but leaving everything behind—leaving Dad behind—would be torture of a different kind.

Griffin pulled me into his arms, and I leaned against his chest, feeling safe as he held me, his arms around my waist, his chin on my shoulder. The feeling of safety was an illusion, I knew that in my head. Still, my body stopped trembling.

All too soon, Griffin pulled away. "I swear to you, I'll figure this out."

Three days later, my stitches were removed, a smaller cast was put on my wrist, and I was discharged. I wrapped my arm in plastic and took a shower. After I wrung out my hair and put on my jean shorts and T-shirt—which, despite being washed, probably more than once, still bore faint brown blood stains—I felt like a person again.

I waited impatiently for Griffin to get to the hospital. I'd barely even seen him these last few days. Between more reports to the Council and meetings with his attorney, he'd been busy. When I did see him, he seemed distracted. Whenever I asked about the Council or the investigation into the Serpent Society, he answered matter-of-factly, his face stony. I thought—more than once—about pressing the matter, but each time I saw him, he looked worse: his shoulders more stooped, his eyes more shadowed. I decided to wait until we were back at Bradford Manor, where we could spend more time together and he couldn't so easily dodge my questions.

I said goodbye to Dad—who claimed he felt better even though his bruises had darkened to a deep eggplant color—and promised him I'd visit every day until he was released. Then, I called Dr. Harrington. Surprisingly, our conversation went well, despite the fact it lasted as long as a session.

Finally, Griffin knocked on the door.

"Out here!"

Richard had brought my art supplies a few days ago, so I was sitting on the balcony, trying once more to capture the setting sun. Long shafts of pink light sliced through the woods, and for a moment, it seemed as if the birch trees had burst into flames. My fingers worked furiously, but all too soon the forest was cast in shadow as the fiery bands of sky kissed the mountains and twilight descended.

Griffin peered over my shoulder. "I wish I could see what you see."

I smiled up at him. "I wish I could capture what I see."

"How are you feeling?" he asked.

"Much better," I said, even though my bruises had blossomed into a gruesome shade of green. "Despite the fact that I look like an extra in a bad alien movie."

Griffin smiled, but it didn't reach his eyes.

"What is it? What's wrong?"

Despair flittered across his face for just an instant, before he rearranged his features into the mask of indifference he was so good at hiding behind. "Annabeth, we need to talk," he said in a deadened tone.

My chest constricted as if I'd had the wind knocked out of me. I stared at Griffin—searching for reassurance in his eyes—but instead he looked at me with detachment.

My heart plummeted like the hawk that swooped past, diving after its prey.

"I promised you that I'd figure this out, and I have," he said softly. "There's a way out."

"What?"

"A fresh start in a safe house, far away from here, with new names, new identities, where there would be no need to worry about the Serpent Society or the Brasilites."

For a moment, I could see myself, along with Griffin, Dad, Richard, and Camila, in a cottage by the sea on a rocky coast somewhere. Dad would write; I would paint; Griffin, Richard, and Camila would work on a cure for Griffin. Maybe Zach and Lucas could visit. I couldn't deny that part of me longed for it, longed to leave everything behind, to live in a small, safe world, with the people I loved. But I knew now that wasn't really living. Living was taking risks. Dangerous ones. Like driving in a car. Like letting yourself care about someone so much that when that person leaves, a part of you goes with them.

"No, Griffin. I'm not running away. Not again."

"Annabeth, please listen to me. The Serpent Society knows you have information about the island. That's a fact. The Brasilites are advanced. Very advanced. They've developed all kinds of technologies. Most are great, helpful, but some are designed to protect the island. Like a machine that can wipe your memory, completely, and insert another person's memories so you don't even know it happened."

"They wouldn't!" One look at Griffin's ashen face told me that they would. That they *had*. "That's crueler than torturing someone. I'd rather have my hand cut off than have my memories of Mom ripped from my mind."

"I know. Believe me, I know. I just want you to know what you're dealing with."

I couldn't take that risk. I wouldn't. Maybe we did need a sanctuary, at least for a little while. "First, we have to get those documents back, even if we have to steal them."

Griffin shook his head, his dark hair lifting in the soft breeze. "It is not worth the risk."

"Yes, it is. Otherwise, the sheriff will figure out he only needs your DNA or bone marrow or whatever. Then, if the Brasilites look like they pose a risk, we'll take off. Until it's safe again." I threaded my fingers around his neck. "As long as we're together."

His muscles tightened beneath my palms. Holding my wrists gently, Griffin removed my hands. If I didn't know him so well, I might have missed the deep emotions that played across his face. Longing . . . regret . . . resolve. My breath hitched.

"No, Annabeth. You don't understand. It wouldn't be all of us. Just you and Sam would leave. And it wouldn't be for a little while. You'd leave for good."

CHAPTER *Nineteen*

It felt as if the balcony had tilted beneath my feet. I stared at him, dumbfounded.

"Some members of the Council are on their way here to investigate." Griffin's tone was even, his face expressionless. "They want to speak to you and Sam."

My heart bounced against my rib cage and up into my throat. "I'll lie. I'll tell them the Serpent Society asked me about an island, but other than that I don't know anything."

"The truth serum the Brasilites use isn't something you can fight against," Griffin said grimly. "Richard will take you to the airfield. Now. Your father will go in the morning, with a medical team."

Gripping the railing so tightly my knuckles turned white, I tried to keep my legs steady while processing what he was saying. I must be missing something. I must have heard him wrong. "Wait. So Dad and I will go, you'll deal with the documents and the Council, and then you'll meet us."

"No, Annabeth. I won't." His voice was cold and impassive.

"Why the hell not?"

Griffin clutched the silver orb in his hand. "Because of this. The Council doesn't know about you. Sure, they'll be pissed you and Sam took off, but they won't *hunt* you. If I left . . ." He shook his head. "I know too much to be allowed to roam free with no tracker. Besides, I made a vow. The Brasilites saved me. I promised to wear this necklace. I owe it not just to them but to Mom and Dad."

"So that's it? This is goodbye?" The terrible ache in the pit of my stomach was spreading, making my legs feel heavy and my chest tight.

His expression softened. "It has to be. Annabeth, please don't cry." Griffin softly traced the wet skin from my cheek to my jaw with his finger.

"I thought—" I swallowed hard, closing my eyes tightly to cage in the rest of my tears. "You said you cared about me."

Griffin cupped my cheek with his palm, his eyes harrowed. "Of course I do. I've always cared about you. I always *will* care about you."

"Then we'll figure this out. Together," I whispered, my voice trembling.

He dropped his hand and looked away. A long minute later, Griffin inhaled a deep breath and swiveled his head back toward me. "You were right. That night we kissed, you were right. We are both going through so much right now, emotionally, that of course we turned to each other. And I'm so grateful you were there for me. I honestly don't think I would have made it through without you. But now—"

"Now what? What are you saying?"

He scrubbed a hand across the back of his neck. "Now, we need to go and live our own lives. You need to finish high school and enroll in art school. I need to work with the Council on what's next for me. Those two paths can't cross, Annabeth."

I tried to shutter the emotions raging inside me: confusion, anger, sorrow. My own heart breaking. Something deep inside me cracked, like a block of ice splintering into sharp pieces. I'd endured physical pain and mental anguish, but this was suffering of another kind.

Griffin captured my hand in his. I looked up at him, and again, I saw a fleeting expression of regret on his face.

Snatching my hand away, I stared at him with narrowed

eyes. "Are you saying this to protect me, or is this what you really want? Because I've made it pretty clear that I don't need protecting."

Griffin rubbed his forehead. "What I want doesn't matter. It stopped mattering when Mom and Galena brought me back."

"What you want always matters, Griffin. You're a person, not an experiment."

"Maybe I'm both." He looked off into the darkening woods, his gaze unfocused. "You need to get away. While you still can. Paint the world as only you see it. Fall in love. Go on with your life, Annabeth."

I grabbed his arm and made him face me. "You're good at dodging questions, but I'm good at getting to the bottom of things. What do *you* want, Griffin? That's the question."

He caught his lip in his bottom teeth, his face conflicted.

"Just tell me! What do you want?"

"I want to stop worrying about you," he answered without hesitation. "It's too much. Right now, I need to focus on myself."

I inhaled a sharp breath—that, I didn't expect. But in the long, silent moments that ensued, I began to understand.

Griffin felt responsible for all that had happened to me. I had, maybe we both had, confused his protectiveness with something different. Something more. The simple truth was, with Dad and me away somewhere safe, Griffin would be relieved.

"I'm so sorry, Annabeth. I never meant to hurt you. We were distractions for each other. Someone who knew what it was like to have your heart torn to pieces. Someone safe to flirt with. And then . . ." He shook his head. "If Sam hadn't been taken, I would have dropped you off at school, we would have promised to call, and neither one of us would have. I would have seen you at Thanksgiving, or over the holidays."

That was true. There was no denying it.

"We would have each gone to school, and this— whatever it is—would have just ended naturally."

True again.

But none of that mattered. Because what should have happened, didn't. The ghost road doesn't matter. Each decision we make affects so many different potentials. Wondering about our phantom selves, our phantom lives—those damned what ifs—causes nothing but heartache.

Griffin clutched the railing with his uninjured hand. "All we're doing now is prolonging the inevitable."

His words pierced me, like shards of glass. "Do you really mean that, Griffin? I deserve the truth. No bullshit."

He nodded. "You do deserve the truth. Which is why I'm telling you how I honestly feel. I'm just sorry it took me so long to figure it out."

As always, Griffin's eyes didn't lie. He cared for me, I knew that. I also knew that he hated to see me suffer. That he felt responsible for my suffering. But he didn't feel what I felt. He didn't feel enough. He didn't love me.

But I loved him. I knew that now.

For some reason, I had just assumed it would be recip-rocated, as I had assumed so many things in my life. Like I'd have another drive to school with Mom, with her listening to an audiobook and getting me to class late because there was a long line at the coffee shop. Since the universe took Mom, I assumed Dad was off-limits. Nothing bad could happen to him. Then it did.

Why was I treating love as something given in exchange for something taken? Love wasn't just a transaction—I love you, so you love me. It wasn't the equivalent of a couple of dollars for a loaf of bread. I had told Griffin that love and sacrifice were intertwined. Were those hollow words? Or did I mean them?

"Annabeth. The plane is waiting. It's time to go."

It took all my strength, but I swallowed back my tears and looked up at him. "You don't get to order me around, Griffin. I'm not leaving my home, my school—maybe my country—just because you say so."

His forehead wrinkled like a musical score. "It's the only way to keep you—and your father—safe." His words were sharp and pointed.

Anger prickled across my skin, and I was glad for it. Glad to feel something, anything, other than hollow. "For the last time, I don't need protection. And I think I've proved I can look out for my father. You worry about yourself and get those damn documents back. Let me worry about me."

"Forget the documents. There's no getting them back, unless we break into a police station, loaded with cameras and security."

Why wouldn't he listen to me? Why was he more worried about the Brasilites than the Serpent Society?

Richard peeked his head through the door. "Annabeth?"

Without tearing his eyes from mine, Griffin called, "We're out here. I told her."

Richard crossed the room, smiling at me sadly. "I'll stay

with you for a few days, to make sure you and Sam are settled and all the security is in place. I've arranged for you to attend a very prestigious art school. I think you're really going to love it."

Like hell.

Richard put his arm around my shoulder and steered me inside. I was trapped. Yet, I had learned something from being the only person to escape from the Serpent Society. Every trap had a weakness. Every trap had a way out. *Think, Annabeth, think.*

Then I had an idea. It was beautiful in its simplicity. Better still, it just might work.

"I'm not going anywhere until I say goodbye to Holly. She texted this morning. She's here visiting her father. I'll meet her in the cafeteria."

Richard nodded. "I'll go with you."

Holly and I texted back and forth, and then I quickly deleted the texts before surreptitiously stashing my phone in the pillowcase.

"I'm ready." I could feel Griffin's gaze on me. Although I wanted to turn, to see his expression, to look into his green eyes and memorize every detail of his face, I didn't. Right now, I needed to be clearheaded. With my chin tipped forward, I walked out the door a few steps ahead of Richard and focused on the details of my plan as I made my way to the cafeteria.

Richard stayed by the cashier, where he was flanked by two burly guys—the security guards he had hired, I supposed—while I joined Holly. She was sitting at a table near the emergency exit, as I'd instructed, a Red Sox hat perched on top of her mane of red hair and two coffees on the peeling brown laminate before her. Sliding into the seat next to her, I whispered, "Put the keys on my lap when I hug you."

"Come on, Annabeth, you have to give me something. Why do you need to see those documents so badly?" Holly's expression was an odd mixture of worry and curiosity, with a dash of excitement thrown in.

I couldn't help but smile. I would miss her. Terribly. "I told you. If everything goes according to my plan, I'll give you something, I swear it. Something that hopefully will get your mother off your back about college." And I would. I just wasn't sure what yet. "How's your father? Is Deputy Clarke still visiting?"

She smiled. "Dad's much better. The two of them are compiling a list of everyone who has a motive. And guess what? A whole lot of people don't like Dad." She adjusted her fuchsia glasses. "They're going to be a while. And I'm pretty sure the boxes are still at Deputy Clarke's house."

I was counting on both. Still, my stomach lurched. Little did Holly know, the person they were searching for was sitting right beside her.

"I wish I could stick around and let you know when Deputy Clarke leaves, but Mom's picking me up and taking me to dinner."

"Hopefully, I won't be long."

Leaning toward me, Holly placed her hat on the table and pulled her wild curls behind her ears. "I made the call to my boss and told him your father was being discharged tonight, so everything should be all set. Annabeth, be careful, okay? Stealing evidence is a felony."

"Promise."

As I put my arms around her narrow shoulders, she dropped the keys onto my lap before hugging me back. "You've been a great friend," I whispered. "I don't know what I'd do without you."

Holly laughed. "Right back at you. Believe it or not, making friends isn't exactly my strong suit. Mom's always telling me I'm too abrasive."

"Don't listen to her, and don't change. I'll bring the car back here when I'm done."

Without so much as a glance back at Richard, I secured the hat to my head and bolted out the emergency exit, the alarm screeching in my ears. I tore down the service road in Holly's car, past the teams of reporters and news vans swarming around the main entrance and clogging up the parking lot. I only hoped the diversion would buy me enough time to get away without being followed.

My eyes kept flashing to the rearview mirror as I drove down the twisting country roads, repeating the directions Holly had given me in my head. So far, so good. Dark storm clouds were all that followed me, rolling across the sky, extinguishing the starlight. No sign of Richard and his guards. No sign of Mac and Galena. No sign of the Serpent Society. I ran a finger over my jagged cut, my throat tightening. Was this my new reality? Always looking at what was behind me? I had focused so much on my plot to get the boxes that I hadn't stopped to consider the risks. What if Python ran me off this desolate road? I had no phone, and no one but Holly knew where I was. My hands shook, and the car jerked into the dirt and then back.

To calm myself, I recited the Hudson River School artists, until I was suddenly transported back to that night Griffin showed me his mom's study. I could see it all clearly—his sad smile, the paintings that reminded him of the island. I could even hear his deep voice, like a whisper in my ear, reciting the poem. The poem that was about Hy-Brasil. I pushed aside my fears. I had to do this to protect Griffin.

My purpose firmly rooted in my heart and my head, I looked forward, not back. First, I'd take the documents and destroy them.

Then, I'd figure out what to do about the safe house and the Council.

I drove past Deputy Clarke's driveway—the house wasn't visible from the road—and killed the lights. The sudden darkness was absolute: The sky, woods, and ground all melted into each other. I shrugged off my anxiety like a coat, unbuckled my seat belt, and exited the car, trying not to think about the last time I was in the woods alone.

Fingers of fear clawed up my throat as I ducked beneath thick tree limbs, my head spinning in every direction, my feet crunching on the gravel. A flash of lightning illuminated the outline of a small log cabin and a detached garage. I hurried toward it, yet the air was so thick and heavy that it thwarted my way as I climbed the brick walkway. The house was dark, but I peered through an oversized window, just to be on the safe side. Deputy Clarke couldn't have beaten me here, but what if the Serpent Society had? What if I opened the door, only to find Python concealed in the shadows?

A dreadful sense of foreboding washed over me and the muscles in my legs clenched, aching to listen to the voice inside my head telling me to turn around and run away as fast and as far as they could take me.

Aching to abort my plan.

With a deep breath for courage, I knocked on the front door and then tried the handle. It was locked. Making my way around to the back of the house, I shielded my eyes from the sudden downpour, climbed up the steep deck stairs, and tried the back door. Naturally, it was also locked—with a deadbolt, like the front door. I was looking for something to pick the lock with, when I spotted an open window a foot or so beyond the deck. I slid a chair over to the railing, and with my fingers in the grooves of a log for balance, I reached for the sill with my good hand. I tried not to look down as I hoisted myself through the window and onto a kitchen counter. After fumbling around in the dark until I found a light switch, I put on the plastic gloves I'd swiped from the hospital and got to work.

The worn hardwood floors complained with each step I took as I surveyed the combination kitchen/living room. Deputy Clarke was certainly not into decorating—the sofa was old and threadbare, a leather recliner was being held together by duct tape, and the few pictures hanging on the walls were of hockey players. It was hard to believe the cute long-haired guy laughing with a teammate was Deputy Clarke.

In the kitchen, I found piles of police documents on the table and a few boxes stacked against the knotty pine paneling. My hands tingled as I sat down on the stiff wooden chair and started reading. A flash of lightning made me jump and a low grumble of thunder spurred me on. I quickly flipped through the pages, but the folders were about different cases. "Damn it!" I slapped the last one shut.

My eyes flashed to the clock—I'd been here twenty minutes already. I peered into a neat-as-a-pin bedroom that was bare except for a mismatched bed, nightstand, and dresser. No pictures decorated the walls, and no curtains framed the two windows. One framed photo sat on the dresser—of a younger Deputy Clarke and an older man who was clearly his father. They had the same wide, serious face, the same kind brown eyes. Lighting exploded in the room, soon followed by a peal of thunder. My heart hammered even faster. After a quick peek under the bed, I made my way down the hall. I passed a dated but spotless bathroom, a small room filled with exercise equipment, and then finally, a study.

There, in the corner, were about a dozen boxes labeled Bradford Manor, the date, and a case number. My muscles softened and I blew out a sigh. I left the kitchen door slightly ajar, pulled Holly's SUV down the driveway, folded down the back row of seats, and stacked all the boxes inside. Just as I was about to shut the trunk, I noticed numbers on the lids: 1 of 11, 2 of 11 . . . I counted the boxes; I only had ten.

Shit.

I hesitated for a moment. Maybe that last box contained nothing important. But what if it did? All of this would've been for nothing. I drove down the driveway, leaving the car on the side of the road again, and raced back through the pouring rain, careful to wipe my shoes on the mat so I wouldn't track mud into the cabin. The wind shut the door for me.

Blood pounded behind my ears as I double-checked the study . . . searched through the bedroom closet . . . the bathroom cupboard . . . the kitchen cabinets.

Then the garage door rattled open.

My heart was in my throat as I searched for a way out. Would Deputy Clarke come in through the kitchen door or the front door? The window. I'd go back out the way I came in. I was climbing up on the butcher block counter when a key clicked in the tarnished brass kitchen doorknob—only half a dozen feet away. I'd never make it.

As quietly as possible, I darted into the bedroom and looked out the window. It was way too high up for me to jump. The kitchen door creaked open as I slid beneath the bed. Maybe, just maybe, Deputy Clarke wouldn't check the study. And when he went to bed, I'd find that last box and get the hell out.

I waited. And waited. The fridge door opened, the microwave beeped, and the smell of tomato sauce and mozzarella cheese wafted down the hall. The faucet turned on, a cupboard door slammed, and then Deputy Clarke was headed this way. My muscles wound as tight as the springs poking through the box-spring inches from my head. The echo of approaching footsteps grew louder and louder, and then softer, as Deputy Clarke walked past the bedroom, past the bathroom, past the exercise room, toward the one remaining room—the study.

"Goddamn it!" he bellowed. Moments later, he was shouting to someone on the phone.

I had to escape before I was caught and charged with a felony. After rolling out from under the bed, I poked my head out the door. No sign of Deputy Clarke. I tiptoed down the hall and into the kitchen. All I could hear was the rain clopping against the roof. Hoping it would mask any noise I made, I climbed up on the counter and was just about to shimmy through the window when a deep voice startled me.

"Well, hello, Annabeth."

Swallowing hard, I jumped down. "I can explain."

"This, I'd love to hear."

I followed him over to the kitchen table. Deputy Clarke motioned for me to sit.

"I'm listening."

My thoughts were scattered as I ran through a handful of explanations—but each was more preposterous than the last. Finally, I decided I had no choice but to stick with the truth—or as close to the truth as possible. "I was worried you'd find something in the documents and tell the sheriff."

Deputy Clarke leaned back in the chair and crossed his arms. "As a matter of fact, I did find something strange in the papers. As I knew I would, given the way Griffin completely overreacted to the search warrant. Not to mention, the amount of money he's spent in attorney fees just trying to get them back. Although money doesn't worry Griffin, does it?" He thrummed his fingers on the table. "I find it very interesting that someone went to great lengths not to identify the subject of the tests. Maybe you know who it is?"

The phone in his holster rang.

Deputy Clarke watched me from the living room as he took the call. My brain worked overtime to come up with something—anything—to tell him. As soon as he sat back down, I blurted out that the Bradfords were doing classified research on an experimental drug. Malcolm tested it on himself, but it didn't work. God, it sounded ridiculous even to me. And apparently it was equally ridiculous to Deputy Clarke, if his smirk and quirked eyebrow were any indication.

He stood, removed a photograph from the wall above the sofa, and opened a safe. Why hadn't I thought to look for a safe? He kept his eyes trained on me as he tossed a folder on the table. "Looks to me like they created a creature with remarkable cell regeneration and increased strength. The question is, who is this creature and where is it now? I think you know the answer to both questions."

"The experimental drug caused those side effects. Malcolm was the subject, like I said," I stammered. "He had blackouts, headaches—it was terrible. That's why he was on the lake that night. And that's what Griffin and Richard are hiding. They don't want to tarnish his legacy. It means so much to them. Please, you can't go to the sheriff with this."

Deputy Clarke sat down, leaned his elbows on the table, and steepled his hands. "How about you tell the truth, or I arrest you for breaking and entering?"

I splayed my shaking fingers across the beat-up wood. "Can I have some water first?"

Never taking his eyes off me, Deputy Clarke turned on the faucet and then handed me a glass. As I took a long sip, my pulse slowed and my mind chilled. And then it came to me. I would tell him what I had believed. The facts fit my theory.

"Well?" he demanded.

"You see, Malcolm did discover a strange creature. He was studying it." I licked my lips. "It got loose, so Malcolm and Sarah ran after it and—"

"Enough."

I was stunned by the vehemence of his voice.

"Suzette reported to the police that *Griffin* ran out of the house that night, not some creature. *Griffin* was the person the Bradfords were searching for the night they drowned. She also reported that *Griffin* has migraines and blackouts, not Malcolm Bradford. What is going on with Griffin, Annabeth?"

Damn, Suzette. My mind whirling and my anxiety rising, I wiped my sweaty palm on my thigh. "Okay. It's true. Griffin has a problem with sleepwalking. He did leave the house that night without even realizing it. His parents went looking for him and they drowned. It was pouring and—"

"Why lie to the police?"

"Because we don't trust the sheriff and neither should you!"

He leaned forward. "Why not?"

"Because he's involved!"

"In what? Annabeth, you're not making any sense."

"In . . ." What could I possibly say? I couldn't tell him about the Serpent Society without telling him about Hy-Brasil. "In corporate espionage. I think he had something to do with Camila's kidnapping." The words tumbled out of my mouth in rapid succession.

Deputy Clarke narrowed his eyes, but he didn't seem surprised or angry. Rather, it was as if he expected me to implicate the sheriff. Did he suspect him, too?

"Explain yourself, Annabeth." He cupped his chin with his palm—showcasing his leather watch strap. It was torn, right above the gold buckle.

I felt as if there was a fist clenched around my heart as I looked into his dark eyes.

The same eyes that had stared at me through a blood-red mask.

The sheriff wasn't Cobra—Deputy Clarke was.

CHAPTER *Twenty*

Deputy Clarke leaned closer to me. "I have an obligation to tell the sheriff what I've learned. Griffin and Richard will be questioned, of course. Interrogated."

Did I imagine the emphasis on terror? It wasn't possible for me to feel more terrified.

I cleared my throat, trying to force in some air. "Like I told you, I'm worried the sheriff was involved in Camila's kidnapping, but you do what you need to do." I worked so hard to keep my voice steady that even to me it sounded oddly robotic. Standing, my shoulders squared, I crossed the floor in measured steps. The thirty-some-odd feet felt like a mile and my legs ached again, longing to run. With trembling hands, I clutched the cold metal doorknob and twisted it. The door wouldn't budge.

Slowly, I turned around. Deputy Clarke stood but a

foot away, a long serated knife in his hand. "Do not move."

The cold menace in his voice froze my blood in my veins. I tried to do as he ordered, but my entire body shook. Was he going to kill me right now? No. Of course not. The Serpent Society wasn't done with me yet. *Be brave, Annabeth.*

"It seems you and I have been keeping secrets. You now know mine. Your turn."

"My father and I haven't been there! Why are you doing this?"

"Clearly, we thought your father knew more than he did. Initially, it was Camila who we were after. Her research notebooks indicated she had been to the island. During the execution of the search warrant, I fed the security footage from Bradford Manor to my laptop, waiting for our chance to grab her, but her husband wouldn't leave her side. When we saw your father—a Magellan, with the symbol of Hy-Brasil tattooed on his shoulder—wandering in the woods by himself, the opportunity was too good to pass up."

"You won't get away with this. Griffin will find me," I said with more bravado than I felt.

He gave me a carnivorous smile. "I'm counting on it."

My heart sank. They were going to use me as bait. And

Griffin would take it. "He doesn't know anything, either!"

Deputy Clarke threw back his head and barked out a laugh as sharp and hard as breaking glass. "Please. After he was struck by the car, his diagnosis was sepsis with multiple organ dysfunction syndrome. It was terminal. Medical records do not lie. Yet here he is. How do you explain that?" Deputy Clarke tapped the knife on my cast. "Start talking."

Panic flooded through me at the wicked glint in his eye; I couldn't move, let alone think. Yet as I stared at his wolfish smile, the weight of his betrayal hit me like a blow, anger eclipsed my fear. "All this time, you've pretended to care about me and Dad while you've been working with the sheriff. Bravo. I actually thought you were a decent person."

"The sheriff?" He snorted. "That idiot doesn't work with us. But stabbing him in the stomach outside of Kendall's was the easiest way to keep your suspicion focused on him."

The room spun around me, and I leaned against the door to steady myself. I played right into his hands, as if I were a puppet and he, the puppeteer. "Who did I knock out in the cellar?"

"A very good friend of mine. He has a concussion, but he's recovering."

I rubbed my forehead, trying to connect the pieces.

"So it was you who stole Dr. Harrington's phone. You texted me that night."

He nodded. "Whether you believe me or not, I had grown fond of you, Annabeth. I tried to get you to leave Bradford Manor on multiple occasions. You wouldn't listen." A trace of regret softened his voice. "Once Suzette gave me the sheet with your questions, I knew you had stumbled upon the secret, leaving me no choice but to lure you out of the house. I was actually going to break protocol and leave you alive. If you had cooperated, we would have administered some psychedelic drugs and brought you back to McLean."

His plan to twist my illness into a weapon filled me with red-hot rage. I hauled off and slapped him across the face without a care or a thought.

His head snapped back, and for a moment, he looked stunned.

"Am I supposed to thank you for that?" I yelled. "My doctors would have thought I suffered a relapse! I might have thought the same!"

Deputy Clarke rubbed his crimson cheek. "At least you would have lived." His tone was hard and cold again. "It's too late now, Annabeth. You saw to that when you escaped. You only have yourself to blame for what's about to happen."

"Do you hear yourself? You and your gang kidnapped me, tortured my father, and were about to kill him! And what about Jack?"

"We didn't touch Jack. If those who knew about Hy-Brasil answered my questions, there would have been no need for violence or torture. Why should the Brasilites hoard the Fountain of Youth while the rest of the world suffers? Why should they give the healing water to a select few, like the Bradfords, and not to everyone?"

"I don't know why you want to get to Hy-Brasil so badly, but I'm sure it isn't to ease the world's pain and suffering. My father and I know nothing about the island; we've never been there. So what are we? Collateral damage?"

"As I said, I didn't want to see you suffer. That was before you did this." He lifted his shirt, revealing a stained and foul-smelling bandage covering his stomach. "The dagger was coated in poison designed to eat away at the surrounding tissue. Thanks to you, that poison is now destroying my insides. There is no antidote. But I won't die from this injury. You did it and you will save me."

The door flew open, causing me to stumble into Deputy

Clarke. My breath froze in my chest at the sight of the man who loomed in the doorway, a red mask fastened to his face. "How nice to see you again, Annabeth." Python's voice was smooth and pleasant, as if we were discussing the thunderstorm. As he watched me back up against the paneled wall, my legs quaking like jelly, he laughed softly. "I'm not going to hurt you. At least, not yet. I brought you a present."

Deputy Clarke helped Python lay a sheet of heavy plastic across the braided rug. I tried not to think about why they needed the plastic, but of course I knew. How long would I keep the secrets I vowed to protect if they tortured me?

I tugged at my collar, bitterly wishing I had a necklace like Griffin's. If only I could press a button and send a distress call. Or if all else failed, take that little pill—and not have to worry about betraying the people I loved.

Deputy Clarke held the door open while Python dragged a shackled, unconscious Griffin—soaking wet and bloody—onto the plastic. I ran toward him, but Deputy Clarke shoved me back.

As I stared at Griffin—bound like an animal, his face swollen, cut, and bruised, welts crisscrossing his arms and chest, and duct tape covering his mouth—I let out a low, guttural sob. "What have you done to him? You're monsters!" My heart flailed like a captured bird, beating against my rib cage, when I realized his chest was bare.

"I couldn't believe you were foolish enough to come here alone, Annabeth," Deputy Clarke said. "But we knew Griffin would search for you." He turned to Python. "Ready to test our theories?"

Griffin had tried to save me, while I delivered him to the Serpent Society like a shiny present, gift-wrapped with a bow on top.

"Here's proof that Griffin has not only been to Hy-Brasil but he's also drunk from the Fountain of Youth." Python pulled a knife from his belt and dragged it across Griffin's torso.

His skin pulled apart, blood welling darkly. My knees buckled, and although I clapped a hand over my mouth, it barely muffled my scream. How much more could Griffin's battered body withstand?

Python and Deputy Clarke stood over Griffin, staring at him intently. As Griffin's skin began to knit together, Deputy Clarke gasped incredulously, his eyes shining brightly. They both looked upon Griffin hungrily, as if he were a hunk of meat and they were starving.

Griffin tugged one swollen eye open. His gaze flicked from me to the door and back again. I knew what he was asking, but how could I leave him like this? What would they do to him when he didn't reveal the secret? He stared at me, his open eye pleading.

I needed to escape and get help. It was his only chance. There had to be a house nearby. As Python and Deputy Clarke stood transfixed, watching Griffin's body heal itself, I inched my way slowly toward the kitchen. Griffin moaned loudly, muffling any noise I made, as I climbed onto the counter. With my head and torso through the open window, I reached a hand toward the deck railing, praying I'd make it. My fingers slipped on the wet wood, and I faltered.

A pair of strong hands clutched my hips and pulled me back through the window. Python's open palm came down hard and swift across the side of my head, and the snake ring that coiled around his pointer finger sliced into my ear.

Stumbling to the kitchen floor, my ear rang while warm drops of blood dripped down my neck. Python yanked me to my feet and shoved me toward Griffin.

With his boot on Griffin's stomach and his hand around

my neck, Python said, "Time for you two to switch places. Take a good look at Annabeth, Griffin. I don't think she'll heal quite so quickly when I slice and dice her, do you?"

Griffin's eyes were wild, his rage almost palpable as his muscles clenched.

Deputy Clarke dragged Griffin's bloody body over to the edge of the sheet while Python pulled me onto the plastic. With his hot breath on my cheek and the cold, hard mask pressed against my skull, Python slowly pressed the edge of his knife along my skin from my ear to the base of my neck. The cut, although not deep, stung, but I kept my lips fastened together. *I will be brave. I will be strong*, I said over and over in my head, like a mantra. With a sigh of satisfaction, Python pushed the point of the blade into the small of my throat and twisted it. I gasped, a thin stream of blood trickling down my chest.

I will be brave. I will be strong.

And then, with his hand around a fistful of my hair, Python snapped my head back—my neck burning—and poured something simultaneously cold and searing hot against my exposed throat. It felt as if my skin was on fire and I screamed, tears stinging my eyes.

Python let me go, and my legs crumpled beneath me.

I fell to the plastic on my hands and knees, lifted my head, and reached for Griffin. He was struggling against his bindings, fury flashing darkly in his eyes—but he was too far. I crawled toward him, but, with another fistful of hair, Python wrenched me to my feet again. My fingers went to my throat, and I was surprised to still feel skin.

"That was a cocktail of my own creation, Annabeth, meant to cause pain, but not disfigurement."

I will be brave. I will be strong.

"How much Annabeth suffers is entirely up to you, Griffin," Python said in a perilously silky voice. "I hear she's an artist. I'll start by removing her fingers. One. By. One. If that doesn't work, I'll cover her face in hydrofluoric acid, which causes liquefaction necrosis. If I were to use that, her cells would actually liquefy and dissolve. She might survive, but she'd wish she hadn't."

My legs gave out again as a paralyzing fear quaked through me, but Python held me firmly. Griffin thrashed against the ground, his words sounding like a growl behind the tape, as Deputy Clarke dragged a table to the middle of the plastic sheet. Python wrapped his thick arms around my chest while Deputy Clarke held my wrist against the whiskey-colored wood. My head lolled to the side and I felt light-headed; I was sure I was going to faint. Griffin screamed something—and Deputy Clarke's mouth turned up in a small smile. "We will start with her pinky, to make sure you're properly motivated, Griffin. If you tell us everything we want to know, we will stop there."

Griffin was going to talk. He would say something to try to save me. Agony over what it could be—what it could mean for him—sliced through my mind-numbing panic and gave me an idea. "Stop! I'll tell you what I know. I can save you, Deputy Clarke. Please."

"This better not be another lie." Python *tsk*ed in my ear.

I met Deputy Clarke's gaze. "Even if Griffin agreed to bring you to the island right now, what makes you think you'll still be alive when you get there? The poison could destroy your kidney or your liver, and once that happens, there's no fixing it. Look at Griffin's hand—his fingers didn't regrow." I had no idea if that was true or not, but I could tell my bluff was working. Deputy Clarke's face paled. "If I get you some of the healing water now, will you let Griffin and me go?"

"They brought some back?" His flat tone belied the excitement in his eyes.

I nodded, wincing in pain. "Griffin is given some each

week, to—to help with the side effects from his accident."
Did that even make sense?

Deputy Clarke tipped his head and studied me intently.
"Where do they keep it?"

I kept my expression fixed as I raced through my
options. Would he risk taking me to Bradford Manor? "In
the boathouse," I finally said, my mouth dry. "Beneath a
section of floorboards. Griffin and Jack hid it there the day
you searched the house." I was glad my voice didn't shake
like my body.

Python's chest tensed against my back, but he said
nothing. I held my breath as the silence stretched on and
on, watching Deputy Clarke for any sign of a reaction.
He drew his eyebrows together, his wide face brittle, as he
considered my proposition. I could almost hear the gears in
his mind working, looking for a hidden trap. Finally, relief
softened his sharp expression, and he gave me a curt nod.
"If you get me the water, I'll let you both go."

I almost believed him. Not that it mattered. He stood,
and I snatched back my hand, rubbing the inside of
my wrist.

Python took a step back, releasing me. "Those aren't the
orders we were given."

"I'm following orders. It's only a short delay." Deputy Clarke's tone left no room for argument.

From beneath his mask, Python sighed. "You should at least—"

"Lest you've forgotten, I'm the one who discovered the connection to the Magellans. I'm the one who got us into Bradford Manor. You killed Kathy and Paul without gaining any information or leads, while I'm the one who developed a relationship with Annabeth and put all the pieces together. I'm the leader of this cell. I make the decisions. Not you."

"What if she's lying again?"

In one sudden movement, Deputy Clarke ripped the duct tape off Griffin's mouth. "Do everything I say, or I'll let Python get creative with how Annabeth pays the price. Understood?"

Wearing a look of sheer and utter hatred, Griffin nodded.

Deputy Clarke opened the safe and removed a small glass vial I recognized instantly as the truth serum they had force-fed me before. My chest constricted so tightly I could only take a shallow breath. I had tried to find a way out, and I'd just made things worse. White spots clouded my vision as I played out the most likely scenario in my mind: Griffin admitting there was no secret stash of water, admitting there was no Fountain of Youth, admitting how he could heal so fast.

"Leave Griffin out of this. Give me the serum," I pleaded.

Deputy Clarke gave me a wry, sidelong look. "After you resisted last time, I don't think so. Now that I have Griffin, you're expendable. You do realize that, don't you?" Crouching on the ground, he ordered Griffin to open his mouth.

His nostrils flaring, Griffin looked at me, and as his eyes met mine, he moved his lips as if to mouth something, but Deputy Clarke grabbed him roughly by the chin and poured the violet liquid down his throat. With a grimace, Griffin swallowed. Deputy Clarke ripped off another piece of tape and slapped it over his mouth.

Deputy Clarke's phone buzzed loudly from his pocket. His eyes lit up with excitement as he listened. "And you're sure customs won't be a problem? . . . Good. We'll be there in a little over an hour." His eyes flashed to me. "We have them both."

"Is the plane ready?" Python asked, sounding disappointed.

Deputy Clarke nodded.

"You promised to let us go!" I shouted.

Deputy Clarke looked at me, a hint of pity in his eyes.

"We will. A private plane is waiting to take us to Ireland. From there, we will board a boat. You'll both be in shackles and will be injected with truth serum. Griffin will tell us how to get to Hy-Brasil. If he resists, he can watch us torture you." He cleared his throat. "Once we're on the island, we will let you go."

Griffin snorted loudly from behind his gag, which was all the encouragement Python needed to kick him, hard, in the gut. I covered my mouth, muffling the choked sound that gurgled in the back of my throat.

"The serum will be effective in an hour. In that time, we need to wipe down the cabin. Bind her and gag her," Deputy Clarke ordered.

Python shoved me onto a stiff wooden kitchen chair and twined rope so tightly around my calves and torso that my arms and legs went numb. All I could do was sit in the corner and watch as Python and Deputy Clarke shredded the documents I had stashed in Holly's car, burned the boxes, and wiped away any trace that I'd been there.

It was by far the longest hour of my life. Without adrenaline surging through me, the pain was almost unbearable. My head and ear throbbed from Python's blow, my throat felt like it was on fire, and my muscles were clenched so tightly against my bindings that every part of my body ached. Worse still, once Griffin admitted there was no healing water in the boathouse, I was sure Deputy Clarke would be true to his word. I'd be killed, and Griffin would be taken to Ireland.

What had I done?

I couldn't bear to look at Griffin, certain I'd see my fear reflected in his eyes. Certain I'd see that he regretted ever meeting me.

Deputy Clarke stared at the clock above my head, clutching his side, his face contorted in pain. "Time's up."

I swallowed the bitter bile stuck in my throat as Deputy Clarke jerked Griffin up to a sitting position and removed the tape. "Where is the liquid from the Fountain of Youth?"

Griffin's expression was almost serene, with a far-off look in his eyes.

Deputy Clarke shook him roughly by the shoulders. "Where are you keeping the healing water?"

I held my breath as he opened his mouth.

"In the boathouse."

My entire body exhaled.

"Where in the boathouse?"

Griffin described the location in such detail that I wondered if there really was a secret compartment.

"Can you and Annabeth both open the gate?" Deputy Clarke asked.

"Yes," Griffin answered at once.

"Take Griffin to the airport," Deputy Clarke ordered Python. Annabeth and I will meet you there." He walked over to me, unfastened my bindings, and removed the gag from my mouth. He gave me a stern look. "Don't even think about crying for help. If you do, Python here, who I will be in constant contact with, will make sure Griffin pays the price. With his ability to heal, think of how much torture his body could withstand. We can't kill him, but we can separate him from his limbs."

I drew in a deep breath to steady myself.

"Throw Griffin in the trunk. We'll meet you at the airfield."

With Deputy Clarke's revolver pressed into my back, I stepped outside. The storm raged around us. Deputy Clarke said something, but I couldn't hear him over the howling wind. He shoved me into his car, then called Python. They talked on and off, the rain pinging off the windshield as Deputy Clarke navigated the wet roads. I huddled on the vinyl seat and rubbed my temples, trying to think of something—anything—but came up empty-handed.

"I never wanted to hurt you," Deputy Clarke said, a touch of remorse in his voice. "I did warn you to leave Bradford Manor. You should have listened."

"Trying to ease your conscience? You tortured my father. Jack is dead because of you. I'm sure you killed the Bradfords, too."

"I've never killed anyone. Suzette called me to report Griffin, and Python and I found the Bradfords searching for him on a boat. I tried to reason with them, but they took the poison, just like your aunt and uncle."

Tears stung my eyes. So many people I loved had died protecting Hy-Brasil. I wished the Magellans never went on that damn expedition. How different all of our lives would have been. The secret was like the Minotaur of Greek mythology; it required sacrifice. Who would be sacrificed next? Most likely, me, when Deputy Clarke learned I was lying. Then it would be Griffin. He would never bring them to the island.

Python's voice crackled from the phone. "Annabeth was right, by the way. Body parts don't regrow."

"What did you do?" Deputy Clarke asked.

"I had a little fun with Griffin. But now he's in the trunk. We're on our way."

I wrapped my arms around myself, feeling as raw and splintered as the lightning slicing the darkness. I glared at Deputy Clarke. "Did you hear him? That's your buddy's idea of fun: torturing and killing people. The Serpent Society is nothing but a bunch of sadistic thugs with a catchy name."

Deputy Clarke's hands tensed on the wheel. "My father never killed anyone. He followed the ancient code. For all the good it did him."

I thought back to what Deputy Clarke had told me about his father. "He was in the Serpent Society?"

He nodded. "He was a librarian at Trinity, which has the largest collection of documents and maps regarding Hy-Brasil. He couldn't believe it when someone started taking out books on the island." His voice was tight. "He and Malcolm became friends. He didn't kill Griffin when he hit his bike, although he could have. But the Brasilites play by their own rules—and now my father is dead. So don't you dare lecture me."

The horror of his words smothered me. "Your father hit a kid on purpose. A fourteen-year-old boy. Griffin almost died!"

Deputy Clarke's eyes narrowed to slits. "Almost . . . but he didn't. Father played a hunch. The fact that Griffin is alive and well proved the Bradfords had been to Hy-Brasil and knew how to return. Griffin lived; my father didn't." With each word he uttered, his tone and expression became harder. "When the Bradfords left Ireland, Father followed them. That's the last we heard from him." His voice rang with bitterness. "His boat was found near the Aran Islands, but he and the crew he took with him were gone." He gave me a sharp sideways glance. "And you call us monsters."

A loud thud sounded on the other end of the phone.

Deputy Clarke put it to his ear. "Python? What the hell is going on?"

I couldn't hear Python's response, but whatever it was, Deputy Clarke wasn't happy. He swore repeatedly and hit the gas.

"What happened? Is it Griffin?" I clutched my churning stomach and pulled my knees to my chest. I could think of only one reason for Deputy Clarke to be this pissed off: Griffin was dead. Python, the sadistic bastard, must have hurt Griffin so badly that his body couldn't heal fast enough.

Ignoring me, Deputy Clarke called someone named Mamba as he gunned the car around bends and twists in the road. We were almost at the bridge leading to Bradford Manor when a car—without its headlights on—pulled alongside us.

A hand of lightning crackled into the river, and in that blinding flash I saw Griffin behind the wheel of the car.

So did Deputy Clarke. In an instant, he had his seat belt unbuckled and his gun drawn.

My heart hammering, I made a split-second decision. I grabbed the steering wheel and turned it. The car hydroplaned, spinning around and around. I braced my hands against the dashboard, but my head still slammed forward and ricocheted back as the car broke through the barrier and plunged into the raging river.

Deputy Clarke lay slumped across me, bloodied beyond recognition. Tentatively, I felt his neck for a pulse. He was dead. Guilt washed over me like the water rushing into the car. But this wasn't a what if moment. Griffin was innocent. Deputy Clarke wasn't.

I pushed him over, unbuckled my seat belt, and grabbed the door handle, but I couldn't get it open and the window wouldn't budge. I tried again and again, the water quickly rising around me. When it was almost up to my chin, I had little choice but to take one last deep breath and duck my head under. I turned the handle, pushing against it, but it still wouldn't move.

As the air in my puffy cheeks deflated and exhaustion covered me like a heavy blanket, my panic ebbed and I became oddly clearheaded. I stopped thinking about my own survival. Instead, I thought about what it feels like to be the one left behind. How I would fight with everything I had so that Dad wouldn't have to go through that again.

I clutched the door handle again and pushed my shoulder and hip against it as hard as I could while slamming my cast against the door frame. Pain seared up my arm.

Yet, it wasn't enough.

Both ears were ringing, but all of my pain floated away on the murky water; not even my throat hurt anymore. I was growing more and more light-headed, and the white spots blotting my vision swirled together. It was as if I were floating in a cloud. I must have been delirious, because Griffin's face appeared before me for just an instant. I tried to reach him, but he was gone.

And then, the blackness at the edges of my vision grew, swallowing the mist. A bone-chilling darkness surrounded me. I was utterly alone.

Until the door curled back, and I saw Griffin's face

again, mere inches from mine. As he gathered me up in his arms, I felt like I was flying through the water. Cold bullets of rain stung my skin, and I was hoisted onto the grassy hillside. I don't know how long I lay there, coughing out water, my chest heaving as thunder erupted all around us, reverberating through my body. The feeling slowly returned in my limbs, bringing with it the pain.

I heard a groan and then realized it was coming from me. Griffin cradled me in his arms, and as I looked up at him, I gasped. Half of his face was covered in blood—his left eye was gone. I ran my fingers across his wet cheek. "Oh, Griffin."

"Shhhh." He nuzzled his face next to mine, burying his head in my shoulder. "It's all right, Annabeth. We're both safe now. Let me get you home." He gently scooped me up, as if he were holding a bird with a broken wing, and carried me up the steep incline to an unfamiliar black sedan. With a glance behind him, he said, "Python's dead. I didn't have a choice."

I followed his gaze and could see straight into the trunk—the back seats had been ripped out—and a red mask gleamed in the darkness. Shuddering, I leaned my head against his shoulder. "Neither did I."

CHAPTER *Twenty-One*

As the veil of sleep slowly lifted, images assaulted me in rapid succession: Griffin's bound body, his chest torn open; Python hitting me in the head; Deputy Clarke's dead body; my heavy limbs, weighed down by the river . . . Griffin. My teeth chattered and my body shivered uncontrollably. I was afraid to open my eyes. Afraid of what I'd see.

"Annabeth. Sweetheart. Wake up." It was a woman's voice, but I couldn't place it. It sounded as if she was far away. "You're having a bad dream."

I only wished it was all a nightmare.

"You're safe. I'm right here." It was Camila.

As she rubbed my back and repeated soothing words, her voice quelled my fears and gave me the courage to lift my eyelids. I was in my suite of rooms at Bradford Manor. My body relaxed against the soft pillows, and I burrowed deeper beneath the fluffy comforter. Glancing at my cast—which appeared to be new—I vaguely remembered a doctor examining me, giving me something for shock, and Richard, Camila, and Griffin hovering over me, watching me, like a trio of hawks.

Camila, who was sitting on the edge of the bed, pushed my hair off my face and kissed my forehead.

"Have you been here since last night?" I asked.

"Of course. How are you feeling?"

"Okay."

She wiggled an eyebrow and handed me a cup from the nightstand. "Liar. Drink this."

I took one look at the thick brown sludge and wrinkled my nose. "Looks yummy."

She laughed. "It will reduce inflammation, diminish your bruising, and help with the pain as well. And before you ask, it is perfectly safe. Although, it isn't FDA approved. At least not yet."

"Cheers." Pinching my nose, I chugged the disgusting thing down in two gulps. "You might want to add some cherry extract or something?"

She shook her head, smiling. "What are we going to do with you?"

My smile faded. What were we going to do without Jack? How was Camila going to survive it? "I'm sorry. So sorry. About Jack. About everything."

Camila wrapped her arms around herself, her eyes glistening with the tears she held back. "I still can't believe he's gone."

Neither could I. My thoughts turned to Mom. Sometimes, I still couldn't believe I'd never see her again. But the gaping hole in my heart didn't ache quite so much anymore. A few months ago, that would have made me feel guilty. Now, it made me feel closer to her. She wouldn't have wanted me to endure my self-inflicted penance. She would have wanted me to heal.

"Seeing the boys helped." Camila gave me a thin smile. "Galena arranged a meeting. But that's a secret."

I nodded. So, so many secrets. Now, that was part of my life, part of my world.

"Since you've had your medicine, you can have this." Camila picked up a tray from the window seat and placed it on my lap.

On it was a coconut iced coffee, pastries in a pink bakery box, and a vase of peonies. After all I'd put him through, Griffin was still being kind. Guilt stole my appetite, and I pushed the tray aside. "When I went to steal the documents . . . I didn't think. It never occurred to me that Deputy Clarke was Cobra. I messed everything up. And Griffin—" I looked up at the beadboard ceiling, swallowing my sob.

Camila squeezed my hand. "Griffin is doing just fine. Brasilites have better senses than we do. His vision, even with one eye, is still better than twenty-twenty."

"Will it heal?"

"It hasn't yet. He was injured so badly it will take time for his body to repair, and by then . . ." She forced a cough, catching herself.

But I could fill in the blanks: *By then, it may be too late.*

"Where is he? I need to talk to him." There was so much I had to say—how sorry I was for what happened, for putting him in that position in the first place.

Richard appeared in the doorway and said, "Griffin's resting. How are you? Do you need anything?"

"No." I looked down at my hands. I couldn't bear to see the compassion in Richard's eyes. Not after what I had done. Instead of sitting in this beautiful room, being pampered, I could be on a boat headed to Ireland, chained and beaten, my fingers gone, while having to watch Griffin being tortured. The secret we both vowed to protect disclosed. All because I thought I knew better. Because I was convinced I could steal back the documents on my own.

The delicate vanity chair scraped against the floorboards as Richard pulled it beside the bed and sat down. "Listen to me, Annabeth Winters, no one blames you for what happened. Once again, you risked yourself to save someone else. And now, two members of the Serpent Society are dead, and we have both of their cell phones."

"But Griffin's eye," I choked out.

"Clarke knew about Griffin before last night. It wasn't a matter of *if* the Serpent Society got to him, it was a matter of *when*." Richard inhaled a deep, shuddering breath. "You saved Griffin from a far worse fate. Your mother would be so proud of you. We all are."

Camila squeezed my hand again. "We love you, sweetheart. But no more going it alone. Family is there for each other, no matter what."

Wiping away the tears that clung to my lashes, I thought about Mom and smiled. She would be proud of me, I knew that. She would never have wanted me to live a safe life, a life with no risk, no adventure, no mistakes. After she died, I made my world so small—there was only room in it for me and Dad. I couldn't bear to care about other people and to disappoint them or hurt them or be hurt. I believed love made you vulnerable, but really, love makes you strong.

I hugged Richard and then Camila, and as she stroked my hair the way Mom used to, a warmth radiated through my chest. I wouldn't shut this family out again.

"Now I need you to listen to me very carefully," Richard said in a sudden shift of tone. He explained that Galena and Tristan were waiting to interview me on behalf of the Council. Griffin had kept me out of what happened with Deputy Clarke last night, so I only had to explain how I rescued Dad. After I recited what he told me to say, twice, he made me go through three rounds of role-playing, all with different questions to trip me up, until finally Camila told him I was ready.

But I wasn't. Not by a long shot. I hoped the Council believed I didn't know anything, but lately my hopes hadn't panned out. I had to prepare for the worst. And the truth was, they may take me to Hy-Brasil and swap out my memories before I could even say goodbye to anyone. "I need to see Griffin first."

"That's not possible. Sometimes, when Griffin exerts himself like he did last night, it triggers an episode." Richard's tone was calm, but I could see the worry in his eyes.

"Did he have one?"

He shook his head. "But he's asked to be locked in a safe room, just in case."

My heart ached for Griffin. After all he'd been through, he still kept his wits about him during an interview with the Council, lying about why he was even at the cabin, and now he was all alone. "Richard, it's important. Please."

He sighed. "I'll go check on him."

Camila stood. "I better go with you."

I pinched my lips together. Why were they treating Griffin like a rabid animal, when he was a hero? "The Serpent Society is responsible for Malcolm and Sarah's deaths, *not* Griffin. He's never hurt anyone who didn't deserve it." And he wouldn't. I knew he wouldn't. Episode or not, Griffin would never hurt anyone he cared about. "He risked his life to save me. Twice. I would have drowned if he hadn't pulled me out of that car. There's no reason to lock him up."

Camila gave me a sad smile. "That's not how Griffin sees it. Besides, if he has an episode, we're worried he'd hurt himself."

After I took a quick shower and changed into cotton gym shorts and one of Mom's old RISD T-shirts, I paced back and forth in the kitchen, waiting and worrying. Did

Griffin have an episode? Or did he simply not want to see me, after what I'd done? When I couldn't stand it another minute, I picked the lock to the basement door and made my way to the gym. The door to the safe room was open, and Richard and Griffin were arguing.

"I'm not seeing her, Richard, and I won't change my mind."

I froze, my chest tight.

"You're not being fair to her, Griffin."

"That's the understatement of the year. She almost died—again—last night. She was tortured—again—and I had to watch; I couldn't do a thing to help her. Then, she almost drowned. Next time, she may not get away. Next time, I may not be there in time. The sooner she leaves, the better. The farther she is from me, the safer she'll be."

"Sweetheart, listen to me . . ." Camila said.

I stepped into the room. "No, listen to me."

Inhaling a sharp breath, Griffin raked me over with his one good eye, from my freshly bruised face, to the bandages around my throat, to my new cast. "You shouldn't be here."

"Yeah, yeah. I've heard that line before. Can I talk to you alone?"

"No," he answered quickly and unequivocally. "I may

have an episode. It's not safe."

"That's bull," Camila said. "If you haven't had an episode yet, you're not going to."

Griffin slipped a hand through his long hair, now almost skimming his shoulders. "But what if—"

"You're fine. The new medication is working. You haven't had an episode since the memorial. Suck it up and talk to Annabeth. We'll give you two some privacy. Come on," Camila said, jerking Richard away by the arm.

After they left, I sat beside Griffin on the mattress pushed into the corner. A black patch covered his injured eye, and the shadows beneath the other one were a deep plum against his sallow skin. He wore a lacrosse pinnie and gym shorts, revealing angry red welts and raised scars crisscrossing his arms and legs. Right then, I could have killed Python myself for what he had done to Griffin.

"Did you get any sleep?" he asked.

"Some. You?"

Griffin pulled his arms around his knees and shrugged. "A little." He slid his gaze over to me, flinched, and quickly looked away. "How much pain are you in—and don't lie to me."

"Camila gave me some sludge to drink, so it isn't too

bad. I'm more bone-tired than anything else, and my muscles feel like Jelly. How about you?"

"About the same. Weak, exhausted."

We sat in a heavy silence, weighed down by words unsaid. From the corner of my eye, I watched Griffin, but he continued to stare at the patterned rug as if he had never seen anything more interesting.

"Griffin, I'm sorry."

Snapping his head back, he finally looked at me. "For what?"

Where to begin? I ran my fingers through my damp hair and let the words tumble out of me. "For blackmailing you into breaking your vow to the Council and telling me about Hy-Brasil. For taking off in Holly's car without telling anyone. For leading you straight into a trap. For all the torture you endured last night. For making you feel like you had to lie to the Council, again, to protect me. I'm sure there are other things, too. I just can't think of all the ways I put you at risk."

Griffin leaned toward me, and then away. "You've got it all wrong. I'm the one who's sorry. Because of me . . ." He shook his head. "Richard thinks Tristan and Galena will believe the story you're going to tell them. They're friends, they were—hopefully, still are—on our side. It isn't too late. After you talk to them, you and Sam can still leave. Disappear. Live your lives free of all this."

Disappear. The word terrified me. After Mom died, I had disappeared. Now I felt like I was finally back. I hadn't fought so long and so hard to give up so easily. "Griffin, after I was released from McLean, all I wanted was to live the rest of my life in a safe place—emotionally, physically, and mentally. But I don't want that kind of life anymore. I want a big life. A life filled with mysteries and adventures and magic. I won't trade that for anything. It cost me too much to get here. And I'm done hiding and retreating."

Griffin exhaled a long, weary breath. "You said something, something I keep thinking about. You couldn't have predicted what happened to your mom. I couldn't have predicted what happened to my parents. But this—" he swallowed hard "—you being in danger from the Brasilites and the Serpent Society, *that* we can predict. I need to protect you from it."

"No one can protect anyone, Griffin. That isn't how life works. Dad feels guilty he didn't go with Mom that night to pick me up. But if he had, she'd still be dead, and he probably would be, too. I know you're worried, and I know you feel responsible, just like I feel responsible for what happened to you. But you don't get to make decisions for me. The Serpent Society is still out there, somewhere. I am not going to hide and hope they don't come for me. And I'm not going to worry about Dad every time he leaves the house. I'm not going to live in fear of what might be lurking in the shadows. I won't. I'm going to do whatever I can to bring them down. Every single one of them."

Griffin shook his head furiously. "No, Annabeth. Please. Don't say that. Don't even think that. You need to stay far away from the Serpent Society."

"Because of them, your parents are dead. Jack is dead. My aunt and uncle." My nails bit my palms as a surge of anger pulsed through me. "I won't let them get away with it."

"God, Annabeth. You don't listen when you should." His eyebrows furrowed as he stared at me, and then they shifted into a pained expression. He looked down at the carpet again. His curled shoulders make him look almost small. "I keep wondering how we even got here. How you got caught up in this. It's just . . ." His voice was soft and laced with pain. "I wish you never came here. Then, at least, you'd be safe."

I'd be safe. I just wouldn't be living—I'd be going

through the motions. "Remember what you told me about the land of what ifs. Don't go there. I don't know why things happen the way they do, but I don't regret it."

Griffin's eyes softened for just a moment before he rearranged his expression into something hard. Something cold. "Well, I do. Every single day."

I had suspected that was how he felt. So why did it still feel like someone was cutting me up from the inside? I slid my trembling hands beneath my thighs and opened my mouth to speak, but then stopped, worried I wouldn't be able to control what came out. I shut my eyes tightly—I would not cry—and cleared my throat as I forced myself to look at him. "I wanted to talk to you for one reason, and one reason only. If the Brasilites don't believe me, if they take me away and swap out my memories . . ." I paused for a beat, until I could continue with no risk of blabbering. "I want you to know that what I said was true. I don't regret any of it. Not coming to Maine, not spending time with you, not . . ." I stopped. I couldn't tell him how I felt, not when he stared at me with a look of sheer horror, his eyes wide and his mouth gaping open. "You're not a monster, Griffin. You're special. You're beautiful. Don't let anyone tell you differently."

I had vowed to myself that I would be calm, no theatrics. But I could feel the tears welling up in my eyes and the sob about to explode in the back of my throat. I jumped to my feet and darted out the door, through the gym, and down the hall. Griffin called after me, but I knew if he really wanted to, he could catch me.

Which meant he could also let me go.

CHAPTER *Twenty-Two*

Pushing through the French doors, I ran right into Camila's outstretched arms. "Oh, Annabeth. What happened, sweetheart? What is it?"

My sob froze in my throat, for right behind her was Galena and a man who I could only assume was her brother. They were walking down the path from the guesthouse toward the patio. Like Galena, Tristan had an aquiline nose, dark red hair that skimmed his shoulders, and a long, lean physique that exuded the same kind of power as a panther prepared to strike.

Camila turned, her eyes widened, and then she squeezed my arm. "I'm sorry, but you need to pull it together. I'll try to buy you a few minutes," she whispered in my ear as she kissed my wet cheek.

"Tristan! I heard you were here, and I was just looking

for you. It's so good to see you!" Camila had her arms around his neck in an instant, chatting nonstop and laughing nervously. I almost cringed. If it were Jack, he'd have pulled off this delay tactic seamlessly, but she had no finesse.

While Camila kept them busy talking, I retreated into the kitchen and poured myself a large iced coffee. Looking out the window, I clicked my nails against the plastic glass as I watched them talking. Twice, I ran through the version of events Richard had me memorize, and still they were huddled together. I appreciated Camila giving me time to steel my nerves, but now I just needed to get it over with. To calm my frayed emotions, I ran through the Greek Gods: Aphrodite, Apollo, Ares, Artemis, Athena . . . It was fitting that I was on Dolos, the god of deception, when the doors opened. That didn't feel like a good omen.

Chugging the last dregs of my coffee, I smiled politely as Tristan and I were introduced.

"Why don't we go upstairs to the study," Galena said in a conversational tone, as if I had a choice.

With a deep breath to slow my racing pulse, I walked up the stairs, my head held high, trying not to feel like a prisoner. But of course, I was. Galena directed me to Malcolm's study, locking the door behind her with a resounding click.

Whereas Sarah's office was bright and airy, Malcolm's was dark but comfortable, with a faded Persian rug laid across the dark hardwood floor and his beloved guitar in the corner. I couldn't help but look for some indication of the hidden closet, wishing I could disappear inside it. Instead of artwork, his study was decorated with old maps and a large whiteboard, his theories and notations still scribbled across it. It was almost as if he had just gone downstairs for coffee.

"Do you know why we've asked to speak to you privately?" Tristan asked pleasantly.

I burrowed my nerves behind a more appropriate expression—a relaxed smile mixed with a dash of curiosity thrown in for good measure. "You want me to tell you how Dad and I escaped from that cellar, right?"

They exchanged a dark look that made my skin prickle.

"How old are you, Annabeth?" Galena asked.

"Seventeen." My voice quavered, making me sound younger.

She frowned. "Too young, I think, to understand the implications of what you've learned about the island."

My heart gave a thud. "Island? What island? I was never questioned by the guys who kidnapped me. I tried to get away, and one of them . . ." I bit my lip, trying to block the memory of me lying on the cellar floor, with Python's arms and legs caging me in. "One of them did this." I pointed to the scar zigzagging around my eye. "I was knocked out. Then—"

"We don't want to hear a repeat of the lie Griffin told us," Tristan said, an edge to his voice. "We want to know exactly what happened in that cellar. And we want to know what happened last night. A surveillance camera we installed at the bridge shows you in the car with Deputy Clarke."

I froze. I felt like a rabbit in a wolf's den.

"You don't need to be frightened. We are only asking you to tell us the truth." Galena's voice was commanding, her stare piercing.

I shuddered. I had plenty of cause to be frightened— my freedom, my memories, my very life were on the line. "Are you ordering me or asking?"

"Ordering." Tristan's tone was imperious.

My heart thudded. There was no way out of this.

"The secret of Hy-Brasil is more important than any one life," Tristan continued.

Elizabeth's final words flashed in my head: *Our secret died with me.* She willingly died to protect the island. As did my aunt and uncle, Jack, Malcolm, and Sarah. My life was insignificant compared to the threat exposure posed. "I know."

Another unspoken look passed between them and the silence stretched on and on. I couldn't stand the waiting. I opened my arms in surrender. "Ask away."

Galena sat at a round table and motioned for me to sit across from her. "It's simple, really. We want to know every detail about the journey that brought you here."

As if anything about that was simple.

With my finger, I traced the jagged line where my sutures had been. Not all my scars were visible.

Walking past Galena, I stood at the window and stared at the lake, painted violet in the fading light. I said a silent prayer that I'd always remember it. That I'd always remember this summer, my parents, Griffin. Then I told them everything. Well, almost everything. What I felt about Griffin—that was none of their business.

"We appreciate your candor, Annabeth," Galena finally said.

"Now we must communicate with the High Council. Wait here." Tristan locked the door behind them.

My fears multiplied uncontrollably as I wondered what

would happen next. Would I be eliminated as too high a risk? Certainly my past would play a factor in that. Would I be whisked off to Hy-Brasil like the man Griffin had met there? Would I even get to say goodbye to Dad? To Griffin? Would my memories be swapped with someone else's—if that happened, would I still be me?

The doorknob jiggled, and I backed against the paneled wall, blood pounding behind my ears. It turned again, faster this time . . . and again . . . and then the door cracked open, right off its hinges. Griffin stood before me, his shoulders tense, the veins in his neck throbbing as he looked helplessly at me. "What's going on? Why are you locked in here?"

"They knew," I said in a defeated voice. "I told them everything. I had no choice."

He hissed in a breath. "What did they say?"

"They're communicating with the Council."

His face was ashen. "We're leaving. Now." Griffin's tone left no room for argument, not that I wanted to argue. He snatched my hand and pulled me into the hall, where we ran straight into Tristan and Galena.

"I thought I was clear, Annabeth, that you needed to wait in the study." Tristan scowled. "Why don't you join us,

Griffin, as this pertains to you as well?"

I squeezed Griffin's warm calloused skin, tethering myself to him. He was, first and foremost, my friend. He would always be my friend. Whatever I had to face, at least I wasn't alone.

Galena and Tristan sat at the table, and Galena motioned for us to take the two remaining seats. Griffin remained rooted in place, his hand tightening around my palm.

"As I'm sure you understand, Hy-Brasil is a very unique island." Galena's words were slow and measured. "I can count on my hand the number of people who know of its existence, outside of its inhabitants. It is crucial that Hy-Brasil remain a secret. Sometimes that secret requires a sacrifice."

"Don't you dare threaten Annabeth," Griffin said through gritted teeth.

"Listen to me, Griffin," Tristan said calmly, though his glare sent a shiver down my spine. "Annabeth *is* in danger, make no mistake about it. She was kidnapped, twice, by the Serpent Society. It is *you* who has endangered her, not us. Let me remind you, you owe your life and your allegiance to the Brasilites."

Griffin shook his head, his green eye narrowed to a slit.

"My allegiance is to Annabeth and Richard, above anyone or anything else."

Galena shot to her feet. "If it weren't for Hy-Brasil—if it weren't for *me*—you'd be dead. Your parents were our very dear friends, but it is more than friendship that binds us. We are connected by our genetic makeup. You have as much a responsibility to protect the island as I do."

Griffin dropped my hand and slammed his palm on the table. "Don't you dare bring my parents into this! My responsibility—"

"Wait," I interrupted. "Griffin did tell me about Hy-Brasil, but only because I'd already figured out most of it on my own, and I threatened to call the police. I left him no choice. I didn't know then how important it was that the island remain secret. I do now. I swear to you I'll never willingly tell anyone what I know. I hope you believe me and let me live. I give you my full permission to monitor me. Frankly, I'd like a necklace."

Griffin inhaled sharply. "You don't know what you're saying."

"I do. When the Serpent Society had me and Dad cornered in front of the cave, before the aonbharr saved us, I decided I would kill us both. I far preferred a quick death

over what awaited us in that cellar. The poison isn't a burden.
It's a gift."

Galena's lips turned up slightly at the corners. I wondered
if that was her version of a smile. "Well said, Annabeth."

"I also want to help you find the rest of the Serpent
Society. They need to be stopped. They need to be held
accountable for what they've done."

"Annabeth!" Griffin's eyes were dark, his voice forbidding.

Tristan gave me an appraising look, as if he was really
noticing me for the first time. "You can tell that to the
Council yourself—on Hy-Brasil. They want to speak in
person with everyone who has been attacked by the Serpent
Society, including your father. A thorough investigation
must be launched. We believe the Serpent Society is working in small cells and the old cells have been re-activated.
We are more at risk now than we have ever been."

"Annabeth is going back to school. She is *not* going to
Hy-Brasil." Griffin's voice was as taut as the strings of the
guitar perched behind him.

Galena put her hand on his shoulder, and for the first
time, I saw that in her own way, she cared about Griffin.
"Think that through. Do you really think she'd be safe
at school?"

His face was conflicted. "I'll hire guards. She'll wear the necklace and a tracker. She's never been to the island—the Serpent Society knows that."

"They also know how you feel about her," Galena said gently. "She's a way to get to you."

Griffin's face crumpled, as he came to terms with what I already knew—my *before*-life was over.

"How long will we be gone for?" I had so feared what the Brasilites might do to me that I never considered visiting the island. But as I thought about the paintings in Sarah's office, I couldn't help but smile. Maybe I could paint it, too.

"That will depend on the Council and the investigation," Tristan said. He removed a small wooden box from his pocket. The lid was carved with Dad's tattoo—with the symbol of Hy-Brasil. Galena opened it and placed a gold link chain around my neck. Although the metal felt light, I knew the heavy responsibility it represented. Knowledge is power, but knowledge is also a burden.

"Wear it well," Galena said.

And with that, we were dismissed.

Griffin stormed through the door ahead of me. I raced after him, pausing to listen to his footsteps, and followed the sound through a door at the end of the hall. It led to a circular staircase and up to a roof deck. It was surprisingly intimate, with a table and four chairs, two chaise lounges, a love seat, and three telescopes attached to the railing. Vines and plants covered the chimneys on either end. Griffin stood with his back to me, his elbows on the railing.

"What the hell, Griffin? Why are you running away from me—again?"

With a deep sigh, he hung his head, his fingers floating to his eyepatch. "Honestly, I don't know what to do with you, Annabeth. I've never met anyone as exasperating."

I rolled my eyes. "Well, we can't all be easygoing like you."

To my surprise, he laughed, the tension in his shoulders ebbing as he reached his hand out to me. I gladly took it. "Mom and I used to spend hours up here, stargazing." Griffin gave me a sad smile. "Maybe she sent you my way, too."

I returned his smile and thought about Sarah and Mom. "Maybe they both knew we needed each other."

The thick clouds that wrapped around the sky parted, and all at once, the moon shone down on the lake and distant mountains. Fog swirled in the light breeze like spirits dancing across the water, and my stomach rolled like the waves as I tried to summon the courage to tell Griffin how I felt. It was strange how many different types of courage there were: the courage to stand up for someone, the courage to stand up for *yourself*, the courage to fight when the situation seems hopeless, the courage to not worry about what other people think. Yet finding the courage to offer up your heart, knowing how easily it could break, took a different type of strength.

With a great leap of my heart, I looked up at Griffin— his full lips, sharp cheeks, crooked nose, the deep dimple in his chin, and his cat-like green eye watching me with a burning intensity that made me feel off-balance. "Tonight, when I worried what Tristan and Galena would do to me, my biggest regret was that I hadn't told you . . . I love you. It doesn't matter that you don't feel the same way . . . I still wanted you to know."

Griffin stared at me for a long moment, his eyebrows drawn—I could see him struggling with what to say as confusion, fear, and regret played across his face. He turned away from me and stared off into the gathering night.

"Anyway," I said in a small voice. "I just wanted you to know."

My shoulders squared, my head held high, I walked toward the stairs. Both my gait and my nerves were steady. I would leave with my dignity intact.

"Annabeth. Wait." His voice was deep and gruff.

I took a deep, steadying breath and faced him.

Griffin slowly closed the distance between us. I couldn't think straight, not when he was this close. Not after what I'd just said.

"In your hospital room, the things I said—it was so you'd leave."

"I know."

He caught his bottom lip in his teeth, his dimple disappearing, and raked a hand through his hair. "No. You don't. Not really."

"Then explain it to me."

"I'm not fully human, Annabeth."

"I know that."

"Do you?" His face was open and unguarded, his green eye pained as he removed the patch. He stepped into a pale shaft of moonlight. "You need to look at me. Really look at me. Not all the eye tissue was cut out, so it's beginning to repair."

I moved closer to him and peered at his eye socket.

Although it was dark, I could still see tiny fibers knitting together. "Does it hurt?"

He slid the patch back down. "No. It feels sort of strange, though. As if tiny spiders are dancing around in there." Griffin smiled at my shuddering shoulders. "Bad analogy. Ants. It feels like tap-dancing ants."

Hesitantly, I cupped his cheek. "I'm sorry."

"It's not your fault." His fingers gently encircled my wrist and pulled my hand away. "But it's proof of what I am. Who I am. I'm dangerous. I killed someone." Once again he looked down at his hands, as if they belonged to a stranger.

A pang—not of regret, exactly, but of something akin to remorse—radiated through my stomach. "I did, too. Does that make me dangerous?"

He stared up at the trees silvered by the moon. "That was different. You didn't kill Clarke with your bare hands."

"Why does that matter?"

Griffin expelled a plume of warm breath that shimmered in the cool air. "It just does. Besides, you know how I feel about you."

"I do." I bit the inside of my cheek, trying to keep my eyes from watering. I knew he wanted to protect me. I knew he loved me. But not in the way that I loved him.

Griffin slid his gaze to me. He was struggling with something, and then his expression softened. "Oh, hell." His eye roved over my face, and the corners of his lips curved. Even now, I struggled to keep my feet rooted in place, wanting only to crash into him. "I've dated quite a few girls."

This, I really didn't need to hear.

"But something always seemed to be missing. I realized, this summer, what it was. Even though I thought you were a pain in the ass, without even realizing it, I still compared every other girl I met to you. No one has ever infuriated me like you have. Or gotten under my skin the way you do." He gave me one of his roguish smiles. "This isn't really coming out right."

My heart was thumping furiously. "You're doing great. Keep going."

His smile widened, and he put his hands on my hips, pulling me closer, his lean muscles shifting against mine. My breath caught in my throat.

"You're incredibly insightful, too curious for your own good, stubborn, kind, and like no one I've ever met before. I love your fierce heart and that you follow it no matter where it takes you. It feels like I've loved you my whole life."

Something flexed and opened deep inside of me, and I felt vulnerable and happy and terrified all at once. I held Griffin's face in my hands. "I know," I whispered. "I feel it, too."

Griffin lightly traced my lips with his thumb and my heart hammered even faster, like a dragonfly trapped inside my chest, until at last his head dipped, his mouth finding mine. There was nothing hesitant about it—his kiss was deep and sure. I leaned into him. I could feel his ragged breath as his kiss grew deeper. "I love you, Annabeth," he murmered against my neck.

Lying on the chaise lounge with Griffin's arms around me, we listened to the night music—the owls, tree frogs, and cicadas, all singing out in their distinct voices, combined to make a beautiful song. The moon was almost full, just a sliver missing, and I thought that maybe life had cycles just like the moon, waxing and waning, full and new. When I arrived in Maine, I was a mere sliver; now I was just like the moon that filled the sky.

Almost full.

CHAPTER *Twenty-Three*

Sitting on the tufted cushion of the window seat, I packed the pillow Mom had made for me in my overnight bag. It was my last night in Bradford Manor for who knows how long. Sliding open the window, I inhaled the cool, crisp air as it caressed my face. Already, the wind carried with it notes of autumn, notes of change. So many things had changed this summer. I had changed. I was no longer the Annabeth-*before*, or the Annabeth-*since*.

I was just Annabeth.

Staring down at the forest, I wondered, for just a moment, what—or who—was concealed within the shadows. I supposed I would always wonder.

As I cast my gaze up at the star-pricked sky, a flash of light spiraled across the horizon, followed by another and another—and then dozens of stars flew across the sky in unison, a celestial dance so breathtaking it didn't seem real. The last time I saw a meteor shower was on the beach long ago—I was curled up at my mother's side, feeling safe, feeling loved, feeling that I belonged.

After she died, I didn't feel safe, I didn't feel worthy of love, and I felt alone. My fantasy world had been my only refuge then, and now my life was in danger because I knew the truth about the magical forces at work in the world. Maybe the world is woven from threads we can see and touch, bound together by a magical border that most people live their entire lives completely unaware of.

"Annabeth?" Griffin said from the door. "All packed?"

"Almost." On the dresser was a framed photo of all of us—the Magellans, Mom, Lucas, Zach, Griffin, and me—on a camping trip in search of Bigfoot. I rubbed a finger over the image of Mom and Aunt Kathy—their arms looped around each other—before sliding it in my bag, between two sweatshirts. "Ready."

Griffin brought my hand to his mouth and kissed my knuckles. "Whatever the future holds for us, we'll face it together. Okay?"

I squeezed his hand in response.

"Come with me. I have a surprise for you."

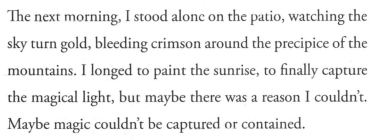

The next morning, I stood alone on the patio, watching the sky turn gold, bleeding crimson around the precipice of the mountains. I longed to paint the sunrise, to finally capture the magical light, but maybe there was a reason I couldn't. Maybe magic couldn't be captured or contained.

Griffin joined me and handed me coffee in a Bruins travel mug. His eyepatch was slid up on his forehead. Although his eye was almost fully healed, sunlight irritated it, so he still needed the eyepatch for most of the day. The trade-off was that his night vision was even keener. I stared into his injured eye, which was several shades lighter than the other, like a shimmering piece of sea glass, and it occurred to me that Griffin wasn't just a biological chimera—he was part of the real world and the fantasy world. A perfect mixture of both.

His arms around my waist, Griffin rested his chin on my head. "The plane is waiting and the convoy's ready. Niamh is not happy about being in that horse carrier. Camila had to sedate her."

"Poor baby." My new charm bracelet clanked against the stainless steel as I lifted the mug to my mouth. It didn't matter that it wasn't the same bracelet Mom had worn; they were the same exact charms: the whale from their honeymoon in Nantucket, the miniature painting, and the very thin #1MOM I had bought with my babysitting money when I was twelve. Griffin had found a way to replace what I thought was irreplaceable.

I rubbed my finger against the new charm—a mermaid—and took a long sip of the steaming, heavenly liquid. "Please tell me there's coffee in Hy-Brasil."

He laughed. "I've packed your favorite kind. I wouldn't want you to go into shock or something without it."

I took one last look at the lake, trying to memorize the view. "I just need to drop that folder"—I pointed to the table—"in Holly's mailbox first. We drive right by her house."

"Dare I ask?"

"I'm fulfilling a promise. Camila was suspicious about the CEO of a company she had some dealings with. She was going to go to the police, but she gave Holly enough information to get her on the right track. I'm sure Holly will write a scathing exposé." Maybe it would convince her mother that college wasn't for her. Or maybe it would help Holly get into a good journalism program. Either way,

I hoped she'd be happy. It was nice having a friend again, a best friend. I was going to miss her.

The next day we boarded a ship from Galway to Inis Mór, one of the Aran Islands, where a Brasilite yacht was waiting for us. Once land was just a distant speck on the horizon, my entire body shuddered, expelling all the tension and adrenaline that had been stored in my muscles. I didn't need to look over my shoulder every time we left Bradford Manor or wake up in the middle of the night worried that someone was in the house. I hoped the nightmares would stop, or at least, happen less frequently. The worst was the same recurrent one, with me lost in the forest, which was now even more terrifying as the monster had a face. Or rather, he wore a red mask.

Richard, unfortunately, didn't share my sense of well-being. As we tossed and turned in the rough Irish seas, he spent most of the journey with his head hanging over the side of the boat. Tristan often stood next to him, rubbing his back or getting him another Dramamine, which didn't seem to help.

On the evening of the third day, Galena told us we were almost there. Griffin and I sat out on the deck, holding each other and shivering as a thick fog encircled the boat. The farther we traveled, the thicker it became, like an opaque curtain that hung from the sky. Jutting out around us was a labyrinth of razor-sharp boulders. As we sailed, I lost track of time. Had it been ten minutes or ten hours?

The closer we sailed to Hy-Brasil, the more my nerves jangled and my stomach fluttered—like the second after the bar comes down on a roller coaster, and the cart starts its slow ascent. I didn't know what was coming, but I knew, without a doubt, it would be a trip I'd never forget.

Griffin pulled me against his chest, his arms holding me tightly.

"Please tell me about the island," I said.

Griffin laughed. "I told you, I want you to discover it as I did, without any preconceived ideas."

I sighed. "Are there myths and legends on Hy-Brasil?"

Griffin nodded. "I'll tell you the story of the goddess Niamh, as the Brasilites tell it. The legend is depicted on a mural in the museum."

"I'm glad there's a museum."

Griffin twirled a strand of my hair around his finger.

"The story goes that Niamh crossed the sea on her aonbharr, Embarr, and asked Fionn mac Cumhaill, a mythical Irish hunter-warrior, if she could bring his son, the great warrior, Oisín, to the Land of the Youth, Tír na nÓg. Oisín fell in love with the beautiful Niamh and wanted to go with her. He promised his father he'd return soon, and so his father agreed. Although Oisín and Niamh were very happy, Oisín missed his family, and he wanted to return to Ireland to see them. Niamh agreed as long as Oisín promised to stay on Embarr and not touch the soil. But what had seemed like three years on Tír na nÓg to Oisín was really three hundred years, so when he returned to Ireland, his family was all dead. He got off Embarr to help some men and aged immediately. While he was gone, Niamh gave birth to their daughter. When Oisín didn't return, Niamh returned to Ireland to find him, but he was dead."

"Is Tír na nÓg Hy-Brasil?"

Griffin nodded.

"Why are all love stories sad?"

Griffin pulled me closer. "Only the legendary ones are sad. Ours will be perfectly ordinary."

Shaking my head, I laughed. "Ordinary? Do you actually think—"

Griffin's head swooped down and he kissed me. "I've decided the only way to keep you from asking so many questions is to keep your mouth otherwise engaged."

Before I could say a word in response, he kissed me again.

We fell asleep, and when we woke up, the mist had thinned and a rocky island appeared before us. It reminded me of a glacier made of stone, black and impenetrable.

Griffin rubbed the goosebumps that had erupted on my arms and whispered in my ear:

"On the ocean that hollows the rocks where ye dwell,
A shadowy land has appear'd, as they tell;
Men thought it a region of sunshine and rest,
And they call'd it 'O Brasail—the Isle of the Blest.'
From year unto year, on the ocean's blue rim,
The beautiful spectre show'd lovely and dim;
The golden clouds curtain'd the deep where it lay,
And look'd like an Eden, away, far away.

Don't be nervous, you will love Hy-Brasil."

We sailed into a narrow gap that I didn't even notice until we were upon it. The rift opened into a large underground cavern. Tristan and Mac tied the boat to giant hooks embedded in the rock, adjacent to a stone plateau about two feet wide that curled around the side of the cavern. Everyone climbed out, but I hesitated for a moment.

Unlike the night I snuck out of the house and Mom died, and the day I left school for Maine, times when, unbeknownst to me, the course of my life was about to be forever altered, this time I knew that once I stepped on Hy-Brasil, things would never be the same. But I was no longer afraid of *after*.

Griffin held out his hand. As our fingers entwined, I inhaled a deep breath and stepped into the uncharted territory.

The End

Acknowldgements

First and foremost, thank you to my incredible editor, Ashley Hearn, whose guidance, creativity, insight, and keen editorial eye made this book SO much better. Thank you for pushing me, encouraging me, and for making me laugh during edits! You are a rock star editor, and I am just so very grateful that you believed in this story.

I also want to thank the incredible team at Page Street Publishing! Everyone was wonderful to work with it—they are all my heroes! Thank you to Will Kiester, publisher extraordinaire, whose passion and vision are truly inspiring, editor Marissa Giambelluca, designers Sara Pollard and Meg Baskis who created this beautiful book, contracts manager Meg Palmer, and copyeditor Sheelonee Banerjee for her sharp eyes. And thank you to my amazing publicists Lauren Wohl and Deb Shapiro. I am so lucky to have you all, and I very much appreciate all of your hard work, enthusiasm, and support!

I owe a huge debt of gratitude to my wonderful critique

partners. Thank you to my dear friend, the wonderful author, Diana Renn. Without a doubt, *Uncharted* would still be a file in my laptop, if not for Diana. Not only did she read many versions of this novel, it was Diana who still believed in this story when I had lost faith, and convinced me to go back to it. It was also Diana who encouraged me to submit to Page Street Publishing. I also want to thank the generous and brilliant Martina Boone, who figured out I was starting in the wrong place (as usual!), and helped me see the mistakes I hadn't realized I had made. Thanks go to the hugely creative Rob Vlock, for his wonderful advice (as always), and pushing me to dig deeper into my characters. I don't know what I would do without the three of you—the world's best critique partners and friends!

To Jaida Temperly, thank you for taking the time to speak with me about *Uncharted*, and for your excellent notes. They were invaluable to me as I revised!

A number of people read early drafts of this book, and pointed out what was working and what wasn't. Thank you to my writing group, Diana Renn, Eileen Donovan Kranz, Patrick Gabridge, Ted Rooney, Julie Wu, Gregory Lewis, and Rob Vlock. Also, a big thank you to Danielle Forshay, for her wonderful suggestions.

Thank you to Annalise McDonald, whose research on chimeras and tracking devices was so helpful!

Writing can be a solitary endeavor, and so I also want to thank the wonderful writing communities I am so fortunate to be a part of; The 1st 5 Pages Writing Workshop, Adventures in YA Publishing, and Book Pregnant. You guys are the best!

Thank you to my parents. To my mother, Josie, for inspiring me with her love of (and belief in) myths and legends, and for introducing me to her version of Celtic mythology. To my father, Tim, who certainly inspired my love of reading, and of fantasy stories, and for always letting me pick out as many books as I wanted during our frequent trips to the bookstore. I hope to make you both half as proud of me as I am of you. To my sister, Kathy, and her husband Paul, for their limitless love, encouragement, and support.

And to my wonderful husband John, thank you for always believing in me, even when I stopped. To my darling children, Sean, Maggie, and Danny, you inspire me everyday with your kind hearts, humor, insight, and creativity. Thank you all for your endless love and support. In particular, thank you for putting up with the many car rides and Saturday afternoons that turned into brainstorming sessions, for listening when I needed to read a few lines (or pages), and for always encouraging me—especially when I was ready to throw in the towel on this whole writing thing. You guys are my heart.

Lastly, like Annabeth, my mother was hospitalized and underwent treatment for depression, including electroconvulsive therapy. She was so grateful for the care she received, telling me without it she never could have returned home. I am so very grateful to all those who work in the field of mental health.

About the Author

Erin Cashman is a Young Adult author living in Massachusetts. Her debut YA fantasy, *The Exceptionals* (Holiday House) was named a Bank Street College of Education Best Children's Book of the Year. She is also the workshop coordinator and a mentor at the 1st 5 Pages Writing Workshop through the blog Adventures in YA Publishing. Visit her at erincashman.com and follow her on Twitter @etcashman.